"WE'VE BEEN HIT!" THE CAPTAIN OF THE MERCHANT VESSEL SHOUTED.

"We are under attack! Mayday! Mayday!"

On the bridge of the *U.S.S. Enterprise,* Captain Picard responded swiftly to the distress call. "Mr. Worf," he ordered, "tell them we're on our way. Mr. Data, engage."

"Sir," Data put in, "I do not believe we will reach them in time. . . ."

Look for STAR TREK Fiction from Pocket Books

Star Trek: The Original Series

Star Trek: The Next Generation

Star Trek: Deep Space Nine

STAR TREK
THE NEXT GENERATION®

BLAZE OF GLORY

SIMON HAWKE

POCKET BOOKS
New York   London   Toronto   Sydney   Tokyo   Singapore

An *Original* Publication of POCKET BOOKS

POCKET BOOKS, a division of Simon & Schuster Inc.
1230 Avenue of the Americas, New York, NY 10020

This book is published by Pocket Books, a division of
Simon & Schuster Inc., under exclusive license from
Paramount Pictures.

ISBN: 0-671-88045-4

First Pocket Books printing March 1995

10 9 8 7 6 5 4 3 2 1

POCKET and colophon are registered trademarks of
Simon & Schuster Inc.

Printed in the U.S.A.

For Mike Stackpole, with special thanks to Bruce and Peggy Wiley, Megan McDowell, Robert M. Powers and Sandra West, Jennifer Roberson, Emily Tuzson, Tudor and Angelo Marini, Adele Leone and her staff and associates, and Tracy Ashleigh, all of whom provided valuable assistance and moral support during the writing of this novel. Live long and prosper.

BLAZE OF GLORY

Prologue

COMMANDER WILLIAM RIKER leaned back in the command chair on the bridge of the *Enterprise* and touched the insignia on his chest. "Riker to Captain Picard."

"Picard here," the captain responded from his quarters. "What is it, Number One?"

"Sir, we're making our approach to Starbase 37," Riker replied. "We should be ready to begin docking procedures in about five minutes."

"Very good, Number One. Thank you. I will be there shortly."

Riker looked up at the main viewer. Starbase 37, revolving in orbit above Artemis VI, filled the screen. It was the first time the *Enterprise* had ever visited this sector, and Riker was painfully aware that he had not read anything about the K'tralli system since his days at the Academy. He had intended to refresh his memory before they arrived at the starbase, but his duties had left him with no opportunity to do so. What with a backlog of crew efficiency reports to complete; having to go over and sign off on one of Geordi's exhaustively detailed, periodic maintenance reports; then having to see Dr. Crusher for an overdue physical that he had already put off at least a dozen times until she finally insisted that he had to do it *now,* there had simply been no chance to consult the data banks. Now they were here, and almost ready to begin docking procedures.

The commander of Starbase 37 was an old friend of the captain's. Riker knew Picard would want his crew to present their usual spit-and-polish, and it wouldn't do for the first officer not to be adequately briefed. Fortunately, Riker had access to a unique last resort in Lieutenant Commander Data.

"Mr. Data," he said, "access your memory under the subject headings of Starbase 37, Artemis VI, and the K'tralli system and give us a brief summary overview, if you please."

"Very well, sir," the android replied, from his forward console. He cocked his head slightly to one side, an affected mannerism Riker knew well. Data had picked it up from observing humans and often did it when he was processing information or as an interrogative expression. Riker listened carefully as the android launched into a summary of his programming concerning the subjects specified.

"Starbase 37 was established thirty-five years ago in orbit above Artemis VI, the only Federation colony planet in the K'tralli system. There are five other inhabited planets in the sector. A'tray, L'ahdor, D'rahl, and S'trayn were all colonized from the K'tralli homeworld, N'trahn. First contact with the K'trall occurred approximately forty years ago, and led to the treaty which resulted in the colonization of the planet now known as Artemis VI.

"The K'trall are descended from the same racial stock as the Vulcans and the Romulans," Data continued, "but they are a distant, offshoot civilization, with a culture all their own, having hardly anything in common with their racial forebears save for their physical appearance. Unlike Vulcans, they express emotion, but are far less aggressive than the Romulans.

"For much of their history, the K'trall had a monarchical form of government," Data went on, "but approximately ten years before the Federation made contact with them, a revolution had occurred that brought about a dictatorship. At the time of first contact, their economy was in a state of near total collapse, and their provisional government was having difficulty effecting the promised democratic reforms. They welcomed contact with the Federation, and were eager for economic aid and establishing trade. Following the negotiation of the treaty that made them members of the Federation, the K'trall invited the colonization of Artemis VI, the last of the easily habitable planets in their system. Starbase 37 was established as a diplomatic outpost, and to administer the Federation colony on Artemis VI, in addition to all Federation shipping in the sector. For the past thirty-five years, that has remained the primary mission of Starbase 37 and its personnel. There is, at present, no Federation ambassador to the K'trall. Ambassador Bowman, who last held the post, died of natural causes recently and his replacement has not yet been appointed. Until a new ambassador is designated, those duties are being filled by the current commander of Starbase 37—"

"Captain Ivan Valentinovitch Gruzinov," said Picard, as he came onto the bridge.

Riker immediately got to his feet.

"Yes, sir, that is correct," said Data.

"Captain Gruzinov is an old friend, Mr. Data," said Picard, as Riker moved aside to let him assume the command chair. "He was in his last year at the Academy when I was just a plebe. There were many times I stood braced at attention before him while he called me on the carpet." Picard smiled at the memory as he sat down.

Data cocked his head slightly to one side. "If I understand the reference correctly, sir, you mean to say that he upbraided you for some perceived flaw in the performance of your duties?"

"Yes, indeed, and most vociferously," replied Picard.

"Were there frequent flaws in your performance at Starfleet Academy, sir?" asked Data.

Riker cleared his throat softly. Picard gave him a sidelong look. Riker was staying out of this one. "In certain matters pertaining to discipline, yes, I re-

4

gret to say," Picard admitted. "Especially during
my first year. Cadet First Lieutenant Gruzinov
made it something of a personal crusade to whip
me into shape. And though I resented him for it
mightily at the time, looking back, I am grateful for
his efforts. He provided me with no small amount
of motivation, if for no other reason than to deny
him the satisfaction of finding fault with me."
Picard smiled as he remembered. "At the time, I
absolutely loathed him, but following my gradua-
tion, we served together aboard the *Antares* and
became good friends. I have not seen him now in
over twenty years."

"Captain, we are being hailed by Starbase 37,"
Lieutenant Worf said, from his console.

"Onscreen, Mr. Worf," Picard said.

Riker turned toward the main viewscreen. The
image that appeared on the screen was that of an
officer a few years Picard's senior, robust and fit,
with broad shoulders and a thick chest, close-
cropped gray hair and a wide, rugged-looking face
with broad features and pale blue eyes. "Greetings,
Enterprise," he said, with a slight Russian accent,
then smiled. "Welcome to Starbase 37, Jean-Luc."

"Thank you, Ivan," Picard replied, and Riker
noted that he gave the name the correct Russian
pronunciation, saying the "I" as a long "E" and
accenting the first syllable. "It's been a long time,
old friend. You're looking well."

"Flying a desk agrees with me," replied
Gruzinov. "I'm getting soft in my old age. You are

cleared to begin docking procedures. Try not to bump anything on your way in. I'll see you when you come aboard."

He signed off, and the image on the screen was replaced by that of Starbase 37, its docking port filling the viewer.

"Try not to bump anything?" said Worf, glancing at Picard in a puzzled manner.

Picard looked slightly irritated. "A rather annoying reference to the first time I ever directed a docking procedure on an Academy simulator, Mr. Worf," he replied. "I ordered the helmsman to engage starboard forward maneuvering thrusters, when I should have said starboard *rear* maneuvering thrusters."

"Ah, *that* kind of bump," said Riker, with a grin. He recalled his own early experience at simulated docking procedures at the Academy all too well. Docking a Galaxy-class starship was a great deal more difficult than it looked, and it looked damn near impossible to a first-year cadet. "I think we've all done at least one of those," he added, with a smile.

"Correction, Number One," Picard said. "There was *one* cadet at the Academy who aced the simulation first time out, isn't that right, Mr. Data? She's all yours. Why don't you show them how it's done?"

"Yes, sir," the android replied, lining the ship up for its approach.

Data executed the docking maneuver with unbelievably smooth precision. Riker smiled as he thought how the crew of the starbase would be impressed at the way Data brought the ship in, computing the approach so accurately that they were simply able to drift into the docking port completely without the use of maneuvering thrusters for minute course corrections, except merely to slow the ship's drift as they locked into berth. It was a very showy display, the sort of thing the starbase crew would talk about for quite some time to come.

A short while later, they were being escorted down the companionway leading to the central hub of the starbase and the commander's office. Picard had chosen Riker, Worf, Data, and Troi to accompany him. Riker noted how all the starbase personnel they passed saluted their party smartly. Generally, military protocol was not so formally observed in Starfleet. The salutes were not required, but they were being given as a courtesy. It spoke well of Captain Gruzinov's leadership, thought Riker.

Gruzinov rose from his chair and came around his desk to greet them as they came into his office. He was a large man, big-boned and powerful-looking. Riker thought he must have made an intimidating upperclassman in his days with Picard at the Academy. "Jean-Luc!" he said, extending his hand to Picard warmly.

"It's good to see you, Ivan," Picard said. "You've put on a bit of weight."

"And you look depressingly fit," Gruzinov replied, with a grin. "It's good to see you, too, old friend."

"Allow me to present my officers," Picard said. "My first officer, Commander William Riker; ship's counselor, Deanna Troi; Lieutenant Worf, chief of weapons and security; and my helmsman and navigator, Lieutenant Commander Data."

Gruzinov greeted each of them in turn. When he came to Data, he said, "I saw the way you brought the ship in, Mr. Data. Most impressive. I see the stories I've heard about you have not been exaggerated."

"Thank you, sir," said Data.

"Well, I'd be pleased if you'd all join me for a drink," Gruzinov said.

"We'd be delighted," said Picard.

"I think you'll find the adjoining briefing room a bit more comfortable," Gruzinov said, beckoning them toward a connecting door. They went through into a small and very comfortably appointed briefing room, similar to the one they had aboard their own ship, Riker thought.

"Please, be seated," said Gruzinov. "I have asked a member of my staff to join us. She will be arriving shortly."

He poured them drinks, enjoying playing the host, and then proposed a toast. "To old friends," he said, to Picard.

"Old friends," Picard echoed.

"How long has it been, Jean-Luc?" Gruzinov asked. "About twenty years since we served on the *Antares?*"

"A bit more than that, I think," Picard replied, as they all sat around the table.

"You've done well for yourself," Gruzinov said, approvingly. "I've seen your record. You've come a long way from the hell-raising plebe you were back at the Academy."

"Yes, well, in no small measure, you bear some of the credit for that," Picard replied.

"It's kind of you to say so," said Gruzinov, "but you pulled yourself up by your own bootstraps. You've come far, and you will go further still, I have no doubt of that. Me, I'm just an old warhorse getting ready to be put out to pasture."

"Surely not," Picard said, with a frown. "We are not *that* far apart in age!"

"Perhaps not, but I have no illusions about my prospects for further advancement, Jean-Luc," Gruzinov said. "I have had a good career, but hardly a distinguished one. I was passed over for promotion several times. If I had waited to receive command of my own ship, I might be waiting still. This opportunity arose, and I leaped at the chance. I have never regretted it for a moment. I've put in enough years to be eligible for retirement, and I have already picked out some land down on Artemis VI. A few months from now, I will take my pension, build myself a small home, get married, and settle down to a quiet life devoted to fishing and raising children. I've had a good run and I'm ready for a change." He shook his head. "I have no complaints."

"Well, I'm pleased to hear that," said Picard.

"However, I want to leave things in good order for my successor," said Gruzinov, "and right now,

I've got something of a problem on my hands. And it's a problem I am not really equipped to handle on my own."

"I must confess that I was anxious to know why we were dispatched here," said Picard. "Our orders were curiously unspecific."

"Well, that is partly my fault," Gruzinov admitted. "I informed Starfleet that I thought it best, under the circumstances, that this mission be kept low profile, and they agreed."

"Our orders said nothing about this being a classified mission," said Riker, with a frown. He knew from experience that Starfleet was usually quite specific about such things.

"No, not really classified, Commander Riker," Gruzinov replied, "merely . . . how shall I put it?"

"Low profile?" said Riker, repeating Gruzinov's own term for it.

"Perhaps I had best explain," Gruzinov said. "Are you familiar with the background of Federation involvement in this sector?"

"Reasonably so," said Riker, thankful for the briefing Data had given him.

"Good," said Gruzinov. "That will save some time, then. You see, what we have here is a somewhat sensitive political situation that is being exacerbated by a problem I am, unfortunately, not really capable of dealing with, given our limited resources. But perhaps I should back up a bit, so that you will better understand the context of the situation."

He touched a button set into the tabletop and a

section of the bulkhead slid aside to reveal a viewscreen. "Computer," said Gruzinov, "run *Enterprise* Briefing Program One, visual display mode only," he said.

A moment later, an image of an old K'tralli male appeared upon the screen. His hair was white, and down to his shoulders. Despite his obviously advanced age, he had a forceful look about him, Riker thought.

"Hold it there, computer," Gruzinov said. "This is General H'druhn, the hero of the K'tralli revolution and, for the past fifty-some-odd years, military overlord of the K'tralli Empire. He's a tough old bird, but he's getting on, and recently he has turned the reins of power over to his son, J'drahn. Computer, next visual."

The image of H'druhn was replaced by that of a much younger man, but the family resemblance was immediately apparent. J'drahn looked every inch his father's son, thought Riker. Proud and forceful-looking, but with a more arrogant set to his sharply defined features. Like his father, he wore his dark hair long, down to his shoulders, and he wore a military uniform festooned with decorations.

"J'drahn is the current overlord of the K'trall," Gruzinov said. "Since being appointed to his father's post, he's moved quickly and decisively to consolidate his power. And ever since, he's been something of a thorn in my side. His father was tough, but fair, and he was someone I could work with. But now J'drahn is the one who wields the power, and he is as unscruplous as he is ambitious. On the surface, he makes all the right diplomatic noises, but though he keeps promising more democratic reforms, they seem very slow in coming. That is, of course, strictly none of our business. The K'trall are entitled to run their own government any way they choose, but J'drahn is an unpredictable maverick who looks to his own self-interest first and, frankly, I'm no longer certain where he stands."

"In regards to what?" Picard asked.

"I was coming to that," Gruzinov replied. "Despite the fact that J'drahn postures as a loyal and devoted member of the Federation, there have been recent rumors of secret contacts with the Romulans."

"The Romulans!" said Riker.

"We are not far from the Neutral Zone here, Commander," said Gruzinov. "It would be a relatively simple matter for them to cross over beyond the range of our scanners, and it is impossible for us to police the entire sector. That is, after all, not within the scope of our mission. The K'trall have that responsibility. Our job is merely to administer the colony on Artemis VI, maintain relations with the K'tralli government on their homeworld of N'trahn, and administer Federation shipping in this sector. Which brings me to that problem I mentioned earlier.

"I have reason to believe," he continued, "that J'drahn, or at least one of his military governors, has been providing sub-rosa support for freebooters who have been preying upon merchant shipping in this sector. If J'drahn is not directly involved himself, then at the very least he looks the other way. Officially, he condemns the freebooters, and he's promised us his full support in dealing with the problem, but I haven't noticed that he's done very much to stop them. I have managed to put a dent in some of the piracy with the two light cruisers I have at my disposal here, but there is one freebooter in particular who presents a problem that has gotten completely out of hand."

At that moment, the door to the briefing room opened and Riker turned to see a young, attractive, dark-haired woman enter. She had a severe, no-nonsense look about her, but Riker still found it difficult not to stare.

"Ah, Lieutenant," said Gruzinov. He turned to the others. "Allow me to present Lieutenant Angela Dorn, my senior base security officer." He quickly introduced the others to Lieutenant Dorn. "Please sit down, Lieutenant," he said. "I was just getting to the main point of the briefing."

"Thank you, sir," said Lieutenant Dorn, taking her seat.

"Computer, next visual," said Gruzinov. The image of an old Federation starship came on the screen. *"This* is the problem I was referring to earlier."

"But that's a Constitution-class starship," said Riker, with a frown.

"Correct, Commander," said Gruzinov. "At one time, this *was* a Starfleet vessel, though I have no

13

idea which one. I realize the quality of the image is poor, but if you look closely, you may notice that the ship now bears no markings."

"A decommissioned vessel?" asked Picard.

"Yes," Gruzinov replied, nodding. "It is one of the old, outmoded ships that were stripped of their warp drives and all military ordnance and sold off as surplus many years ago. Before Starfleet discontinued their policy of disposing of their old ships in this manner, a number of them were sold and privately refitted as impulse-powered merchant vessels. This one, on the other hand, is considerably more interesting. It is called the *Glory,* and it belongs to Captain Blaze, a notorious pirate who is part human and part K'trall. And he has been using it to wreak havoc with Federation merchant shipping in this sector. He fancies himself something of a modern swashbuckler, right down to the flamboyant, piratical-style outfits he affects along with his crew."

"And this is why you've sent for us?" Picard asked, with some surprise.

"Wait," Gruzinov said. "There's more. Lieutenant Dorn has been assembling a file on Captain Blaze. Lieutenant?"

"Thank you, sir," Lieutenant Dorn said, her tone clipped and businesslike. She turned to Picard and his officers. "Until fairly recently, Captain Blaze has been something of an engima to us. However, in the last few weeks, we have managed to make some progress with our investigation. Regrettably, we have no image of Captain Blaze on file, but we've managed to discover that his real name is Diego DeBlazio, and he was born on Artemis VI approximately thirty years ago. Computer, next visual."

Riker saw the images of two people appear on the screen, a human male and a K'tralli female.

"His parents were Dominic DeBlazio, a retired Federation diplomat who was one of the original colonists on Artemis VI, and his wife, M'tala, a woman from a prominent K'tralli family," Lieutenant Dorn explained. "They are now both dead. Blaze, as he is known, grew up and was educated on the K'tralli homeworld of N'trahn, so that records regarding him are sketchy. However, we know that he had access to Federation tutors in his childhood on Artemis VI and, more notably, he has served apprenticeships in both the K'tralli fleet and aboard several Federation merchant vessels. He may not have gone to Starfleet Academy, but he knows how to handle a ship. His privateering exploits have become legendary in this sector."

"One moment, please, Lieutenant," Picard said, turning to Gruzinov. "Ivan, I must admit to being a bit puzzled. Am I to understand that this small-time, local freebooter was the *sole* reason for our being summoned here?"

"Blaze is not someone to be taken lightly, Jean-Luc," Gruzinov replied. "I have been completely helpless to do anything about him."

"But you said that you have two light cruisers," said Picard, with a frown. "Surely, they should be more than capable of dealing with a stripped-down and dilapidated Constitution-class ship powered by nothing more than impulse engines."

"If that were, indeed, the case, they would be," said Gruzinov. "But Blaze is a highly skilled ship's captain, Jean-Luc, and what's more, the *Glory* is no ordinary ship. It may not look like much, but Blaze has had it completely overhauled and fully refitted with modern ordnance. What's more, he's had it equipped with a cloaking device."

"A cloaking device!" said Riker, with surprise. "Where and how could a small-time freebooter obtain a cloaking device? And where would he get the knowledge to fit it properly? Are you sure this information is accurate, sir?"

"We have numerous eyewitness reports, including those from the officers of my own cruisers," said Gruzinov. "Somehow, Blaze has not only managed to obtain a cloaking device, but he has found a way to make it operative on his ship. Admittedly no easy task, since Federation vessels were never designed to be fitted with cloaking devices, and it would violate the Treaty of Algeron. It can be done, however, if you've got a crack engineering team."

"The obvious implication is that he's in league with the Romulans," Lieutenant Dorn added. "Federation merchant vessels are easy prey for the *Glory,* and our cruisers are simply no match for it. Blaze attacks, then either cloaks his ship and slips away, or simply outpowers them and escapes."

"Outpowers them?" said Riker, with astonish-

ment. He didn't see how that could be possible for a decommissioned, stripped-down surplus ship.

"That's right, Commander," said Gruzinov. "I don't know what he's got in his engine nacelles, but the *Glory* is capable of considerably more than impulse power. One of our cruisers has already been seriously damaged in an encounter with him and is still undergoing repairs. That leaves me with only one small ship to cover the entire sector and protect both the starbase *and* the colony on Artemis VI. Obviously, I don't dare send my one remaining cruiser out on patrol and leave both the starbase and the colony vulnerable to attack. That's why we're trying to keep a low profile on this mission. I don't want Blaze or any of the other freebooters in this sector to know just how vulnerable we have become. And Starfleet is particularly anxious to have him dealt with."

"In other words, we're supposed to take him into custody if we can, or else blow him out of the sky?" asked Riker, tensely.

"Essentially, yes," Gruzinov replied.

"Ivan . . ." Picard said, somewhat hesitantly. "Forgive me, but you realize this is all highly irregular. We have received no such specific orders regarding this mission. I am afraid that I shall require confirmation."

Gruzinov nodded. "Perfectly understandable," he said. "And there is no need to apologize. I would do exactly the same thing in your position. I will give you access to my communication logs with

Starfleet Headquarters, and you will, of course, be free to confirm them with Starfleet yourself."

"Has this so-called Captain Blaze confined his activities primarily to this sector?" asked Riker.

"So far," Gruzinov replied.

"Then that would suggest he must have a base of operations somewhere nearby," Riker said.

Gruzinov nodded. "Yes, Commander, I agree," he said. "What's more, we even have a good idea where it is. We believe that Blaze has his base on D'rahl, one of the four K'tralli colony worlds. Unfortunately, there's not much we can do about that."

"Why not?" Riker asked, with a puzzled frown.

"Each of the four K'tralli colony worlds is under the administration of a colonial military governor," Gruzinov said, "all of whom are answerable directly to Overlord J'drahn. The governor of D'rahl is a high-handed and dissolute character named T'grayn, who gives only lip service to the idea of cooperating with the Federation. He claims to have been conducting an investigation, but so far, it has yielded nothing. I have tried launching my own investigation on D'rahl, which I have the authority to do under the Federation treaty, but our resources here are limited and our people have received little in the way of cooperation from local authorities."

"You suspect that Blaze has paid them off?" asked Troi.

"Either that, Counselor, or else T'grayn is actively his partner," said Gruzinov, with a wry grimace.

"Personally, I think J'drahn is supporting T'grayn because he's probably receiving kickbacks from the operation. It would amount to a considerable profit. Aside from which, this situation is destabilizing Federation influence in this sector. And who else but the Romulans would stand to gain from that? It seems highly unlikely that Blaze simply happened to stumble onto his cloaking device in some salvage yard."

"A privateer operating on letters of marque from the Romulans," said Riker. He gave a small snort. "That's got to be a first."

"And unless he's stopped, he won't be the last," Gruzinov said. "You can see why I've had to send for help. One freebooter like Blaze is bad enough. Imagine what a whole fleet of them could do."

Picard nodded. "Yes, that would be a disturbing development," he said. "I shall need to confer with my officers, Ivan, and with Starfleet Headquarters before I decide upon a plan of action."

"Of course," Gruzinov said. "I can have quarters prepared for you in the meantime, if you wish."

"No need," Picard replied. "We shall stay aboard the *Enterprise*. It would help expedite matters."

"As you wish," Gruzinov said. "I will assign Lieutenant Dorn to you for the duration. She has my complete confidence, and can provide you with anything you may require."

"Thank you," said Picard. "How soon can you come aboard, Lieutenant?"

"I can have my kit packed in fifteen minutes, sir," she said.

"An hour will be sufficient," Picard replied. "And I would like all the information you have available on this Captain Blaze."

"I already have it here, sir," said Lieutenant Dorn, holding up an isolinear chip.

"Excellent," said Picard. "Mr. Riker?"

Riker took the chip from her.

"I'd like copies of those communiqués as soon as possible," Picard said, to Gruzinov. "In the meantime, I will get in touch with Starfleet and confirm our mission status. I must admit, however, that I have some reservations about this."

Gruzinov nodded. "I know what you mean, Jean-Luc," he said, sympathetically. "None of us joined Starfleet to stalk ships and destroy them. And believe me, no one wants to see Blaze taken alive more than I do. But take it from me, old friend, do *not* underestimate him. The *Glory* may be an old ship, but she's as dangerous as any Romulan battle cruiser."

"The *Enterprise* has dealt with Romulan Warbirds before, sir," said Worf, confidently.

Gruzinov smiled. "Spoken like a true Klingon, Mr. Worf," he said, *"and* a proud and loyal weapons officer. However, if I may presume to advise you, treat the *Glory* exactly as would a Romulan Warbird. Do not be too confident when it comes to Captain Blaze, or you may be very unpleasantly surprised."

A short while later, back aboard the *Enterprise,* Riker and Picard met in the briefing room with the senior officers. In addition to those who had met

with Gruzinov, joining them were Chief Engineer
La Forge and Dr. Crusher. Picard quickly brought
them up to date.

"A cloaking device?" said Geordi. As Riker had
expected, he looked very skeptical. "On a privately
refitted Constitution-class ship? That would require some pretty sophisticated engineering modifications, sir." La Forge frowned and shook his
head. "I'm sorry, Captain, but I just don't see how
an independent operator out here on the frontier
could have come by the expertise to make it work."
He paused. "Unless . . ."

"Unless what?" Picard prompted him.

La Forge grimaced. "Well . . . it just doesn't
seem very likely, sir."

"Mr. La Forge, I asked for speculation," said
Picard.

La Forge took a deep breath. "Well, Captain, the
only explanations I can think of seem pretty far-
fetched. I suppose it's possible he could have found
a first-class engineer to modify the Federation
drives for him, but why would anyone with that
kind of expertise waste his time working for an
independent freebooter? If someone found a way
to fit Romulan drives to a Federation vessel, then
it would be a fairly routine procedure to fit a cloaking device, but then fitting the drives would be
a massive undertaking. From what we know of
Romulan technology, the designs just aren't com-
patible. It would require complete systems reen-
gineering. The modifications something like that
would entail would be very extensive and, well,

it just wouldn't be very cost effective. You might as well design a brand-new ship. But converting an old, outmoded vessel like a Constitution-class starship to Romulan drives?" He shrugged and shook his head. "What would be the point?"

"I must concur with Geordi's analysis, Captain," Data said. "It would certainly seem far simpler for the Romulans to give Captain Blaze one of their own vessels rather than embark on such a questionable procedure."

Exactly, Riker thought, as another possibility suddenly occurred to him. For the moment, he decided to keep it to himself.

"Except that a Romulan vessel would be instantly identifiable," said Picard. "And under the circumstances, the Romulans would hardly wish to advertise their involvement in such a venture."

"You think the Romulans may be using Blaze and his ship in some sort of covert operation, Captain?" Troi asked.

Picard shook his head. "No, I don't believe the Romulans would ever trust an outsider to conduct one of their clandestine military operations," he replied. "However, they might simply have given him the means to disrupt Federation merchant shipping in this sector and then turned him loose to function on his own."

"That would be the classic definition of a privateer," said Riker.

"Excuse me, Commander," Data said, "but I have heard this term used several times now, and I am a bit confused. You seem to use the terms 'pirate' and 'privateer' interchangeably. However, I was under the impression that there was a significant difference between the two."

"Technically speaking, there is, Data," Riker replied. "A pirate is someone who attacks ships and plunders them. The term 'privateer' was originally used to describe privately owned vessels that sailed under special letters of marque during wartime. In effect, they were licensed by their governments to attack the ships of the enemy, or raid their merchant shipping with an aim to disrupting their war effort."

"I see," said Data. "So then, a 'privateer' would be, in effect, a pirate operating with the sanction of a government during wartime. But then, we are not at war with the Romulans."

"No, Mr. Data, we are not," Picard said. "And that is precisely why the Romulans—if they are, indeed, the ones who are behind this—wish to avoid the appearance of being involved directly. I am beginning to realize that this situation may be a great deal more serious than it first appeared. This Captain Blaze may be only a pawn in a much larger game. But apparently a very meddlesome pawn, just the same. Ivan Gruzinov is not the sort of man to ask for help unless he really needs it. And if Overlord J'drahn has been conducting secret dealings with the Romulans, then he has violated his father's treaty with the Federation, and that could have very serious repercussions."

"It sounds as if we have two separate problems here," said Dr. Crusher. "One is the problem of the

Glory, attacking and disrupting Federation shipping, and the other is the problem of Overlord J'drahn, and whether or not he's been in contact with the Romulans in violation of Federation accords. One is purely an enforcement problem, but the other is a sensitive political issue that could have far-reaching consequences."

"And in both cases," said Troi, "the situation poses a danger to the starbase and the Federation colony on Artemis VI."

"And to continuing membership in the Federation for the K'trall," added Riker, agreeing with their analysis. "I can see why Captain Gruzinov had to send for help. He's in way over his head."

"The question is, how best to proceed," Picard said. "The K'trall may be full members of the Federation, but their local autonomy must still be respected. Pursuing freebooters in space is clearly within our purview. The treaty General H'druhn signed with the Federation grants us the authority to conduct operations in K'tralli space."

"It's officially Federation space," Riker pointed out.

"Precisely, Number One," replied Picard. "However, it is also within our authority, according to the strict sense of both K'tralli and Federation law, to participate in local law-enforcement efforts in Federation territory to apprehend any criminals endangering the starbase, Federation shipping, or the colony on Artemis VI."

"Captain Blaze certainly seems to fit those criteria," said Dr. Crusher.

"But we are still faced with something of a gray area," Picard replied. "Strictly speaking, in order to initiate any operations in K'tralli territory, we need the approval of the local government."

"Maybe we already have it," Riker said. "Didn't Captain Gruzinov say that Overlord J'drahn's official position has been to condemn the freebooters and promise the Federation full support in bringing them to justice? That sounds like approval to me."

"Perhaps," Picard said. "Nevertheless, I feel it is necessary for the sake of diplomacy to meet with Overlord J'drahn and receive his official approval directly."

"And what if he withholds it?" Dr. Crusher asked.

"Well, that would place him in a somewhat awkward position," said Picard, "since he has already promised Captain Gruzinov his full support. Mr. Worf, I would like you to contact Captain Gruzinov as soon as we dismiss this meeting and request him to arrange an audience with Overlord J'drahn. We will do this through the proper diplomatic channels."

"Aye, Captain," Worf said.

"And Counselor Troi, I would like you to confer with Lieutenant Dorn as soon as she comes aboard," Picard continued. "See to it that she's properly settled in and familiarized with ship's routine."

"Yes, Captain," said Troi.

"Mr. La Forge, I'd like you to examine Lieutenant Dorn's file carefully and use computer enhancement on the image of that ship. I realize that it's not a lot to work with, but see what you can learn from it."

"Aye-aye, sir," Geordi said.

Picard nodded. "Good. Then if there are no questions, we shall adjourn for the present, until we receive word concerning the meeting with Overlord J'drahn. Dismissed."

Riker lingered while the others filed out. "Sir," he said, when he and Picard were alone, "I know Captain Gruzinov is your friend, but in view of what we've been told, how can we be sure the information we've been given is accurate?"

"Ivan Gruzinov is an experienced Starfleet officer," replied Picard. "He's not an alarmist, and he's never been the sort to leap to conclusions."

Riker took a deep breath. Now was the time to bring up the idea that had occurred to him earlier. "In that case, sir, it occurs to me that it's just possible we haven't been told everything."

"What are you getting at, William?" Picard asked, with a frown.

"If the *Glory* is everything Captain Gruzinov says she is, then there are only two possible explanations that make any sense to me. Either the Romulans performed the modifications for him on the existing drives, or else the *Glory* is a camouflaged Romulan light cruiser, disguised with an artificial hull. And if that's the case, then it's a virtual certainty that she has a Romulan crew. I just can't believe the Romulans would turn over one of their ships to a privateer. Especially one who wasn't Romulan himself. And if what we're dealing with is a disguised Romulan ship, manned by a Romulan crew, then it's an act of war."

"And you think Starfleet isn't anxious to acknowledge that," Picard said.

"This wouldn't be the first time something like this has happened," Riker said. "There are numerous incidents throughout history of battles being fought with no war being declared, battles that no one's ever heard about, officially. One side decides to test the waters and push a little. The other side pushes back. Somebody wins, somebody loses. But if it happens in an isolated area, no one ever hears about it."

Picard nodded. "And you suspect that's what we may be facing here?"

"I think it's very possible, sir," said Riker. "The Romulans take one of their light cruisers and disguise it as an outmoded Federation ship that had been sold as surplus. They manufacture the fiction of some freelance pirate and use it as a cover to raid Federation shipping. Their light cruisers can outmaneuver ours, plus they've got cloaking capability, which Federation vessels are forbidden to use. About the only thing that could stop them would be a Galaxy-class starship, and Romulans are not in the habit of surrendering. If there's a face-off and they manage to escape, then they've got plausible deniability. And if the *Glory* is destroyed in action, then they can claim it wasn't a Romulan ship, but merely an old, decommissioned Federation vessel belonging to some local pirate. So neither Starfleet nor the Romulans acknowledge that there's been any act of war. But it happened, just the same."

Picard pursed his lips, thoughtfully. "And you think that's why this mission is being kept low profile, as Gruzinov said, to avoid openly acknowledging that possibility and creating an incident that might lead to war."

"I think the Romulans may have crossed over the line and it's going to be our job to slap them down," said Riker. "And at the same time, give an object lesson to Overlord J'drahn, without rubbing his face in it. A threat to Federation shipping is eliminated and J'drahn gets put back in his place. All very unofficially, of course."

Picard nodded. "Yes, I had considered that possibility myself," he said. "However, I find it hard to believe that Ivan Gruzinov wouldn't take me into his confidence. And I'm sure Deanna would have sensed it if he was keeping something from me."

"It's quite possible he doesn't know," said Riker. "The Romulans are very thorough. If they've manufactured Blaze's cover convincingly enough, Captain Gruzinov could have bought it. Without taking anything away from him, sir, he *has* been in command of a starbase for almost twenty years. I'm sure he's a highly capable officer, but he's still spent all that time behind a desk."

"All this is still only supposition, William," Picard said.

"That's true, sir," Riker readily agreed. "But it all fits. And if the *Glory* is really a covert Romulan vessel, then we're looking at a very sticky situation.

It means there's little chance we'll be able to take the ship and its crew alive. And Starfleet may not thank us if we do, because then they'd have no choice but to openly acknowledge Romulan involvement."

"And that would mean war," Picard said, grimly.

Riker merely nodded. No further elaboration was necessary.

Picard tightened his lips into a grimace. "I'm not going to be the one to start a war with the Romulan Empire," he said. "Perhaps the mere fact of our presence here will be enough to deter them."

"And if it's not?" asked Riker, watching the captain anxiously.

Picard met his gaze. "Then our options will depend very much on what they do," he replied. "And on how Overlord J'drahn reacts to our arrival."

Chapter One

THE ROYAL PALACE OF N'TRAHN was, indeed, palatial. Located in the center of the capital city of S'drana, it was a gigantic edifice, containing well over a thousand rooms. Its architecture was almost Byzantine, with graceful spires and fluted domes and ornamental buttresses, and there were numerous carvings and sculptures covering the building. The former kings of the K'trall had truly lived in splendor, Riker thought, and the current overlord had made himself quite comfortable in the luxurious domicile of his predecessors.

They had received coordinates to beam down to the palace courtyard, where they were met by a squad of the palace guard and escorted in to meet the overlord. Riker half-expected to see liveried servants in the palace halls, but instead the interior of the palace was a model of military precision.

Everyone they saw wore the uniform of the K'tralli army, which consisted of light gray breeches and a black, high-collared jacket with silver trim and insignia. Their escort brought them in through the gate to meet the captain of the guard, who knew Gruzinov but went through the proper official motions of admitting them, just the same. J'drahn clearly took his military protocol seriously, thought Riker.

After being passed through by the captain of the guard, they were escorted down a long corridor to the main hall, where Overlord J'drahn received them formally. The main hall was once probably a throne room, Riker thought, but if there was once a throne upon the raised dais at the far end of the cavernous room, it had been replaced by a large and intricately carved desk made from some exotic-looking local wood. It was black, with a light yellow figure running through it, giving an attractive swirl effect to the highly polished surface. The massive desk had a communications console built into it, and there was a viewscreen built into the wall behind it.

The effect was interesting, thought Riker. For all its opulence, the desk still looked very businesslike, an effect reinforced by the hardware built into and surrounding it. No monarchical airs, but definitely a feeling of authority. On a slightly lower level, to either side of the desk, there were two other workstations, manned by uniformed personnel. And there was a large, semicircular desk, built in the shape of a giant horseshoe, on the main floor.

Communications and computer consoles covered it, and personnel shuttled back and forth, in and out of the room, with an air of busy efficiency. It looked like a war room, Riker thought.

Their escort marched to the rear of the room and came to a smart, parade-ground halt before the overlord's desk. The ranking member of the escort waited for J'drahn to notice him.

"Your Excellency . . . Captain Gruzinov of Starbase 37, and Captain Jean-Luc Picard of the *Starship Enterprise.*"

"Greetings, Your Excellency," Gruzinov said. "Thank you for agreeing to see us on such short notice."

Overlord J'drahn got up from behind his desk and came down from the dais to greet them. He's established the pecking order with this formal presentation, Riker thought, and now he's going to be folksy. And his guess proved perfectly correct.

"Captain Gruzinov, how good to see you," said J'drahn, coming up to Gruzinov. He inclined his head slightly and touched his right hand to his chest in the K'tralli greeting. "And Captain Picard. Welcome to N'trahn. May I offer you some refreshment?"

"No, thank you, Your Excellency," said Picard. "We do not wish to take up much of your time. This visit will be brief. May I present my first officer, Commander William Riker, and my ship's counselor, Deanna Troi?"

"Welcome," said J'drahn, turning to Troi and Riker.

"Thank you, Your Excellency," she replied, bowing her head slightly.

"Your Excellency," Riker said, taking the K'tralli's measure as he returned the greeting gesture. J'drahn stood about six feet tall, and looked very fit. His features were sharply pronounced. He had long black hair, arched eyebrows, a thin, blade-shaped nose, and a wide, thin-lipped mouth. His physical appearance was midway between that of a Vulcan and a Romulan, which made Riker think that a K'tralli could pass for Romulan without much difficulty. It also meant that the reverse was true. J'drahn's face was a study in insincerity. He smiled, but the eyes were crafty and suspicious.

"To what do I owe the honor of this visit, Captain Picard?" J'drahn asked.

"We have only recently arrived at Starbase 37," Picard replied, "and we wished to pay our respects."

"And the reason for your visit?" asked J'drahn.

"The *Enterprise* has arrived here in answer to my request for assistance in dealing with the problem of the freebooters, Your Excellency," said Gruzinov.

"Ah," said J'drahn, noncommittally.

"We realize that you have already assured Captain Gruzinov of your full support in dealing with this problem," Picard said, "but as a matter of diplomatic courtesy, I wanted to be certain that we had your official approval to proceed."

"Yes, yes, of course, by all means," J'drahn replied, nodding emphatically. "These freebooters have proved to be an annoying embarrassment to my government, and a potential impediment to our continuing good relations with the Federation. We have done all that we could to deal with this irritating problem, but our resources are limited and, as you can see, the recent transfer of authority from my esteemed father to myself has brought about numerous administrative problems. In the last few years, my father's advanced age had made it difficult for him to keep up with all the pressing matters of state that had to be addressed, and as a result, we need to make up a great deal of lost ground."

"I understand completely," said Picard. "And we shall do everything in our power to avoid adding to your burden. Our only intention is to help."

"I appreciate that, Captain Picard," J'drahn replied. "I was concerned that the Federation might not understand our current situation. Needless to say, you have my personal assurances of my government's complete support in your efforts, as I have already told Captain Gruzinov. We will do whatever we can to assist you in this matter."

"Thank you very much, Your Excellency," said Picard.

"Will you be remaining on N'trahn?"

"I am afraid not, Your Excellency," said Picard. "We must be getting back to our ship."

"I see. And what are your plans?"

"We shall be conducting routine patrols of the sector and staying in communication with all incoming vessels," said Picard. "And in the event that any of the freebooters are sighted, we shall respond immediately."

J'drahn nodded. "Excellent. I am sure this will do a great deal to alleviate the complaints we have been receiving from the merchant fleet. I wish you the best of luck in your efforts, Captain. As I said, you have my complete support."

"We are very grateful, Your Excellency," said Picard. "And now we have really taken up enough of your valuable time. With your permission, we will be returning to our ship."

"It has been a pleasure to meet you, Captain," said J'drahn. "And please keep me advised of your progress."

They took their leave of Overlord J'drahn and were escorted back out to the palace courtyard. From there, they beamed back up to the *Enterprise*. They had refrained from discussing their meeting with the overlord in the presence of the palace guard, but as soon as they stepped off the transporter pads, Troi turned to Picard and said, "Overlord J'drahn was not pleased at our arrival, Captain. I distinctly sensed his unease."

"You think he was hiding something?" asked Picard.

"I'll bet on it," said Gruzinov.

Troi shook her head. "I cannot say for certain," she replied. "He was extremely guarded. However, that could simply be his discomfort at the fact that his government has made no progress in dealing with the problem of the freebooters."

"Assuming that he's even tried," Gruzinov said.

"Well, what counts is that we have received his official sanction to conduct patrols," Picard replied. "We have gone through the proper channels, and now he cannot claim that we have acted without his authority."

"I think you can count on acting without his help, as well," Gruzinov said. "Anytime I've needed anything from him, all I've heard about are his pressing 'administrative problems.' It has been his blanket excuse for doing nothing."

They headed down the corridor toward the turbolift.

"Well, so long as he continues to do nothing, then at least he cannot get in the way," Picard said. "In any case, I would much prefer to deal with this problem in my own manner."

"Are you satisfied with Lieutenant Dorn as a liason?" asked Gruzinov.

"Actually, I haven't had the chance to speak with her," Picard replied. "Counselor Troi was in charge of seeing to it that she was settled in."

"She seems most efficient, Captain," Troi said, speaking to Gruzinov. "No sooner had I brought her to her quarters than she requested to be briefed concerning the ship's routine. She strikes me as a very serious and highly professional young woman."

"Yes, she is rather humorless, isn't she?" Gruzinov said.

"Captain, I did not mean to imply—"

"It's perfectly all right, Counselor," said Gruzinov, with a smile. "Lieutenant Dorn is known around the starbase as 'the robot.' They call her that behind her back, of course. I am not supposed to know about this, but I have my sources."

"Well, since you have brought it up, sir," Troi said, "I must confess that I feel a strong sense of defensiveness about her."

"I had reached more or less the same conclusion," said Gruzinov, "though it took me a great deal longer. I envy you your Betazoid abilities, Counselor. They would certainly make my job a great deal easier. But I'm curious. To what would you attribute this defensiveness of hers? Speaking purely off the record, of course."

"I have not spent a great deal of time with her," Troi replied, cautiously, "but my intuition tells me that she is concerned about being taken seriously. She is an very beautiful young woman, and both her age and her beauty, combined with her position of responsibility at the starbase, are probably contributing factors."

Gruzinov nodded. "Yes, I can see that. She is young, even for a first lieutenant, and she is a very attractive woman, which is not really an advantage for a chief of security. She was appointed to that position based purely on her record, which is quite impressive. She graduated from the Academy at the top of her class. When I first met her, I must admit I had my reservations. I was not convinced she would be up to the job. But she has proved

herself extremely capable. She survived a very difficult and dangerous assignment on Artemis VI,
bringing some murderers to justice. The mission
resulted in the deaths of most of the landing party."
He sighed. "Unfortunately, though she has been
a valuable asset to my command, she has not
really been able to develop much of a social life.
She seems to have a certain awkwardness in that
regard."

"You're saying she's all business, and her manner
tends to put people off?" asked Riker.

"For a chief of security, that is not necessarily a
problem," said Gruzinov. "At least insofar as her
performance of her duties is concerned. However,
she strikes me as a rather lonely person. I suppose,
to some degree, I feel a little sorry for her. She does
not seem to have any friends. Only acquaintances.
Perhaps a change of environment aboard the *Enterprise* would do her good."

"We'll try to make her comfortable, sir," said
Riker.

They stepped out onto the bridge.

"Prepare to leave orbit, Mr. Data," said Picard.
He turned to Gruzinov. "Would you care to do the
honors, Captain?" He gestured toward his chair.

Gruzinov glanced at Picard with surprise and
then smiled. "Why, thank you, Jean-Luc. It would
be an honor." He sat down in the command chair,
then took a deep breath and let it out slowly. "I
must admit, it is a nice feeling," he said, with a
smile. "Set course for Starbase 37, Mr. Data."

"Aye-aye, sir."

The ship left orbit and headed back on a course for Artemis VI.

"Captain," said Worf, looking up from his console, "I am picking up a distress signal."

Gruzinov glanced up at Picard.

"Put it up on the screen, Mr. Worf," said Picard.

The image that appeared on the viewscreen was that of a human Federation ship captain, dressed in a dark blue merchant-marine uniform and looking extremely agitated. ". . . ships in the vicinity! I repeat, we are under attack! Our position is—"

"Enter those coordinates, Mr. Data," said Picard, quickly.

Data punched in the coordinates as the merchant captain gave them.

"We've been hit!" the captain said. "Repeat, we are under attack and we've been hit! Mayday! Mayday! Any vessels in the area, please respond!"

Gruzinov immediately vacated the command chair.

"Mr. Worf, respond to that distress call and tell them we are on our way," Picard said, taking his place. "Mr. Data, warp factor six. Engage!"

"Yes, sir."

"Yellow alert," Picard said.

The alert signal sounded throughout the ship as the *Enterprise* accelerated.

"Estimated time to arrival, Mr. Data," said Picard.

"At this speed, I compute that we will shall reach

the stated coordinates in nine point six minutes, Captain," Data replied.

"That's not good enough," Picard said. "Go to warp eight."

"Yes, sir. Estimated time to arrival is now three point seven minutes."

"Warp nine," said Picard, tensely.

"Yes, sir."

"Shields up, Mr. Worf," said Picard. "Go to red alert."

As the alert signal sounded, people throughout the ship hurried to their stations with well-drilled precision.

"Sir, the merchant ship should be in visual range momentarily," Data said.

"Onscreen, Mr. Data."

They watched the main viewscreen tensely. Seconds later, they could see the ship that issued the distress call.

"Prepare to slow to impulse power," said Picard.

"Yes, sir," Data said.

As they approached, they could see that the merchant ship was drifting, but there was no sign of the vessel that had attacked it.

"Slow to impulse power, Mr. Data. Maintain shields," said Picard. "Stand by phasers, Mr. Worf."

As the ship slowed to impulse power, they could see that the merchant vessel had sustained serious damage to one of its engine nacelles. The ship was crippled and drifting.

"Open hailing frequency, Mr. Worf," Picard said.

"Hailing frequency open, sir," said Worf.

"Attention, merchant vessel," said Picard. "This is Captain Jean-Luc Picard, of the Federation starship *Enterprise*. Identify yourself."

"Man, am I glad to see you!" the captain said, as he appeared onscreen.

"Identify yourself, Captain, and report!" said Picard.

"Sorry, sir. Captain Winslow Bryant, of the Federation merchant ship *Wyoming*. We've been attacked by a freebooter, sir. Two direct hits. We've sustained extensive damage to our right engine nacelle. Our left engine is gone. We're plumb disabled, sir."

"What are your casualties, Captain Bryant?" asked Picard.

"None, sir, believe it or not," Bryant replied. "And thank God for that. They just came flat out of nowhere and hit us like a ton of bricks, then disappeared. I guess they picked up your response to our distress call and skedaddled. If it wasn't for you, we would've had it."

"Stand by, Captain," said Picard. "We'll take you in tow." He signaled Worf to cut off communications. "Cancel red alert, Mr. Worf," he said. "Maintain yellow alert and cancel shields. Prepare to activate the tractor beam."

"Aye-aye, sir," Worf said. "Shields down, tractor beam standing by."

Suddenly, the *Enterprise* was rocked by a blast

that knocked Gruzinov right off his feet and threw Picard back against his command chair.

"What the devil?" said Picard. "Shields up! Red alert!"

The alert signal sounded throughout the ship as Worf quickly put the shields back up, just in time as another blast struck them.

"Those were phasers!" Riker said, with astonishment.

"Damage report, Mr. Worf!" Picard commanded.

"Shields holding, Captain," Worf replied, listening to the reports as they came in. "Damage to Decks 12 and 13 from the first blast. Phasers standing by!"

"Where the devil *is* he?" asked Picard.

"Sensors are picking up a ship to the rear starboard, Captain, closing fast," said Data.

"Aft phaser banks, fire!" said Picard.

Worf fired the aft phasers. "Clean miss, Captain. Enemy vessel taking evasive action, but still closing."

"Full about, Mr. Data!"

As the *Enterprise* turned to meet the threat, Picard issued orders rapidly.

"Ready forward phasers, Mr. Worf! Onscreen!"

As they looked up toward the main viewscreen, they saw an old Constitution-class starship closing in fast and firing as it came.

"It's Blaze!" Gruzinov said.

The *Enterprise* was struck by two blasts in rapid succession.

"Shields holding, Captain," Worf said. "Phasers locked on target."

"Fire!" said Picard.

Gruzinov held on to the back of the command chair tensely as he watched the viewscreen. The *Enterprise* fired its forward phaser banks. At the last possible instant, the oncoming ship veered off, disappearing off the screen.

"Damn, he's fast!" said Riker. "Faster than that old hulk has any right to be."

"Report, Mr. Worf!"

"Direct hit, Captain," Worf said.

"Full about, Mr. Data! Stand by to fire again."

As the *Enterprise* came about again, they saw the other ship turning to meet them. It had been struck, but it was difficult to tell the extent of the damage. Apparently, it still had maneuvering power.

"He's putting the *Wyoming* between us," said Gruzinov. "And she can't maneuver out of the way."

"Stand by phasers, Mr. Worf," Picard said. "Open hailing frequency."

"Phasers standing by, Captain. Hailing frequency open."

"This is Captain Jean-Luc Picard of the Federation *Starship Enterprise.* Identify yourself!"

A bizarre image suddenly appeared on the viewscreen. It was the bridge of an old, Constitution-class starship, unchanged from the way Picard remembered it. However, the man seated in the captain's chair and the crew members visible around him looked decidedly out of place on the bridge of a Constitution-class starship. They were a mixed crew, including K'tralli and human freebooters, with an Orion at the weapons console and a Capellan seated at the navigator's station. But as strange as this outlandishly garbed assortment was, it was the man sitting in the captain's chair who immediately commanded attention.

He was neither human nor K'tralli, but some of both, with long, thick, and straight black hair hanging down well below his shoulders. He had a sharp-featured face with high cheekbones, a straight and narrow nose, a cruel-looking mouth, gracefully arched eyebrows, and a piercing, pale gray right eye. His left eye was covered by a black leather patch. He was dressed in a soft, sleeveless, black leather tunic, tight red breeches and over-the-knee black boots. He had a gold ring in his left ear and his bare, muscular arms were colorfully tattooed.

The combination of human and K'tralli ancestry gave him the aspect of a predatory elf, thought Riker. But it was immediately obvious that he was no Romulan, nor were the other members of his bridge crew. Behind him, Riker heard the turbolift door open and he turned to see Lieutenant Dorn come onto the bridge. She took one look at the viewscreen and froze, fascinated.

"This is Captain Blaze, of the *Starship Glory*. I regret to say I cannot see you, Captain. Your phasers have rendered my visual receiving scanners inoperative and caused some damage to my engineering section. My compliments to your weapons officer. His marksmanship is excellent."

Picard shook his head in astonishment at the freebooter's casual insolence and devil-may-care manner. "Captain Blaze?" he said. "Don't you mean DeBlazio?"

Blaze smiled. "So you know who I am? Well, it seems you have the advantage of me, Captain." He gave a slight, mocking bow. "Diego DeBlazio, at your service. But my friends simply call me Blaze. I fear you have arrived at a most inconvenient time. However, the stimulation of this encounter has more than made up for the loss of a fat prize."

"You will surrender your vessel immediately, Captain, and stand by to be boarded," said Picard.

Blaze grinned broadly, then chuckled. "You have a sense of humor, Captain. I like that in a man."

"If you do not surrender your ship at once, I shall be forced to open fire," said Picard.

"And do you plan to shoot through this helpless merchant vessel?" asked Blaze. "That would rather defeat your purpose, would it not? Of course, I could make things easier for you by blowing the *Wyoming* to pieces. Then we could trade broadsides at our leisure, so to speak."

Picard compressed his lips into a tight grimace. "Any further hostile action toward the *Wyoming* will result in the immediate destruction of your vessel," he said.

"Well, we can't have that, can we?" Blaze replied. "I've grown rather attached to this ship. She has served me very well. And it would be a shame to end things so soon when we are only beginning to become acquainted."

Picard glanced at Riker and saw that he was getting a slight facial tic in his cheek. He had seen that mannerism before, and it was a clear signal that Riker was absolutely furious.

"I will ask you one last time, Captain," said Picard. "Are you prepared to surrender your ship?"

"No, Captain, I am not," Blaze replied. "Why don't you come and take it, if you can?"

The image suddenly disappeared as Blaze cut off communications, replaced by the sight of the *Glory,* positioned just behind the crippled *Wyoming.*

"Stand by phasers, Mr. Worf," Picard said, tensely. "Mr. Data, prepare to—"

Suddenly, the *Glory* disappeared from sight.

"He's cloaked!" Gruzinov said.

"I'll be a son of a—" Riker caught himself and stopped.

"Stand by to come about!" said Picard.

"He can't fire when he's cloaked," Gruzinov said.

"But he may try to get around behind us," said Picard. "Stand by, Mr. Data."

"Ready, sir."

"Come about full!"

The *Enterprise* came about, but there was no sign of the *Glory.* They all waited, tensely.

"Scan for drive particle emissions, Mr. Data," said Picard.

"Scanning, sir," said Data. He shook his head.

"I'm picking up rapidly decaying traces of drive particle emissions, Captain. He's gone, sir."

"Maintain shields," said Picard. "It could be a ploy."

Moments passed, and nothing happened.

"He's given us the slip," said Riker. "We may have damaged him more than he let on."

"We did score at least one direct hit, Captain," Worf added.

"Well, at least the *Wyoming*'s safe," Gruzinov said, exhaling heavily as he relaxed.

"So that was Captain Blaze," said Picard. He shook his head. "Well, you've got to give him one thing—the rogue does have a certain style."

Riker frowned. "I'd rather give him the business end of a photon torpedo," he said.

"My apologies, Captain," Worf said, tensely. "I allowed myself to be taken by surprise."

"No more than I, Mr. Worf," Picard said. "It was I who gave the order to lower the shields. I never imagined a mere freebooter would attack when he was so heavily outgunned. I allowed myself to be surprised by a common criminal."

"And a coward, at that," said Riker.

"He may be a criminal, Commander, but he is no coward," Worf said.

"Do I actually detect a note of *admiration,* Mr. Worf?" Riker asked, with surprise.

"Not admiration, sir, but respect, even if it is grudgingly bestowed," the Klingon replied. "It took a warrior's courage to attack a clearly superior foe."

"It was almost as if he were playing some sort of game with us," said Troi. "And he seemed to be enjoying it."

"It was no game, Counselor," Picard replied. "He was testing us. This is the first time a Galaxy-class starship has visited this sector. He wanted to see what we could do. I had foolishly assumed he fled at our arrival, but it seems I underestimated Captain Blaze." He touched the communicator on his breast. "Picard to Engineering."

"La Forge here, Captain."

"What is the extent of the damage, Mr. La Forge?"

"We've sustained some structural damage on Decks 12 and 13, Captain, mostly in the shuttlebay area. I've got the areas sealed off and repair teams are at work in pressure suits. The situation does not appear to be critical, but I'd be a whole lot happier finishing the job at Starbase 37. It looks as if they tried to take out our starboard engine nacelle and missed, but not by very much. That was a bit too close for comfort. A direct hit there would have taken us clean out of action. This guy knows what he's doing, sir."

"What do you make of the sensor readings on that ship, Mr. La Forge?" asked Picard.

"The sensors were able to take a quick reading as he made his pass, sir," said La Forge, "but it wasn't enough time to get any really detailed information. It's a Constitution-class ship, all right, but it's a lot faster than it has any right to be, even if it had its original warp drives."

Riker nodded. It was exactly what he had been thinking. "Is there any possibility the ship might have been disguised by an artificial hull?" he asked.

"Practically none, Commander," La Forge replied. "She'd never be able to maneuver that way if she was. The only things I know of capable of making that kind of speed, aside from us, would be a Romulan light cruiser or a Warbird. Frankly, Captain, I'm at a loss to explain it."

"Work on it, Mr. La Forge," Picard said. "I *want* an explanation. Picard out."

He turned and saw that Lieutenant Dorn was still on the bridge. "Yes, Lieutenant?" he said.

"I . . . Forgive me for barging in, Captain, but when the alert signal sounded, I thought . . . that is, I didn't know if I could be of any help, but . . ."

"But you wanted to see the man you've been gathering intelligence on all this time," Picard said. "I quite understand, Lieutenant. What did you make of him?"

She shook her head. "He was not what I expected, sir."

"I don't think he's what any of us expected," Picard replied, dryly.

"Well, at least you've blooded him," Gruzinov said. "You scored a direct hit on the *Glory*. That's a lot more than anyone else has been able to do."

"It didn't seem to bother him a great deal," Picard said.

"Bluff and bravado," Riker said. "He took refuge behind the *Wyoming* because he had sustained serious damage, enough to make him quit the fight."

"But not enough to cripple him," said Picard. "And speaking of the *Wyoming* . . . her captain must be having a coronary. Open hailing frequency, Mr. Worf."

The captain of the *Wyoming* looked badly shaken when his image came onscreen. "Oh, Lord, is he really gone now?"

"He's gone, Captain Bryant," Picard replied. "Your ship is safe."

"Talk about being caught between the devil and the deep blue sea! I thought we'd had it for sure. Are your people all right, Captain? Did you suffer any casualties in that exchange?"

"Negative, Captain Bryant," said Picard. "Thank you for asking. Stand by, we will take you in tow. *Enterprise* out."

"No casualties," said Troi. "Not aboard our ship, or the *Wyoming*. Captain Blaze picks his targets very carefully. Whatever else he may be, he does not appear to be a wanton killer."

"Whatever else he may be," Picard echoed her, "he is clearly a highly capable ship's captain, and I shall not underestimate him again. What was your impression of him, Counselor?"

"He seemed very confident, Captain," Troi replied. "I sensed no fear in him. Quite the contrary. To use his own words, he found the encounter very stimulating. I would assess him as the sort of man who thrives on risk."

"And that, in addition to his obvious skill, makes him very dangerous," Picard said. "Forgive me, Ivan," he said to Gruzinov. "I must confess that I did not take your warning very seriously. I assure you it shall not happen again."

"I wonder about the timing of this whole affair," said Riker.

"How's that, Number One?" Picard asked.

"We wasted no time getting to the *Wyoming*," Riker replied. "But Blaze had already disengaged and prepared his attack. Maybe he picked up our response to the *Wyoming*'s distress call. But on the other hand, maybe he knew that we were coming."

"J'drahn," Gruzinov said, realizing what Riker was suggesting. "He could easily have communicated with the *Glory* the moment we left the palace."

"Perhaps," Picard said, "but we have no proof of that. It is certainly possible, in fact, highly probable that Blaze intercepted our response to the *Wyoming*."

"Maybe," said Gruzinov, "but I think Commander Riker's right in his suspicions. If you ask me, J'drahn is into this right up to his crooked neck."

"If that's the case, then what does he stand to gain?" Picard asked. "To risk his standing in the Federation, to say nothing of violating his father's treaty with us, merely for the sake of some short-term profit?"

"You don't know J'drahn, Jean-Luc," Gruzinov said. "He and Blaze are both cut from the same cloth. Both egotists, both opportunists. J'drahn believes he can do anything he wants. And he really doesn't think that he can lose."

"He may find out differently," Picard replied. "But we shall have to handle this very carefully. If J'drahn is officially implicated, it could have serious political repercussions."

"I know," Gruzinov said. "That's the truly frustrating part of this whole thing. Whatever we do, we can't touch J'drahn, or he will claim the Federation is attempting to topple his government."

"I think I am going to have another talk with Overlord J'drahn," Picard said. "Mr. Data, set course for Starbase 37. Mr. Worf, engage tractor beam and take the *Wyoming* in tow."

"Tractor beam engaged, sir."

"Take us out of here, Mr. Data, impulse power only. Let's not shake up the *Wyoming* any more than necessary."

"Aye-aye, sir."

"You've got something on your mind, Jean-Luc," Gruzinov said.

Picard nodded. "Yes, but we shall discuss it in detail later. I think the *Glory* may have sustained more damage than Blaze admitted. And that means he will be making for his home base."

"D'rahl," Gruzinov said. "That's where it is. I'll stake my career on it."

"Will you?" asked Picard. "Because that may be exactly what you shall have to do."

53

Chapter Two

WHILE LA FORGE DIRECTED the repairs on the damage to the *Enterprise* in the main docking bay of Starbase 37, Picard, Riker, Troi, and Worf met with Gruzinov in the lounge aboard the starbase.

"Not exactly a very good beginning, is it?" Riker said wryly, as he sipped his coffee.

"On the contrary, Commander," said Gruzinov. "I'd say it was an excellent beginning."

"Outmaneuvered by some small-time, arrogant, frontier freebooter?" said Riker, with disgust. "Pardon me, but I fail to see what's so excellent about it, sir."

"Then allow me to spell it out for you, Commander," Gruzinov replied. "You have managed to save the *Wyoming*'s cargo, the combined insured value of which, according to the manifest, was considerably greater than that of the vessel itself. And you also scored a direct hit on Blaze's ship, which should put him out of commission for a while. I very much doubt that he has access to repair facilities as complete as we have here. He may have considerable difficulties effecting his repairs, while with our maintenance crews assisting Mr. La Forge, the *Enterprise* should be back at a hundred percent in less than forty-eight hours. Frankly, I never expected things to go this well so soon."

"I don't mean to put a damper on your optimism, sir," said Riker, "but for someone who's been put out of commission, Blaze seemed to take it pretty well." He shook his head. "I suspect we may not have hurt him as badly as you think."

"In any case, at least we have managed to learn one thing for certain," Picard said. "The *Glory* is not a disguised Romulan vessel, but a genuine, Constitution-class starship that has been refitted with much of its original equipment. We were fired upon by phasers, not Romulan disruptors."

"I had wondered what you meant when you asked your chief engineer about an artificial hull," Gruzinov said. "I could have told you the *Glory* was not a disguised Romulan ship, Jean-Luc. In effect, I did, when I told you what she was."

"It was not that I doubted your word, Ivan," Picard said, "but I had to consider the possibility of your being taken in by a clever deception."

"I see," Gruzinov said, flatly. "Yes, well, I am an *administrative* officer, after all. It has been a long time since I have seen active duty."

"Ivan," Picard said, placatingly, "I was by no means implying—"

"No, no, I quite understand, Jean-Luc," Gruzinov said. "Explanations are unnecessary."

"Meaning no disrespect, sir," Riker said, quickly, "but it was *I* who made the suggestion that the *Glory* might be a disguised Romulan vessel. In fact, from what you'd told us, I was absolutely convinced of it."

"And you must admit that it *was* a logical assumption," said Picard, "one I simply could not dismiss out of hand."

Gruzinov nodded. "Yes, of course. Forgive me, I did not mean to be overly sensitive. The truth is, when the *Glory* first appeared, I suspected the same thing. However, the reports from the merchant vessels Blaze had plundered, and the testimony of my own cruiser officers who had encountered him, convinced me otherwise."

"There is also the fact of Blaze's mixed crew to consider," Picard said. "It is conceivable that the Romulans might have employed a few K'trall to aid them in their deception, but they would never employ humans, much less Orions or Capellans. I think there is no question but that Blaze is exactly what he appears to be. The question is, where did he get his ship, and how and where was it refitted?"

"He could have picked up most of his equipment on the black market," said Gruzinov, with a shrug.

"Even phaser banks?" said Worf, frowning.

"You would be surprised at what's available out

there, Mr. Worf," Gruzinov said. "Especially here on the frontier, where enforcement, thanks to J'drahn, is rather lax. If you've got enough money, you could probably get your hands on the components to outfit just about anything, short of a Galaxy-class starship. Unfortunately, even Starfleet is not immune to corruption. Supplies and ordnance do disappear from warehouses every now and then."

"Which is precisely why we need to have those questions answered," said Picard. "If someone is peddling black-market Starfleet ordnance in this sector, we must find out who it is and shut the operation down. However, Blaze did not get his cloaking device on the black market."

"Nor his engines," Riker added. "Unless he's somehow figured out a way to adapt a cloaking device to a Federation engine design, which I just don't buy. He's got to have Romulan drives powering his ship."

"That does seem to be the only logical explanation," said Picard, with a frown, "but I shouldn't think they'd fit the existing design. And from what we saw, the *Glory* did not have any obvious structural modifications."

"Then he must have figured out a way to *make* them fit," insisted Riker. "There's just no way I'm going to believe some frontier freebooter has solved a technical problem that's baffled Starfleet's finest engineers."

"Well, according to Lieutenant Dorn's file, Blaze

does not have an engineering background," said Gruzinov. "Of course, that does not preclude his having someone on his crew who does."

"Someone capable of *that* level of engineering skill could write his own ticket," Riker said. "Why would somebody like that sign on with a small-time freebooter like Blaze?" He shook his head. "It just doesn't make any sense, sir."

"Perhaps it was some brilliant, former Starfleet engineer who got in trouble and was cashiered from the service," suggested Gruzinov.

Riker shook his head. "No, sir, that just doesn't wash. If he was *that* good, cashiered or not, he'd be snapped up by the private sector in a heartbeat. And for a lot more money than he could make with Blaze."

"Which brings us right back to the Romulans," Picard said.

"Exactly," Riker concurred. "No matter how you look at it, they've got to be involved. Who would be more qualified to adapt a Romulan engine design than Romulan engineers?"

Gruzinov sighed heavily. "I'm afraid that's a question I cannot answer, Commander. Frankly, I was hoping that you might be able to come up with some other explanation."

Riker nodded. "I understand, sir," he said. "This one is politically very inconvenient. But unfortunately, it's the only one that fits the facts."

"Is it possible that J'drahn is not directly involved in this?" Picard asked.

Gruzinov shook his head. "I suppose anything is

possible," he replied, with a shrug. "But I don't believe it for a moment."

"Overlord J'drahn *was* hiding something, Captain," Troi said. "I am convinced of it. Despite what he said, he was not pleased to learn of our arrival. His attitude was very guarded, and I sensed considerable apprehension on his part."

"Unfortunately, none of this constitutes proof of his involvement," Picard said.

"No, Jean-Luc, that is *not* unfortunate," Gruzinov replied. "If we were to *prove* J'drahn's involvement, then there would be no way the Federation Council could dismiss it. The treaty would be irrevocably broken and the K'tralli Empire would have to be expelled from the Federation. In that event, J'drahn would turn to the Romulans. He'd simply have no other choice. Without Federation support and trade, the economy of the K'tralli Empire would collapse. J'drahn has been bleeding his own treasury dry. And to prevent another revolution that would depose him, he would require the support of the Romulans. We all know what the price of that support would be. J'drahn would become their puppet, and the Romulans would have legal holdings on our side of the Neutral Zone."

"But the treaty of the Neutral Zone specifically marks the boundaries between the Romulan Empire and the Federation," Worf said. "How could the Romulans extend their influence beyond the Neutral Zone without violating the treaty?"

"Very simply, Mr. Worf," Gruzinov replied. "If

the relations with the Federation became strained —and proof of J'drahn's involvement with the Romulans would do that—then J'drahn could argue that he was no longer bound by the treaty his father had agreed to and he would be free, according to his rights, to ally himself with anyone he chose. If he happened to choose the Romulans— and he would *have* no other choice—then the Federation would be forced to recognize that alliance. The effect of that would be a de facto extension of the Neutral Zone to encompass the K'tralli sector. By default, the Romulans would gain territory that is currently under Federation control, and there would be absolutely nothing we could do about it. It would all be perfectly legal."

"In other words, Captain, you're saying we have to stop Blaze, without implicating J'drahn," said Troi, "even if he's guilty?"

"Even if he's guilty," said Gruzinov.

"Well, that's just great," said Riker, and grimaced. "He breaks the treaty by allowing the Romulans to outfit freebooters so they can disrupt our shipping, gets a cut of the profits, thumbs his nose at us, and we're just supposed to look the other way?"

"Believe me, Commander, I don't like it any better than you do," said Gruzinov. "But the alternative is even worse."

"And J'drahn must realize that, of course," Picard said. He nodded. "I think I'm beginning to understand his reasoning. He allows the Romulans to use Blaze to disrupt Federation shipping, and in return he profits from it, while at the same time counting on the Federation to keep the Romulans from making any open incursions into K'tralli territory. He's depending on the strategic value of this sector to keep the Federation from officially recognizing his complicity and expelling him."

"So he's burning his candle at both ends," said Riker.

"And very cleverly, too," Picard said. "The trouble is, stopping Blaze would only solve part of the problem. Even if we took the *Glory* out of action, J'drahn could find himself another freebooter and equip him the same way with covert assistance from the Romulans. So long as we are here, the Romulans may not risk attempting to enter this sector by stealth, but we cannot remain stationed here indefinitely. And J'drahn knows that perfectly well."

"Then we're just going to have to do something about J'drahn," said Riker.

"I don't see how we can," said Troi. "Any attempt to depose J'drahn would violate the Prime Directive."

"Perhaps not," Picard said. He turned to Gruzinov. "You said the former overlord, General H'druhn, was friendly with the Federation, someone you could work with. If we could convince him that his son was acting against K'tralli interests, then perhaps he could be persuaded to remove J'drahn from power."

"I have already thought of that, Jean-Luc," Gruzinov said. "But General H'druhn is an old man and J'drahn is his only son. I tried having a meeting with him once before, and it went very badly. He simply will not listen to any accusations against J'drahn. There was no way I could convince him. I only succeeded in alienating him and J'drahn warned me that if I made any further attempts to see his father, he would issue an official protest to Starfleet and the Federation Council, accusing me of interference."

"Well, I guess that's that," said Riker.

"Not necessarily, Number One," Picard replied. "There is nothing to prevent me, as captain of a Federation starship visiting this sector, from paying a formal diplomatic call of courtesy on the hero of the K'tralli revolution and the Empire's leading citizen."

"That's true enough," Gruzinov said. "And the general will certainly receive you under those circumstances. However, the moment you bring up the subject of J'drahn, the audience is liable to come to an abrupt end, just as it did with me. And then J'drahn *will* issue a formal protest."

"No, I do not believe he will," Picard replied. "I think he was bluffing when he made that threat. Keep in mind that under the terms of such a formal protest, we would have the opportunity to state our case officially, and that is something J'drahn would undoubtedly wish to avoid. If I were to proceed slowly and carefully, seeking out some common ground with the general and gaining his confidence, then perhaps some progress could be made. In any case, I think it's worth a try."

Gruzinov nodded. "If you're right about J'drahn's threat of a protest being a bluff, then we've got nothing to lose."

"Perhaps it would be best, considering your earlier attempt, if you were officially kept out of it," Picard said.

"No, if this should backfire on us, I won't let you take the blame alone," Gruzinov said. "That isn't how I operate, Jean-Luc. Especially with an old friend."

Picard smiled. "I appreciate that," he said. "In the meantime, I would like to proceed on another front. J'drahn is only one part of the problem. There is still Blaze, and whoever is supplying him."

"That would undoubtedly be T'grayn," Gruzinov said.

"The colonial governor of the planet known as D'rahl?" Picard asked.

Gruzinov nodded. "Handpicked by J'drahn," he said. "The original governors of N'trahn's four colony planets were all senior officers in General H'druhn's revolutionary council. Two of them are now dead, and they have been replaced by bureaucrats loyal to J'drahn. One, Governor M'dran of S'trayn, is a feeble old man who is little more than a figurehead. He's surrounded by J'drahn's officials, who effectively run the administration for him. The one remaining governor who was a part of H'druhn's original council was Colonel Z'gral, and he was the only one who tried to stand up to J'drahn. But he is no longer in office."

"What happened to him?" Riker asked.

"J'drahn had him removed from office. If he could have gotten away with it, I'm sure he would have had him eliminated, because Z'gral was a very vocal critic of J'drahn's administration. However, Colonel Z'gral is one of the heroes of the revolution, and he has immense popularity, second only to General H'druhn. J'drahn was too smart to move against him openly. Instead, he had him retired with full honors, and a generous pension, as 'a mark of deference to his age and loyal service to the Empire.' Of course, it didn't fool Z'gral for a moment, but there was nothing he could do about it. J'drahn decreed a national holiday in his honor, and he spared no expense in staging a great celebration, complete with parades and a state dinner and a formal decoration ceremony during which he presented Z'gral with a palatial home on the outskirts of K'trin, the capital city of D'rahl. And that's where Z'gral lives to this day, surrounded by an 'honor guard' that reports his every move to J'drahn. It amounts to nothing more than a luxurious prison."

"I see," Picard said. "Would it be possible to visit him?"

"I doubt it," said Gruzinov. "Z'gral does not receive any visitors. The word is he's in poor health and doesn't wish to be disturbed."

"As a hero of the revolution, and one of his fellow officers, Colonel Z'gral would surely have the ear of General H'druhn, would he not?" Picard asked.

"I'm sure he would, if he was ever allowed to see

him," said Gruzinov. "But J'drahn's too smart for that. If you're thinking of trying to get Z'gral to intercede with H'druhn on our behalf, I'm sure he wouldn't be unwilling. But he'd never be allowed to leave K'trin. J'drahn has done everything in his power to keep him away from his father."

"I think we should make a point of seeing him, just the same," Picard said.

"What have you got in mind, Jean-Luc?" Gruzinov asked.

"The beginnings of a plan," Picard replied. "But first I would like to confer with your intelligence officer, Lieutenant Dorn."

The display panel in the bulkhead outside Holodeck 3 showed that a program was currently running. It said, PROGRAM ENGAGED: DATA— 1322-B. Lieutenant Dorn raised her eyebrows as she read the display. That was a surprising number of programs to be loaded under the designation of one crew member. Lieutenant Commander Data was an android, yet he clearly used the holodecks as much as any of the *Enterprise*'s human crew members. She found that very curious. There was no privacy coding on the display, so she decided to go in and satisfy her curiosity.

She almost lost her footing as the deck suddenly pitched beneath her and the spray from a wave crashing against the bowsprit soaked her to the skin.

"Steersman, hard alee!"

"Aye-aye, sir!" came the shouted response from

above and behind her, over the sound of the wind and explosions.

Explosions? Lieutenant Dorn looked out over the deck railing, across the rolling sea, and saw a tall, four-masted sailing vessel off the port bow. Smoke erupted from the ship as its cannons fired a broadside. As the ship she stood on turned, several of the projectiles fired by the other vessel struck close, sending gouts of water spouting up into the air and soaking her down again. She heard a chorus of laughter and jeers.

"She 'asn't got our range, Cap'n!" someone shouted.

"Bloody Spaniards never could shoot worth a damn, curse 'em to Davey Jones' locker!"

Lieutenant Dorn looked around her at the wood-planked deck and teak railings, at the racks of belaying pins and ropes leading up to the masts and rigging. Wide, square canvas sails luffed briefly as the ship turned, then filled with loud, whip-cracking sounds as the wind struck them, propelling the ship forward.

The men around her on the deck were a coarse and surly-looking lot, bare-chested and tattooed, with gold rings in their ears and colorful bandannas covering their heads. Some were barefoot, in tattered breeches that came down to their calves; others wore tall, square-toed leather sea boots. They all wore cutlasses and daggers, and many had flintlock pistols tucked into cloth sashes at their waists.

"Steersman, steady as she goes!"

"Aye-aye, Captain!" That voice sounded familiar. She turned and looked up at the afterdeck and saw Data standing at a large, spoked wooden wheel, steering the ship. He was barefoot, and wearing brown breeches, a loose-fitting, balloon-sleeved white shirt that laced up at the neck, and a brown leather vest. There were two pistols and a cutlass tucked into a red sash at his waist, and he had a red bandanna tied around his head.

"We're closin' with 'em, Cap'n!" one of the sailors cried.

"Man the guns!" a steely, resonant voice with an English accent cried.

And then she saw him. The captain stood, balanced on the crosspieces of the mainmast and holding on to the rigging, staring out at the ship they were pursuing. His blond hair was blowing in the wind, and his loose-fitting white shirt rippled in the breeze. He had on red-and-white striped breeches and his shirt was open at the neck, revealing a tanned, muscular chest. His classic Saxon features were strikingly handsome. He grinned, revealing flashing, perfect white teeth, took hold of a line, and swung down from the crosspieces, across the decks, and up to the afterdeck, where Data stood behind the wheel.

"Put your backs into it, lads!" he shouted. *"We'll show 'em how it's done!"*

"Mr. Data!" Lieutenant Dorn shouted. *"Mr. Data!"*

The android noticed her for the first time and said, "Computer, hold!"

Everything suddenly came to a standstill. The men hauling the guns up froze, bent over, in the act. The ship stopped rolling and pitching. The wind was gone. The handsome, blond captain stood, immobile, with his arm held out to his crew and his teeth flashing in a dazzling grin.

"Forgive me, Lieutenant," Data said, coming down the steps to meet her. "I did not see you come in."

Lieutenant Dorn stood looking up at him, soaked to the skin, her hair plastered down against her face. She shook her head. "Mr. Data, what *is* all this?"

"It is a new program I have assembled, designed to simulate a pirate sailing vessel circa Earth's Spanish Main in the early seventeen-hundreds," Data replied, as he came down to the main deck.

"But . . . *why?*"

"I was attempting to understand something of the psychology of freebooters, or pirates, as they are otherwise known," Data replied. "I was not due to relieve Commander La Forge in directing the repairs for another four hours, so I decided to take advantage of the opportunity to do some research." He looked her over, up and down. "Forgive me, Lieutenant, but it seems I have inadvertently caused you to get wet."

"It's all right," she said. "I can change into my spare uniform. But you certainly seem to go in for realism in your programs."

"I wanted to capture the authenticity of the experience," Data explained.

"Yes, but . . . *this?* Not that it isn't fascinating, but why wind-driven sailing vessels in the seventeen-hundreds?"

"According to our historical data banks, the time period from 1692 to 1725 was considered the height of the age of piracy," Data replied, "when freebooters such as Blackbeard, Calico Jack Rackam, Captain Kidd, and Henry Morgan plied the seas in sailing vessels such as the one I have re-created here. At no other time in Earth's history, either before or since, has piracy been practiced to such an extent as it was during that brief period."

"Which one was he?" asked Dorn, indicating the dashing, handsome blond captain.

"Actually, he is none of the ones I mentioned," Data replied, "as our data banks do not contain any physical representations of those people. I have taken his likeness from that of an actor who once played the role of a fictional pirate in a cinematic production."

Dorn raised her eyebrows appreciatively as she gazed at the frozen pirate captain. "He must have been a very handsome actor," she said. "But I'm still not sure I understand how all this pertains to our current situation."

"Perhaps it does not accurately reflect the conditions of our current mission," Data said, "but our data banks contain little information concerning the lifestyles of modern freebooters. It is a rare phenomenon these days. However, a great deal had been written about piracy in this particular time period, and while historical conditions are subject to change, I have found that human psychology remains relatively consistent. I thought that by creating this program, I might gain some insight into the personality and motivations of Captain Blaze. Computer, cancel program."

The images around them disappeared, replaced by the darkness of the holodeck, illuminated by its electronic gridwork.

"It's an interesting idea," Dorn said, as Data walked her to the door. "And did you? Learn anything, that is."

"It would seem that greed was a significant motivating factor for these individuals," Data replied, "but it would also appear that the element of risk played an important part, as well."

Several crewmen glanced at them curiously as they walked down the corridor, Data dressed in his piratical costume and Lieutenant Dorn in her soaking wet uniform.

"I have never fully understood it," Data continued as they walked, "but many humans seem to have a desire for what they call adventure, the threat of danger coupled with the challenge of the unknown, which seems to appeal to the human competitive instinct. Many sporting activities that humans engage in incorporate these elements, but then piracy would certainly not qualify as a sporting activity. It seems quite puzzling."

"Why wouldn't it qualify?" she asked.

Data cocked his head and frowned slightly, to indicate confusion. "Because it is a criminal activity," he said. "That is not the same thing."

"You might find it helpful to consult your programming on the subject of aberrant human psychology, Mr. Data," Dorn replied, as they reached the turbolift and stepped inside. "Deck 6," she said. "To certain types of so-called abnormal personalities, criminal activity often takes on the aspect of a competitive sport. The challenge is committing the crime and getting away with it, because it entails not only the risk—or adventure, if you will—involved in the commission of the crime itself, but competition with the authorities, who represent the laws of society. Such people see themselves as being above the law, or outside it."

"I see," said Data. "You are referring to the sociopathic personality."

"That would be one example," Dorn said, "but there are others, less extreme, such as those who are socially maladjusted and resentful, or who consider themselves somehow superior to most members of society."

"You mean the megalomaniac personality," said Data.

"Precisely," Dorn replied.

"And in which category do you feel Captain Blaze belongs?"

The turbolift reached Deck 6 and they stepped out into the corridor.

"To the latter one, I should think," Dorn said. "At least, based on what I've learned of him so far. His ego is certainly a large one."

"I see," said Data. "Then you believe his attack on the *Enterprise* was motivated by his competitive instinct, coupled with his belief in his own superiority?"

"That would be my guess," she said, as they reached the door to her quarters.

"I should let you change," said Data. "Perhaps we can continue this discussion at another time. I find it very enlightening."

"So do I," Dorn said, with a smile. "Why don't you come in? We can talk some more while I change."

"I would not wish to intrude upon your privacy," said Data.

"You're not intruding," she replied. "Come on in." As he came in behind her and the door closed, she smiled and chuckled. "After all, I think I can trust you, right?"

"To do what?" asked Data.

"To, um, behave like a gentleman," she said, as she started to remove her wet uniform.

"Ah," said Data. "If I understand correctly, you are making what is known as a veiled reference in a sexual context."

Dorn tossed her uniform blouse on the bed and started to remove her undershirt. "Your programming covers that, does it?"

"I have extensive programmed knowledge of the mechanics of human sexual behavior," Data said. "And I am designed to be fully functional in that regard."

Dorn paused in the act of pulling off her undershirt. "You *are?*"

"Yes. Completely."

"You mean . . . that is . . . have you ever actually . . . uh . . . you know."

"Engaged in sexual activity? Yes, indeed," said Data.

Lieutenant Dorn pulled her undershirt back down. "You *have?*"

"I found it very interesting," said Data, "but as I am not capable of feelings, I believe that I did not extract the maximum benefit from the experience."

"Oh," Lieutenant Dorn said, somewhat a loss for words.

At that moment, there was a signal on Data's communicator. "Picard to Data."

"Data here, sir."

"Have you seen Lieutenant Dorn, Mr. Data?"

"Yes, sir. I am presently with the lieutenant in her quarters. She is currently removing her uniform."

"I *beg* your pardon?" said Picard.

Lieutenant Dorn covered her eyes with one hand and said, "Oh, boy."

"Have I said something wrong?" asked Data, with concern.

"Lieutenant Dorn here, Captain," she said, quickly. "I was with Commander Data on the holodeck and there was a slight mishap with some water. My uniform got soaked and I needed a dry change of clothing."

"Ah. I see," said Picard, sounding somewhat relieved. "Well, I would appreciate your presence in the starbase main briefing room as soon as you have changed, Lieutenant."

"I'll be right there, sir."

"Very well. Picard out."

She glanced at Data. "Perhaps it would be better if I changed in private, Mr. Data."

"Certainly. As you wish."

The door closed behind him. She sighed and shook her head, then quickly finished changing, dried her hair off, and hurried to the starbase briefing room.

The others were engaged in a discussion when she arrived, and she noticed that they were consulting maps and background files projected on the briefing room viewscreen.

"Ah, Lieutenant," said Picard, when she came in, "good of you to come so soon. I trust your mishap on the holodeck was not serious?"

"No, sir. I was merely soaked."

"What exactly happened?" asked Picard, curiously.

She quickly told them about Data's pirate simulation program.

Picard smiled. "I've always found it prudent to signal Mr. Data first before entering the holodeck while he's engaged in one of his programmed simulations," he said. "With Mr. Data, you never know what you're liable to be walking into."

"It certainly was interesting," Lieutenant Dorn said. "It really did look quite authentic. I felt as if I were surrounded by genuine pirates."

"Funny you should say that, Lieutenant," Riker replied. "How would you like to try it for real?"

She looked at him with a puzzled frown. "Sir?"

"Lieutenant Dorn," Picard said, "during your intelligence-gathering activities, have you ever actually spent any time on the surface of D'rahl?"

"No, sir, I have not. As senior base security officer, I had additional responsibilities aboard the starbase."

"So then how did you gather your intelligence?" Picard asked.

"I had dispatched some of my security personnel to gather intelligence in the field, sir. With rather limited success, I might add. Additionally, I consulted all available data banks, both here aboard the starbase and on Artemis VI, and I assigned several of my staff to interview officers aboard civilian merchant vessels that had been attacked by freebooters, as well as those who had spent any time on the surface of D'rahl."

"I see," Picard said. "In other words, there would be no one on the surface of D'rahl who knew you by sight? Think carefully, Lieutenant."

She shook her head. "No, sir. I have never been down on the surface. Of D'rahl, that is. I attended a formal reception on N'trahn once, and I have been down to Artemis VI, but otherwise I have confined my activities to the starbase."

"What about communications?" asked Picard. "Have you ever communicated by viewscreen with anyone on the surface of D'rahl? Again, Lieutenant, think very carefully."

She paused a moment, thinking. "No, sir." Suddenly, she realized what he was getting at. "Captain, am I to understand that I am being considered for some sort of undercover, intelligence-gathering assignment on D'rahl?"

"'Considered' is the operative word, Lieutenant," said Picard. "I have discussed it with Captain Gruzinov and my senior officers, and we all agree that this assignment should be strictly voluntary. It could entail some personal risk, so no one would hold it against you if you should—"

"I accept, sir."

Picard raised his eyebrows. "You have not yet heard the details of the assignment."

"It makes no difference, Captain," she said. "If my qualifications make me the logical candidate, then I accept. What would you like me to do, sir?"

"You are quite certain that no one knows you on D'rahl?"

"Quite certain, sir."

"Good," Picard said. He snapped his fingers. "Wait . . . what about that reception you attended on N'trahn? Was there anyone from D'rahl in attendance? Governor T'grayn, perhaps?"

"Governor T'grayn was in attendance, sir, but we were never introduced. Lowly security officers do not get to meet colonial governors. We never spoke and I only saw him from a distance, sir. I am quite sure my face would mean nothing to him."

"Excellent," Picard said. "What do you think, Number One?"

"She knows a great deal more about the K'trall than any of us do, sir," Riker replied. "My only reservation was that she might be recognized."

"Lieutenant," said Picard, "I would like you to take part in an undercover assignment on D'rahl. You will be working with Commander Riker and Lieutenant Commander La Forge. Your mission will be to pass yourselves off as freelance merchant spacers in search of crew positions on a new ship. We shall take some pains to give you a somewhat disreputable background."

"I can assist with that, sir," Dorn said. "I could easily arrange for one of the outbound merchant captains who's been hit by Blaze to back us up on that one. We could make it look as if we've been discharged for dereliction of duty, or something even more serious, if necessary."

"Good," Picard said. "Make it so. And we will prepare fake dossiers and papers to back up the deception. Lieutenant Commander Data, Lieutenant Worf, and Counselor Troi will beam down to D'rahl as an official landing party charged with conducting an investigation. They will touch base with the local authorities and remind them that we have Overlord J'drahn's support for our efforts in this regard. However, while they will be actively conducting an investigation in cooperation with local authorities, they will also be functioning to distract attention from Commander Riker's team, which will be working independently.

"While we are in orbit over D'rahl," Picard continued, "we will conduct detailed sensor scans of the planet surface and the surrounding area. Blaze cannot land his ship, so he must be keeping it concealed somewhere in this sector. If he is cloaked, and in orbit with his main engines disengaged, our sensors will be unable to detect him. But he must be resupplying from somewhere on the planet. We shall try to find his base from orbit, if possible. In the meantime, we shall have two teams conducting a search on the planet surface, one openly, one undercover. That way, if the local authorities attempt to hinder one team's investigation, the other will be able to proceed unimpeded."

"I understand, sir," Lieutenant Dorn said. "And if I may say so, sir, it sounds like an excellent plan of operation."

"Thank you, Lieutenant. Let us hope the execution is equally excellent," said Picard. "I would like you to start working with Commander Riker immediately to prepare your cover identities. As soon as Lieutenant Commander La Forge is satisfied that the repairs are proceeding accordingly, I will assign Mr. Data to relieve him and he will join you."

"May I ask a question, sir?"

"Ask, Lieutenant."

"Why Mr. La Forge, sir? With all due respect to Lieutenant Commander La Forge, surely a security officer would be better qualified for such an assignment than an engineer."

"Under ordinary circumstances, Lieutenant, I would agree with you," Picard said. "But this is a rather extraordinary situation. We need to find out exactly what sort of drives are powering the *Glory*. And if they are Romulan drives, as seems to be the case, we need to know how they were modified. Mr.

La Forge would be the most qualified officer aboard the *Enterprise* to ascertain those facts. Engineers talk to other engineers, and with a ship as unusual as the *Glory,* surely someone must have heard something. D'rahl is a liberty port, and I want your team to mingle as much as possible. Particularly among the more disreputable merchant spacers. Blaze has to recruit his crews from somewhere. Freelance spacers are a rough-and-tumble lot. They might hesitate to speak with Starfleet personnel, but not with other freelance spacers."

"I understand, sir," Lieutenant Dorn said. "And I appreciate your confidence in my abilities."

"Thank your commanding officer," Picard said. "Captain Gruzinov speaks very highly of you. That's good enough for me. Very well, this briefing is dismissed. Let's get to work."

Chapter Three

GOVERNOR T'GRAYN RECEIVED THEM in the rotunda of the State Palace in the capital city of K'trin. As Picard and the other members of the landing party crossed the wide, circular meeting hall, T'grayn waddled out to meet them, accompanied by his entourage. *Waddled* was the only word to describe the way he walked, Picard thought. The governor was immense, and in his loose-fitting white robes, he looked like a tent coming toward them.

"Ah, Captain Picard!" he said, holding out his hands as he approached. "It is an honor, sir, truly an honor! Allow me to welcome you and your illustrious party to our fair city!"

"Thank you, Governor," Picard said. "I appreciate your seeing us on such short notice."

"Short notice? Short notice? Why, everyone in the Empire is aware by now that a Federation starship has arrived! News travels fast, even here in

the colonies. We have completely modern communications, you know. Yes, yes, we knew of your
arrival, but we scarcely expected to be honored by a
formal visit! May I offer you and your party some
refreshment, Captain?" He clapped his chubby
hands, and a member of his entourage came forth
with a tray holding what appeared to be some sort
of globule-shaped fruit.

"No, thank you, Governor," Picard said. "May I
have the honor to present my officers? Lieutenant
Worf, chief of security, and ship's counselor
Deanna Troi."

"Such a distinguished retinue!" T'grayn said,
barely glancing at them. "You are sure I cannot
tempt you? These really are delicious." He picked
one of the globules up between a thumb and
forefinger and popped it in his mouth. Purple juice
dribbled down his chin as he bit into it, and
instantly, a member of his entourage stepped up
with a cloth to wipe his face before he could dribble
on his robes. Worf grimaced with distaste at the
sight. "Oh, and at the absolute peak of ripeness!"
said T'grayn, his face transported with ecstasy.
"Really, Captain, you should try just one!"

"Thank you, Governor, perhaps another time,"
Picard said.

"Pity, pity," said T'grayn, with an elaborate
shrug. "You really don't know what you're missing.
Ah, well, I shall not press you. Not everyone's
tastes are the same. Come, come," he said, beckoning as he turned, "we shall talk out in the garden. It
is such a pleasant day. And the *talla* vines are in full

bloom. A spectacular display, truly spectacular. And, ah, the scent of them! It surpasses description!"

"This is the governor of this entire planet?" said Worf, with disbelief, as they followed T'grayn and his retinue out into the garden. "He cannot even govern his own appetite!"

"Softly, Mr. Worf," said Picard. "We do not need to antagonize him. We merely need to secure his official cooperation, whether he follows through on it or not."

Worf growled softly, but said nothing, clearly disgusted.

The garden was, indeed, spectacular. They walked out through an archway onto a path of glazed, hand-laid brick that wound through several acres of lushly planted foliage. It was a gigantic greenhouse, covered by a clear dome, and the temperature inside was hot and oppressive. Fronds more than six feet across draped over the pathway, providing some shade, and flowers with huge, sickly-sweet-smelling blooms proliferated everywhere. Worf wrinkled his nose at the smell. They followed the governor and his entourage down the path to a circular plaza with a fountain that had carved stone benches placed around it. T'grayn chose a bench and sat with a contented sigh, fanning himself slightly with a chubby, beringed hand. Immediately, two attendants with large, feathered fans on poles materialized and began fanning him gently.

"Ah," T'grayn sighed, with contentment. "Now

isn't that much better? My garden is my pride and joy, you know. I personally picked out all the plants myself. It is always so deliciously fragrant here." Someone appeared at his side with another tray, containing what looked like a pile of small crystals. T'grayn took several and popped them in his mouth. He closed his eyes and sighed again. "Do at least try one of these, Captain," he said. "They are called *kanna* crystals. They dissolve slowly in your mouth and fill you with a wonderful, cool, tingling sensation. Too many and one can get quite intoxicated, you know, but the sensation is delightful."

"No, thank you very much, Governor," Picard said, waving aside the proffered tray. "We really do not wish to take up much of your time."

"Yes, yes, there are so many demands upon my time," said T'grayn, wearily. "Still, it is not every day a Federation starship captain pays me a visit. Most of the dignitaries call on the overlord at N'trahn. Sadly, they don't pay very much attention to us out here in the colonies."

"Well, we did pay our respects to Overlord J'drahn, but I also considered it important to pay a call of courtesy on you, as well, Governor," Picard said. "D'rahl is an important planet. N'trahn may be the K'tralli homeworld, and a beautiful world it is, but D'rahl is a major shipping center and K'trin a thriving port city. As such, it bears great importance for the Federation."

"Yes, yes, we are always so busy here," T'grayn said, with a dismissive wave. "There is no end to all the aggravation. So much traffic, so much business, so many things to see to. I scarcely have any time to myself at all."

"Yes, Governor, we realize you must be very busy," Picard said, keeping a straight face, "so I shall get directly to the point. We have been dispatched here to assist the commander of Starbase 37 with the problem posed by the freebooters in this sector."

"Oh, yes, how very tiresome," said T'grayn, with an expression of distaste. "Freebooters, freebooters, that is all Captain Gruzinov ever seems to talk about. You would think I had nothing else to do but drop everything and concentrate on his problems alone. As if I could do anything about the freebooters! I have no ships with which to pursue them! Here we have only small transports and merchant vessels. The K'tralli fleet is under the direct authority of Overlord J'drahn, and he assures me that everything in their power is already being done to address this vexatious problem. I honestly don't see what more *I* could do. I do hope you understand that, Captain."

"Yes, of course," Picard said. "Doubtless, you have many more problems taking up your limited time."

"It is not as if I am unsympathetic, after all," T'grayn said. "But I understand these freebooters are well armed, and one of them even has a cloaking device! Can you imagine! How could my small and lightly armed patrol vessels stop a ship they cannot even *see?*"

"Precisely, Governor," Picard said. "Which is

why Starfleet has dispatched us to assist you with this problem. A cloaking device in the possession of a freebooter like Captain Blaze is an alarming development, indeed, and raises the likely possibility of Romulan involvement."

"Captain Blaze, Captain Blaze, I am sick and tired of hearing about Captain Blaze! He is the bane of my existence! Who knows where Blaze got his infernal cloaking device? Perhaps he got it from the Klingons. They also possess cloaking device technology, do they not? And there is no telling *what* Klingons would do!" He popped two more crystals, apparently oblivious to the fact that he had just insulted Picard's chief of security. Worf stiffened, but at a sharp glance from Picard, kept his peace with an obvious effort. "Ah! Delicious! I truly wish there was something more that I could do to be of help with this annoying freebooter situation, but they plague the shipping lanes in space, and I have my hands full with problems on D'rahl, as it is. I am limited in my resources, after all."

"I understand entirely," said Picard. "Which is why I have instructed my investigative team to use their own resources and avoid troubling you with their work."

T'grayn frowned. "Investigative team?"

"Overlord J'drahn has assured me of his complete support in our efforts to apprehend the freebooters," said Picard, "so I was not going to trouble you with any unreasonable requests. I realize you are a very busy man, Governor, and Overlord

J'drahn has already officially granted his approval. However, I did feel it was incumbent upon me, given your esteemed position, to call upon you formally in this regard before we began our work."

"I see, I see," T'grayn said, looking a bit distracted. "What sort of work?"

"Well, D'rahl is a center for commerce in this sector," said Picard. "And as such, the city of K'trin sees a great deal of merchant traffic. I thought it might be helpful to assign an investigative team to conduct interviews with some of the transient merchant crews, as well as local businesspeople and perhaps some of your law-enforcement personnel, in an effort to gather information that could help us learn something more about these freebooters."

"Yes, yes, I understand," T'grayn said. "But I was under the impression that Captain Gruzinov had already conducted a similar sort of investigation."

"Indeed, he has, Governor," Picard replied, "but I fear that it has not yielded any significant results."

"Well then, I fail to see the point in repeating the entire dreary process," said T'grayn, with a frown.

"Perhaps it would be merely a duplication of effort, Governor," Picard replied, "and it may well produce no better results, but I have my own superiors to answer to and they shall want to see reports that every possible effort was made to conduct a thorough investigation. I must at least go through the motions, purely as a matter of form, you understand. We cannot remain in this sector indefinitely, after all, and I am anxious to get my ship back out on patrol. That is where I feel we have the best chance of success."

"Yes, I see, I see," T'grayn replied. "Well, do whatever you feel you must, Captain Picard. I will see to it that our law-enforcement officials are advised of your effort and extend their fullest cooperation." He clapped his hands and spoke to a member of his entourage. "See to it that Captain Picard receives whatever he requires."

"Thank you very much, indeed, Governor," Picard replied. "And now we really have taken up enough of your time. I do appreciate your seeing us."

"My pleasure, Captain, my pleasure. Do feel free to call upon us again."

"Thank you, Governor, you are most kind. Oh, there is one other small matter. I understand that the distinguished Colonel Z'gral, a hero of the K'tralli revolution who was instrumental in the signing of the treaty leading to your membership in the Federation, resides here in K'trin. I would be remiss in my duties if I did not pay a call on him as a courtesy."

"Regrettably, Captain, Colonel Z'gral is in very poor health these days," T'grayn replied, "and is not receiving any visitors. It would be quite a strain on him, at his age, and he has requested that his desire for privacy be respected. I am sure you will understand. He is one of the Empire's leading citizens, and has devoted a lifetime of service to our people. It is the very least that we can do to allow him to live out his final days in the peaceful solitude he craves. However, I will be certain to pass on your respects to him."

"Thank you, Governor, I understand, of course," Picard said. "And now we really must be going. You have been most accommodating. I will be sure to mention that in my report."

T'grayn inclined his head and made a grand gesture with his hand. "It was my pleasure, Captain Picard. I am always glad to be of assistance to the Federation."

As they left, Worf growled deep in his throat. "That man will be about as much use to us as a phaser to a Denebian slug!"

"Which is about what I expected, Mr. Worf," Picard said. "What did you make of him, Counselor?"

"A most unappealing man, Captain," Troi replied, "and thoroughly duplicitous. He was not at all pleased to learn of our presence here, and even less pleased at the idea of our conducting an investigation. I distinctly sensed that he saw it as a threat. However, his concern seemed to abate somewhat when you told him that you merely had to go through it as a matter of form, for the sake of your reports."

"Yes, I thought that would be wise," Picard said. "If he thinks that we are only going through the motions here, and counting on stopping the free-booters in space, he may be lulled into a false sense of security."

"Perhaps, Captain," Troi replied, "but despite his manner, he is a devious individual. When he told you that Colonel Z'gral was in poor health and did not wish to receive any visitors, I sensed it was a lie."

"I thought as much," Picard said. "However, I was in no position to press the issue. The important thing is that we received his official sanction to conduct our investigation. Were you able to get all that, Mr. Data?"

"Loud and clear, Captain," Data replied, from the ship.

Worf glanced at Picard with surprise. "Your communicator was active the whole time?"

"Yes, Mr. Worf. We now have recordings of both my conversations with Overlord J'drahn *and* Governor T'grayn."

"So they will not be able to protest that you interfered and conducted an investigation without their prior approval," Troi said. She smiled. "Very clever, Captain."

"I, too, can be devious, Counselor," Picard replied. "And I was very careful not to state what sort of investigation it would be, or how many people would be involved."

"So the governor's approval could be construed to apply to Commander Riker's undercover team, as well," said Troi.

"He did say, 'Do whatever you feel you must,' and that was a direct quote," Picard replied. "I would interpret that as a carte blanche, Counselor.

We may be walking a rather fine line here, but since T'grayn is not telling us everything, I see no reason to be completely candid with him, either."

No sooner had they left the garden than an abrupt change came over Governor T'grayn. He clapped his hands and dismissed his entourage, and his expression grew very serious as his eyes narrowed and he swore softly under his breath. He reached into the folds of his robe and withdrew a Romulan communicator. "You heard?" he said.

Footsteps sounded behind him on the path. "Yes, I heard," said the figure who stepped into the plaza. Physically, he resembled a K'tralli, but his Romulan military uniform labeled him as something else entirely.

"He could be trouble," said T'grayn.

"A Galaxy-class starship is always trouble," said the Romulan. "But trouble can be dealt with."

"Must you wear that uniform?" T'grayn said, tensely. "Your presence here is risky enough as it is."

"With a Federation starship in orbit above this planet, if I am caught in civilian garb or K'tralli uniform, I could be executed as a spy."

"The Federation does not execute its prisoners," T'grayn replied.

"So they claim," the Romulan replied. "I have no intention of finding out for sure firsthand. If something should go wrong and I am captured, it will be as a Romulan military officer."

"And if you are captured as a Romulan military

officer, it could mean war," T'grayn said. "This Captain Picard is nobody's fool. He wanted to see Z'gral."

"You handled that very well," the Romulan replied.

"A call of courtesy," T'grayn said, scornfully. "A likely story! I see Gruzinov's hand in this. He must have told Picard that Z'gral is the only one who would stand a chance of convincing H'druhn of J'drahn's involvement with the freebooters. I know what Picard's after, but I could not very well refuse to let him conduct his investigation. Especially since he has already secured J'drahn's approval. And J'drahn could hardly have withheld it, under the circumstances. This Captain Picard is a more skillful manipulator than Gruzinov. I should have had Z'gral eliminated a long time ago."

"That could easily be arranged," the Romulan said. "Z'gral is old and has not appeared in public for a long time. You have already circulated stories about his supposed ill health. Death at his age would not appear untimely."

T'grayn compressed his lips into a tight grimace. "It must be handled quietly and efficiently," he said. "If I am tied to Z'gral's death, it would mean the end of me."

"Trust me," said the Romulan. "I will see to it. Have you heard from Blaze?"

"Yes, blast him for a fool!" T'grayn said, viciously. "He attacked the *Enterprise* and compounded his mistake by suffering damage to his own ship. He said some of the drive components were badly damaged and will have to be replaced. He barely managed to escape. And how are we going to resupply him now, with the *Enterprise* here?"

"Leave that to me," the Romulan said. "This possibility was foreseen. Blaze will not be out of action very long."

"The longer he is out of action, the better I will like it," said T'grayn. "The other freebooters have all suspended operations while the *Enterprise* is here, but Blaze is impossible to control. I told him to keep out of sight until the *Enterprise* departs, and he just laughed at me. At *me!*"

"Blaze is the sole reason the *Enterprise* is here," the Romulan said. "Picard will not leave until he has either captured Blaze's ship or else destroyed it."

"So then what are we to do?"

"Send Blaze back out to finish what he started," said the Romulan.

"Are you mad? You want him to destroy the *Enterprise?* Do you realize what that would mean? They would only send more ships to replace it! Besides, Blaze has never destroyed a ship. He cripples them and loots them."

"If he were to cripple the *Enterprise,* I certainly would not object," the Romulan said.

"And what if Picard should cripple him, instead? If he were to capture the *Glory,* then Blaze would implicate me!"

"And you would doubtless implicate J'drahn," the Romulan replied. "And me. I have no illusions about your keeping heroically silent, T'grayn. But if

Blaze were to cripple the *Enterprise* and take her, it would give us access to all the secrets and technology of the most potent weapon in the Federation's arsenal. A Galaxy-class starship would be quite a prize, indeed."

"On the other hand, if Blaze is captured, our involvement will surely be exposed!"

"True. But the Federation is weak. They shall not go to war over this. They will not be able to remove J'drahn from power, because their own Prime Directive would prohibit it, so they will have no choice but to expel him from the Federation. And then J'drahn will turn to us, for without the backing of the Federation, he could not survive. The K'tralli sector will become part of the Romulan Empire, and the boundaries of the Neutral Zone will be extended to cover it. Either way, we cannot lose."

"But *I* could lose!" T'grayn said, with dismay. "I could lose everything!"

"You should have thought of that before you decided to support the freebooters for your own gain," the Romulan replied. "You are in this much too deeply to back out now, T'grayn."

"But there is still H'druhn," T'grayn said. "He does not believe his son capable of corruption, but if it were proven beyond a doubt, and the K'tralli Empire faced expulsion from the Federation, H'druhn himself would remove J'drahn from power, for the good of the Empire."

"That would, indeed, be unfortunate for you," the Romulan replied. "If H'druhn were to return to power, or name a successor to replace J'drahn, then the K'tralli Empire would remain in the Federation, which means that J'drahn and his accomplices would be punished according to their crimes. However, I do not think J'drahn would go so easily, and General H'druhn is old. His death, like Colonel Z'gral's, would not seem at all untimely."

"You are talking about the assassination of the most revered figure in the Empire!" said T'grayn, in a low voice. "That is not the same thing as eliminating Colonel Z'gral! Z'gral is here, and under our control. H'druhn is on N'trahn, and protected by his own guard!"

"That is not my problem," said the Romulan.

"Surely, you cannot be suggesting that *I* . . . ?" T'grayn's voice trailed off as he stared at the Romulan with disbelief.

"It would make no difference to me how it was done. You are the one with the most to lose, T'grayn. You and your partner in crime, J'drahn. He would be the most logical choice to carry it out. I am sure you could convince him of the necessity."

"But . . . his own *father?*"

"If H'druhn is everything you say he is, then he would be no less sparing of his own son," the Romulan replied. "Especially considering the extent of his betrayal. J'drahn knows that perfectly well. Why else would he have gone along with imprisoning Colonel Z'gral?"

"But suppose the Federation does not expel J'drahn?" T'grayn asked. "They have a starbase in this sector, after all, and the colony on Artemis VI. To keep them out of Romulan hands, they might be willing to pardon him and merely impose some sort of sanctions."

"I am afraid they would not have that option," the Romulan replied. "Open acknowledgment of J'drahn's involvement with the Romulan Empire would mandate his expulsion, according to their own laws. They could not depose him and violate their Prime Directive, the very foundation on which the Federation stands, nor could they pardon him, for that would violate their own Federation Accords and render them meaningless. Expulsion would be the only choice left to them, whether they liked it or not. And we would graciously allow them time to move their starbase and evacuate Artemis VI."

"By the gods! You have planned all this from the beginning!" said T'grayn.

"Of course," the Romulan replied. "And very carefully, too."

"You have played me for a fool," T'grayn said, bitterly. "And J'drahn, as well."

"You and J'drahn have played yourselves for fools. It was merely your own greed that made you think our motivations were similar to yours. We did not go to so much trouble and expense merely for a percentage of the profits in your freebooting operation."

"No, your ambition was considerably greater," said T'grayn. "You were after the whole Empire. And you accuse me and J'drahn of greed?"

"What I have done, T'grayn, I have done for the glory of the Romulan Empire. What you and

J'drahn have done was line your own pockets, and in the process, you have sold out your own people. However, I shall not be ungrateful. For my efforts, I stand to be appointed military governor of the K'tralli Empire, and I shall need pliable administrators. You and J'drahn will have secure positions that will enable you to maintain your decadent lifestyles. You may keep your odoriferous garden, stuff yourself to your heart's content, and administer Romulan law on D'rahl. Your people will not love you for it, but then again, they never did, did they?"

The final mission briefing was always the most important, thought Picard as he strode briskly down the corridor. It was the last opportunity to pick up on anything that might somehow have been overlooked. It was not the first time crew members of the *Enterprise* would be functioning in an undercover capacity to gather information, but it was still an uncommon sort of assignment. He always worried about them. And this time, several missions would be proceeding simultaneously.

Lieutenant Worf and Counselor Troi had already had their final briefing and beamed down to the surface of D'rahl, along with three crew members from ship's security. Picard would have liked to send more, but they were supposed to be an investigative team dispatched to work with local authorities that were ostensibly cooperative. Picard felt that sending a larger landing party might make it appear as if he didn't trust T'grayn. Of course, he didn't, but it had to appear as if he did, even if Governor T'grayn had no illusions on that score. It was all a complicated dance, a dumb show of diplomacy where no one said what he really meant and everyone had his own hidden agenda.

Now it was time for Riker's team to beam down. Picard was a great deal more concerned about them than he was about Worf and Troi's team. T'grayn would make sure that they were safe. He would also try his best to make sure they didn't learn anything of substance, which was why Picard had sent Deanna Troi along. He could count on her to sense any deception, and the K'trall did not realize she was half Betazoid, with empathic abilities. But T'grayn would make sure that nothing happened to them.

On the other hand, Riker's team was going in without any safeguards at all, and they would be circulating in the most dangerous areas of D'rahl's capital city. Merchant spacers were a tough and unruly lot, and many merchant captains were not too particular about who they recruited for their crews. The merchant space fleet had become a refuge for all sorts of borderline personalities— people who were fleeing from their troubles, social malcontents, hardened adventurers, even criminals who had gone to space to escape the authorities on their homeworlds. Taking on a fugitive from justice to serve aboard a merchant ship was a violation of the Federation Maritime Code, but even the best-intentioned merchant captains could be fooled by cleverly forged papers. Some simply didn't care, so long as they could claim that they'd been fooled.

Liberty ports were often tough, freewheeling cities, and if law-enforcement efforts were lax, the neighborhoods where spacers went to unwind often attracted crime. Transient spacers were often easy pickings for muggers and prostitutes, con artists and gambling sharks who knew the territory better than they did. And in many liberty port cities, the local authorities had enough to worry about just with keeping order. If a transient spacer got in trouble, he usually had to fend for himself. And given what he already knew of Governor T'grayn, Picard was fairly sure that local law enforcement was likely to be as corrupt as the administration.

Riker and his party were already waiting in the transporter room when he arrived. They were all dressed in navy blue, like merchant spacefleet officers, but since uniform requirements in the merchant fleet were never observed too strictly, Riker had wisely chosen to personalize their costumes somewhat. They all wore short black boots and blue trousers and shirts, but Riker also wore a short black leather jacket with a wide, open collar and epaulets. He had various merchant fleet patches sewn to it, some identifying ships, others ports of call, and he also had the name STRYKER painted in military block letters over the left breast pocket of the jacket. He had combed his hair differently, as well. He usually brushed it up and back, but now it was more casual, parted on the side and down over his forehead.

La Forge had opted for a dark blue, loose-fitting tech's utility jacket with numerous pockets, just the sort of thing a Merchant Spacefleet engineer would favor, and Lieutenant Dorn had on a brown, Klingon-style armored vest. She had also let her hair down, and wore it in a loose ponytail.

"Well, what do you think?" Riker asked, as Picard looked them over.

Picard shook his head. "You look like three of the sorriest space bums I've ever seen," he said. "On D'rahl, you should fit right in."

"That was the general idea," Riker said. "We're carrying merchant fleet issue communicators, so we won't have anything on us that could be traced to Starfleet."

"What about phasers?" asked Picard.

"I thought about that," Riker said. "But merchant spacers aren't equipped with phasers, and K'tralli law prohibits the carrying of energy weapons without proper authorization. Despite the temptation to carry them concealed, I didn't want to ask for trouble with the authorities. They would also blow our cover if we had to use them. So we're leaving them behind."

Picard nodded. "Yes, that's probably wise," he said. "But I'm not at ease about you beaming down without any weapons at all."

"I didn't say we were doing that," said Riker. Lieutenant Dorn pulled out a wicked-looking alloy knuckleduster, and Geordi had a stun rod. Riker pulled aside his jacket, revealing a huge knife in a leather sheath.

"Good Lord. Is that a *bowie* knife?" Picard said, with astonishment.

"I had it replicated," Riker said. "I think it's the sort of thing my character would wear."

"Your character?"

"Lieutenant Dorn and I created cover identities for each of us, with papers to match," said Riker. "We all chose names reasonably close to our own, so it would be easier responding to them. I'm Lieutenant Bill Stryker, graduate of the Merchant Spacefleet Academy, formerly executive officer aboard the merchant ship *Phoenix,* which called in at Artemis VI two weeks ago and departed for Mars yesterday morning. Geordi's cover identity is Chief George LaBeau, ship's engineer . . ."

"Yo," said Geordi.

". . . and Lieutenant Dorn is Warrant Officer Angie Thorn, a supply officer with a medical rating. We all served together on the *Phoenix,* but were caught stealing ship's stores, selling them, and altering supply records. We were exposed when we got greedy and started diverting cargo, claiming it was damaged and faking insurance reports. Rather than go through the time-consuming process of filing formal charges and all the attendant paperwork, the captain simply had us thrown off his ship when we reached Artemis VI. We managed to hustle a transport ride to D'rahl, and now we're looking for a new berth. If anyone checks our records with either the starbase or the Merchant Spacefleet data banks, that's what will come up. Under the circumstances we've created for ourselves, no legitimate ship's captain would touch us with a ten-foot pole. But having some larceny in our background might make us acceptable to freebooters and black marketeers."

"It sounds like a good cover," said Picard, nodding. "Very well thought out. How do you intend to proceed?"

"We'll be beaming down to a landing strip just outside K'trin," said Riker. "Most of the shuttle landing zones are on the south side of the city, near the warehouse district. That's where all the action's going to be. We'll check in with the Merchant Spacefleet Union office, be told that there's not much chance of our signing on with another ship anytime soon, given our records, and then we'll hit the Combat Zone and start cruising the spacer bars to see if we can turn up anything. In other words, we're going to go through all the motions that people in our situation could be expected to go through. Meanwhile, we'll keep our eyes and ears open and see what we can learn."

"Excellent," Picard said. "Make sure to check in on a periodic basis."

"I've already arranged that with Data," Riker said. "We'll be reporting in at regular intervals."

"Isn't there a risk of being exposed if you use unguarded Merchant Spacefleet frequencies?" Picard asked.

"I've already thought of that, sir," said La Forge.

"I've altered these communicators so that they are capable of broadcasting on a coded Starfleet frequency in addition to their regular channels. Short of actually taking them apart, no one should be able to tell the difference."

"Well, you seem to have covered all the bases," said Picard. "Good luck. And be careful."

"We will, sir," Riker said. They stepped up on the transporter pads. "Energize," said Riker.

Picard watched as their shimmering forms faded from view. He took a deep breath. Well, now both teams had been dispatched. So far, things were proceeding well, but it was still early in the game. Now it was time for him to play his part, and it was potentially even more risky than what Riker's team was doing. He would have to penetrate K'tralli security and see Colonel Z'gral.

Chapter Four

AFTER BEAMING DOWN to an isolated location near a shuttle landing strip, Riker, La Forge, and Dorn made their way to the spaceport buildings and the office of the Merchant Spacefleet Union. In a busy spaceport city like K'trin, there were always openings for crew members listed with the union. Merchant spacers were a transient lot, and few of them ever stayed with the same ship for very long. However, when the union secretary brought up their carefully manufactured records on his monitor, he simply looked at the screen for a long moment, then slowly raised his eyes to Riker.

"This . . . uh . . . last evaluation," he said, clearing his throat slightly, "from your previous commander, the captain of the *Phoenix* . . ."

"Yeah, what about it?" Riker said, in a challenging tone.

"Mr. Stryker, you realize *I* have nothing to do with these things. . . ."

"I know what it says," Riker replied, curtly. "But there were never any formal charges filed."

"Yes, sir, I realize that," the secretary replied. "However, *despite* the fact that there were no charges filed, your commanding officer's evaluation report, all by itself, will make getting you another berth somewhat, uh, problematical."

"Are there listings or aren't there?" Riker demanded.

"Well, yes, there *are* listings," the secretary replied, "but at this point, all I can do is enter your names for consideration and allow the listing captains access to your files. If I receive a positive response, I'll be sure to let you know."

"And how long is that liable to take?" Riker asked.

The secretary shrugged, uncomfortably. "Ordinarily, I'd say anywhere from a few hours to a day or so, but given your, uh . . . recent difficulties . . . " He cleared his throat again. "I simply couldn't say. I mean, surely you realize the situation you're in. It's really out of my control."

"Yeah, right," said Riker, with a grimace.

"If you could check back with me tomorrow, perhaps there might be something. . . . I mean, you never know, sometimes, if a ship is shorthanded and the captain can't afford to wait in port, then . . . " The man hesitated.

"He might get desperate, is that what you're saying?" Riker asked.

"I didn't say that, Mr. Stryker. I will certainly do what I can for you, but under the circumstances, it's going to be rather difficult. Perhaps if you insisted that your previous captain file charges . . . given his report, you certainly have that right . . . then at least you could contest it, and if you won your case, or the captain failed to prove his, then this report could be expunged and—"

"There's no possibility of doing that," said Riker. "The *Phoenix* has already departed this sector."

"Oh . . . yes, I see that," said the secretary, glancing back at his screen. He sighed and shook his head. "Well, I'll see what I can do. But to be perfectly frank with you, it could take quite a while."

"How long?" asked Riker.

The secretary shook his head. "Days, possibly weeks, or even longer. I'm sorry."

"Yeah," said Riker, sourly. "By then, we'll be flat broke."

"I really wish there was something more that I could do," the secretary said. "Look . . ." He cleared his throat again and leaned forward, speaking in a low voice. ". . . I'm not supposed to say this, but you might stand a better chance trying to make connections in the Zone. There are a few bars down there—the Ramjet, the Derelict, the Flying Dutchman . . . just ask anybody, they'll tell you where they are. You never heard it from me, you understand, but word is if you're in a hurry and looking for warm bodies to fill out your crew, and you're not too particular, then you can always find some people there who are anxious to ship out and don't really care what their next port of call is, if you know what I mean."

Riker nodded. "Yeah, I think I do," he said. "Thanks. I appreciate it."

"A word of caution," said the secretary. "We're out on the frontier here, and even though we've got a starbase in this sector, you won't find any Starfleet Security Men down there. And the local authorites don't give a damn what happens in the Zone, so long as it doesn't spill out into the rest of the city. In other words, watch your backs. *Especially* in those places."

"I'll keep that in mind," said Riker. "Thanks again."

"Don't mention it," said the secretary. "And I *do* mean don't mention it."

"Well, that worked like a charm," said La Forge, as they left the union office.

"And we picked up a few possible leads, as well," said Riker. "Now if anyone happens to check with the union office, the secretary will remember us and confirm that we were really looking for a ship." He turned to Dorn. "You know anything about those bars he mentioned?"

"I've heard about them," she replied. "They're bad news. Real slaughterhouses. People have been known to go in there and not come out again. Our jurisdiction does not extend beyond the spaceport. And even if we had permission to police the Zone, we simply lack the personnel to conduct regular shore patrols. T'grayn wouldn't allow it, in any case. The city makes a lot of money off the Zone."

"So what you're saying is we're on our own in there," La Forge said.

"We've been on our own ever since we set foot outside the spaceport gates," Lieutenant Dorn replied, dryly.

The area they were walking through as they moved away from the spaceport was composed of a mixture of warehouses and bars, with various other business scattered up and down the street. Most of the buildings along the crowded street were no more than about five or six stories tall, and just about all of them were garishly illuminated with signs advertising bars and nightclubs, tattoo and piercing emporiums, cyberentertainment salons, and exotic show clubs, some of which openly advertised acts that were illegal throughout most of the Federation. Looking at one of the signs, which displayed a colorful and shocking digital representation of what went on inside, La Forge could only shake his head and mutter, "I definitely get the feeling we're not in Kansas anymore."

Riker nodded as he glanced around. "I've seen some pretty wild liberty ports," he said, "but this one is in a class all by itself."

K'trin was a busy port city and the streets of the Zone were crowded with merchant spacers from all over the Federation, on liberty from their ships stationed in orbit, as well as locals and various transients who made their living from them. In most spaceport cities of the Federation, Riker knew, there was usually a "Combat Zone," a small section of the city where spacers could find the sort of entertainment that would allow them to unwind from their long voyages. Spacers were usually paid when they made port, and when they took their liberty, they had money to spend. Many of them liked to spend it in drinking and gambling and other diversions, and areas like the Zone existed to supply them.

The laws governing the existence of such districts varied with each world. In some cases, local authorities had an agreement with the Federation to allow Starfleet security personnel jurisdiction to police the area and keep things under control. In others, local law enforcement took care of that job, and if spacers got themselves in trouble, they were answerable to local laws. In a few ports, the local authorities tended to look the other way for all but the most serious infractions, tolerating activities that might be illegal elsewhere on their world. However, on D'rahl, it seemed that to all intents and purposes, no laws applied. So long as whatever happened in the Zone *stayed* within the Zone, the authorities didn't seem to care one way or the other. And Starfleet had no jurisdiction. Riker could not imagine a more ideal environment for criminals, particularly freebooters like Blaze.

As they approached the center of the Zone, the streets became more crowded. Small groups of gyro sleds with helmeted riders astride them zoomed up and down above the streets, executing aerobatic maneuvers overhead, then swooping down with alarming speed until a frightening crash seemed inevitable, only to pull out of their dives at the last moment and level off or else zoom back up again. Local youths, thought Riker, out for a bit of hell-raising. He wondered how many of them got killed or maimed performing their daredevil antics, and how many innocent pedestrians they killed or injured in the process.

As they passed a side street, a cloaked figure suddenly stepped out into their path, pulled back her hood, and struck a provocative pose. "Looking for a real *good* time?"

Riker stared, startled, and his hand instinctively reached for the phaser that wasn't there before he caught himself. For an incredible moment, he thought he was confronted by a female Borg, but then he realized that the modifications were considerably different. This woman had extensive cybernetic augmentation surgery, but in addition to that, she'd had biomods, as well.

The upper part of her face, from just below her eyes on up into her thick, lush hairline, was covered with nysteel alloy, so that it looked as if she were wearing a gleaming steel mask through which bionic optics fixed him with their electronic gaze. Through her parted lips, he could see artificial tooth implants extend, resembling the fangs of a vampire. Her right hand and arm were natural, but the left arm, from the shoulder down, was robotic, with unusually complex-looking, articulated fingers. Beneath her cloak, she wore barely enough for modesty, revealing a startlingly muscular body. She wore high, over-the-knee boots and her legs were bare up to what amounted to little more than a thong, above which were washboard abdominal muscles and large, firm breasts encased in a brief halter top. She had thick, lustrous black hair down almost to her waist, but the left side of her head had been shaved and covered with gleaming nysteel alloy studded with tiny microcircuitry receptors and interface jacks. She held up her natural right hand, palm toward her face, and Riker saw an example of her biomods as three-inch needles slid out from beneath her fingernails.

"Natural endorphins, adrenochrome, enhanced biopeptides," she said, with a predatory smile. Then she held up her robotic hand with a flourish, and Riker saw that where the fingernails would be on a normal hand, there were small hypospray injectors built in. "Chinese heroin, K'tralli ice, Rigelian cerebrocain, laboratory-grade morpheto-mine, Orion ambrocide, I've got it all."

The tip of her tongue flicked out to touch her upper lip, and Riker saw a small gland surgically implanted in its underside. She secreted a tiny drop of cerulean blue saliva that glistened on her lower lip. Riker repressed a shudder. The woman wore no weapons, but she didn't need any. All she had to do was trail her robotic fingertips across somebody's skin and she could inject an entire pharmacopoeia of lethal drugs, or else use the needles implanted in her natural hand to wreak havoc on a nervous system with her bioengineered glandular secre-tions. He had no idea what a love bite or a kiss could do, and he wasn't sure he really wanted to know.

"Uh . . . no, thanks," he said.

"Are you sure?" she said, her fangs retracting as she smiled and reached out for him. "For you, I could arrange a special discount. I could take care of your friends, too."

Riker stepped back. "I *said* . . . no, thanks."

"Too bad," she said, looking him over. "I could really enjoy doing you."

"Nothing personal," said Riker. "It's just not my cup of tea."

"Tea is the one thing I *don't* have," she replied with a smile, stepping aside for them. "If you should change your mind, ask for Katana at the Flying Dutchman."

"The Flying Dutchman," Riker repeated. "Where's that?"

"Straight down this alley, last door to your left," she said. "One of the best bars in the Zone. Check it out. Tell the bartender I sent you. He'll give you a free drink, on me. Maybe I'll see you there later." She snicked out her needles once again. "If this isn't your cup of tea, there's lots of other things that I can do."

"I'll think about it," Riker said.

"Do that," said Katana, over her shoulder, as she turned and walked away.

La Forge gave a low whistle. *"What* was that?" he said.

"They're called 'shooters' around here," Lieutenant Dorn said, tersely, "but the proper term is cybrid, for cybernetically augmented, biomodified hybrid."

"What? I've never even *heard* of such a thing," said Riker, with a frown.

"Not many people have," said Dorn, staring hard at the departing cybrid. "They're very rare. Fortunately."

Riker noted her marked stiffness, a hostile reaction indicating there was probably something personal involved. "Come on, let's go," he said, turning down the alleyway. "We've still got work to do."

"What would make people want to *do* something like that to themselves?" La Forge asked.

"It wasn't really their choice," Dorn replied. "Ever hear of Diversified Biotronics Corporation?"

"Wait a minute, that rings a bell," La Forge said. "Wasn't that one of the old industrial conglomerates out in the Belt? I seem to remember reading something about their cybernetic engineering patents back in the Academy."

"That's the one," said Dorn. "They perfected a new generation of cybernetic bioaugmentation procedures, originally intended for medical applications. But then somebody in the corporation decided to diversify into a whole new area. They came up with the idea of cloning biohybrids and augmenting them with various cybernetic implants at key stages in their physical development."

"Wow. Was that *legal?*" asked La Forge.

"I suppose it was a matter of interpretation," Dorn replied, as they walked. "Cloning human cells for commercial purposes has been outlawed for years, but DBC maintained that the cybrids were not, technically speaking, human and therefore they were a patented, bioengineered life-form. The project was already well under way when an injunction was issued against them while the matter was thrashed out in the courts. It took years to settle the whole thing, and by the time it was all over, DBC had lost their court battle and their stock had plummeted. The company did not survive, and several of its officers were convicted on numerous felony charges."

"When did all this happen?" Riker asked, finding it curious that he had never heard of it.

"About sixty years ago," said Dorn.

"Sixty years ago?" said Riker, with disbelief. "But that woman didn't look a day over twenty-five!"

"Looks can be deceiving," Dorn replied, "especially with cybrids. Remember, they're bioengineered. If she was one of the last ones DBC produced, she'd have to be at least fifty years old."

"If she's a biological hybrid, then what exactly *is* she?" Riker asked.

"I have no idea what went into the matrix," Dorn replied. "Chances are she doesn't even know herself."

"How many of them were there?" asked La Forge.

"No one seems to know for sure," said Dorn. "When DBC was brought up on charges, somebody panicked and destroyed all the records. Nobody even knows for certain what their purpose was supposed to be. DBC maintained they were designed for medical applications, and that might even be true for all I know, but there was a widespread belief that they were designed as a mercenary force that the company could hire out. It sounds plausible to me. They certainly fight well enough."

"How do you know that?" asked Riker, glancing at her sharply.

"Same way I know the rest of it," said Dorn. "It was all part of the job. We had some trouble with a few of them on Artemis VI not long after I was assigned here. They came over from N'trahn and there was no law barring them from entry. There is now."

"What happened?" Riker asked.

"Three of them killed twenty-seven colonists and seriously injured another dozen or so."

"My God. Why?" asked La Forge.

"We never could quite figure that one out," said Dorn. "None of the cybrids survived to be questioned. They wouldn't be taken alive."

"What became of all the others?" Riker asked.

"According to my research, when DBC went down, all the cybrids simply disappeared. Rumor had it they were terminated, but some of them obviously got away. And a few apparently came here. We learned that General H'druhn used a number of them in the K'tralli revolution. Now they're K'tralli citizens. Legally, we can't touch them. We don't even know how many of them there are. J'drahn claims he has no idea and hasn't seen any of them in years. He believes they're probably all dead by now. Apparently not."

"Well, they're not really our concern," said Riker.

"They are mine," said Dorn, with a hard edge to her voice. "I lost six of my people taking down those three shooters on Artemis VI."

"Lieutenant . . ." Riker said, stopping and staring at her pointedly, "I *said* . . . they're *not* our concern. We've got a job to do. Is that clear?"

"Yes, sir," she replied, stiffly.

"I can understand how you feel, Lieutenant," Riker said, sympathetically. "It was your first field command, wasn't it?"

She stared at him. "Yes, sir, it was."

"Believe me," Riker said, sincerely, "I know how you feel. I've been there. But if you keep carrying it around with you, it'll eat your guts out. It's over. Let it go."

"Is that an order, sir?" she said, flatly.

"No, Lieutenant, it's merely good advice," he said. "And if you're smart, you'll take it."

"I hate to interrupt," La Forge said, "but we've got company."

They were almost at the end of the alleyway, not quite to the Flying Dutchman, and three figures had suddenly stepped out of the shadows. Their attitude as they stood in the center of the alley to block their way was unmistakable.

"There's three more coming up behind us," La Forge said.

Riker glanced over his shoulder.

"That damn shooter set us up!" said Dorn.

The three in front of them were human. Riker couldn't tell about the ones who had stopped a short distance behind them, cutting off their retreat. The one standing in the center of the group before them spoke.

"We can do this easy, or we can do it hard," he said. He pulled out a double-bladed spring knife and six inches of gleaming nysteel snicked out at each end. "How do you want to play it, mate?"

"I'll see you and raise," said Riker, drawing his bowie with its twelve-inch blade.

The man's eyes grew wide at the sight of the huge knife, and he also saw La Forge pull out his stunner. Dorn had slipped on her alloy knucks and she also pulled a whip baton out from beneath her vest. She pressed the control stud and the flexible alloy whip sprang out to its full length of two and a half feet. It was standard issue to security personnel, and Riker hadn't known she'd brought it with her, but now was not the time to worry about that. The other two men had also pulled out knives, and Riker heard movement behind him, as well. He sincerely hoped that none of them had phasers or projectile weapons.

La Forge quickly turned to face the ones behind them. Riker faced the men in front, and Dorn stood slightly sideways, so she could quickly go either way. Suddenly, the men they were facing didn't look so sure of themselves.

"There's only three of you and six of us," said the

one who had spoken before. "What do you think your odds are?"

"Oh, about even, I'd say," said another voice, and two of the men behind the landing party grunted and stiffened as Katana came up and injected them from behind. As the two men collapsed to the street, the third one turned quickly, but the cybrid grabbed him by the throat with her robotic hand and effortlessly snapped his neck before he could even make a sound. The remaining three men bolted, apparently not caring for the sudden change in odds.

Dorn turned toward the cybrid, holding her whip baton ready. Riker put his hand on her upper arm and squeezed gently. At the same time, he sheathed his bowie. "Thanks," he said. "I owe you one."

"You owe me three," the cybrid replied, glancing down at the bodies at her feet. "I saw them from across the street, going down the alley after you. I just didn't want you thinking that I'd set you up."

La Forge glanced down at the three bodies lying on the ground. "What did you give those two?" he asked, referring to the men she had injected.

The cybrid shrugged. "A mixed cocktail," she replied, with a smile. "And I don't water down my drinks."

"I guess not," said La Forge, uneasily.

"That was fast work," Riker said. "I'm impressed."

"So am I," Katana replied. "I waited to see what you would do. You three don't back down, do you?"

"I never got into the habit," Riker said. "Besides, we haven't got much money, and it's got to last us till we find another ship. I have a feeling this place could get expensive."

"Well, in that case, why don't you let me buy you a round?"

"Thanks, but you've already done more than enough," said Riker.

"Forget it. Like I said, I didn't want you to think I was involved in this. The Zone's not all that large, and I've got a reputation to protect. Come on, hotshot, I'll buy you that drink." She reached out to take his arm. Involuntarily, Riker pulled back. She fixed him with a gaze from those unsettling, crystal clear bionic optics. "Don't worry, lover. I won't sting."

"Yeah. That's what the scorpion said to the frog," said Riker.

"How's that?"

"It's from an old folktale. Forget it." Riker allowed her to take his arm. "Sorry," he said. "Nothing personal. It's just that I've never met anyone like you before."

"There isn't anyone like me," she said, then added softly, "not anymore." She glanced at the weapon still in Dorn's hand. "That's a Starfleet security baton," she said.

"Yeah," said Dorn. "I took it off one in a fight on Abraxis IV. Kept it ever since. It comes in real handy sometimes."

"Abraxis IV, eh?" said Katana, as they walked toward the bar. "I hear that's a pretty rough port."

"I've seen rougher," Dorn replied.

"Well, sister, they don't get much rougher than this," the cybrid said. As if to punctuate her words, as they approached the bar, the door was thrown open and a body flew out into the alley. The spacer landed in a heap on the ground and lay there, moaning. Katana merely stepped over him without giving him a second glance. Riker and the others followed.

From the outside, the Flying Dutchman was marked only by a carved wooden sign hanging over an unpainted steel doorway, illuminated by a small light above the doorframe and displaying the bar's name along with a crude representation of an ancient sailing vessel. Nothing more. No digitronic displays, not even any windows. It was the sort of place that one would have to look for, located as it was at the back of an alleyway, isolated from the glittering main strip of the Zone. But inside, it was another story.

Riker had expected a dark and grim-looking saloon, with men hunched over their drinks at the bar and passed out at corner tables. Instead, as they came in, they were assaulted by flashing lights and the throbbing sounds of loud music played by a live band on a stage protected by a shatterproof polymer shield. The reason for the shield became apparent almost immediately, as a bottle sailed toward the stage, aimed at one of the musicians. The synth player did not even react as the bottle smashed harmlessly on the protective shield, splattering it with foam and amber-colored liquid.

There were several raised stages placed around the room, on which both human and K'tralli females danced, stripping provocatively for the customers seated around them. There were several dancers on the bar, as well. No shields separated them from the patrons, and contact between the dancers and the customers was apparently allowed—for the price of a tip, the size of which seemed to determine the degree of contact. However, as they came in and made their way between the tables, one of the patrons got a bit too friendly for a dancer's taste. She began to struggle, and immediately two very large men descended on the rowdy customer, seized him, and smashed his head against the stage apron. He collapsed, bleeding and unconscious, and the other customers at the stage immediately began to tip the dancer generously.

"Want a table with a view?" Katana asked, raising her voice so Riker could hear her.

"I'd rather have one away from all the noise," he said loudly, in reply.

"Right this way," she said, heading toward the back, where there were private booths enclosed on three sides by dividers, forming small alcoves. The dividers were apparently accoustic mufflers, for the noise decreased enough for them to talk when they sat down.

"So, what do you think?" Katana asked. "Straight-ahead, no-nonsense spacer's bar. No tricks, no gimmicks, no holos, just good booze, good food, and honest entertainment."

"You call that entertainment?" Lieutenant Dorn

asked, looking with distaste at the gyrating strippers.

"Honey, if that's not your style, say the word and I'll get you some nice beef for a private table dance."

"I think I'll pass," said Dorn, sourly. "And *don't* call me 'honey.'"

"Suit yourself. What's your pleasure, hotshot?" she said, turning to Riker.

"You're buying," he said. "I'm not too particular."

"Is that right? You could have fooled me," Katana said, with a wolfish grin. She signaled a server. A young K'tralli woman wearing not much more than the dancers came up to their table.

"Hey, Shooter," she said. "What's up?"

"A pitcher of *bahari,* S'bele, and four chilled mugs."

"Coming right up." S'bele's gaze slid over Riker appreciatively and she smiled suggestively before she left.

"I think she likes you," said Katana, nudging Riker. "If she's more your style, it could be arranged."

"No, thanks," said Riker. "That isn't what I'm after."

"Really?" said Katana. "Wrong gender?"

"Right gender, wrong priority," said Riker.

"Yeah? So what *are* you after?"

"A ship," said Riker. "For me and my crewmates."

"No listings at the union?"

"There are listings, all right," said Riker, "just not for us."

"Uh-huh. I think I'm beginning to get the picture," said Katana. "What'd you do, hotshot? Pull a bad efficiency report?"

"Something like that," said Riker. "Not that it's any of your business."

"Now, is that any way to talk, when I'm the one who's buying?" she asked.

"You're right," said Riker. "I'm sorry. Guess I'm just a little edgy. No offense."

"None taken." She glanced around at them. "All three of you get grounded from the same ship, huh? You facing charges?"

"No," said Riker. He grimaced. "Too much bureaucracy involved. Our captain didn't want to be delayed."

"So he just grounded you and screwed you with his evaluation report, right?"

"You seem to know a lot about it, for a hooker," Dorn said.

Katana turned her bionic optics toward her. The gaze was expressionless and impossible to read, but it was *very* direct. Dorn did not flinch from it. "I know about a lot of things," Katana said. "It comes with the territory. It's just possible that you might even benefit from some of what I know, if you backed off some on your attitude." She turned toward La Forge. "You don't say very much, do you?"

Geordi shrugged. "I do, when I've got something to say."

Katana nodded with approval. "Smart." She turned to Dorn. "You could take a lesson from your mate, here." She turned back to La Forge. "That's a VISOR, isn't it?"

"That's right," La Forge said. "I was born blind."

Katana nodded. "Company I used to work for patented some of that microcircuitry. What's your rating?"

"Chief engineer," said Geordi.

"Really? And your captain *grounded* you? Good engineers are hard to come by. What the hell did you do, try to start a mutiny?"

"You know, you ask a lot of questions, but you don't volunteer much," Riker said.

"No, I just killed three rollers for you, hotshot," she replied. "I figure that entitles me to a few answers. What do you think?"

"Point taken," Riker replied. "What do you want to know?"

"How about your names, for starters?"

"Bill Stryker, formerly executive officer of the Federation merchant ship *Phoenix*. And my crewmates, George LaBeau—" Geordi nodded at her. "—and Angie Thorn, supply officer and med rating."

"With qualifications like that, you must have really stepped over the line to get grounded," said Katana. "So give. What did you do?"

"We got caught diverting cargo," Riker said.

"Diverting, huh? I guess that's one way of putting it," the cybrid replied, with a grin. "Let me guess. You were exec, and with Thorn here a warrant rating, that put you in position to alter cargo manifests and fake damage reports, right?" She glanced at La Forge. "And as chief engineer, you were in an ideal position to stash the hijacked cargo in the tubes until you could make port and arrange to transport it to some buyer. Was it something like that?"

"It was *exactly* like that," said Geordi. "How the hell did you know?"

Katana grinned. "I've been around, LaBeau. I didn't always work the Zone, you know. I've crewed some. It sounds like a pretty good scam to me. How'd you get caught?"

"Submitting too many insurance claims for damaged cargo," Riker said. "Someone got suspicious and planted a tracking device in one of the shipments."

"And cargo that was supposedly damaged or destroyed turned up somewhere it wasn't supposed to be," Katana said. She nodded. "That's where scams like that usually go wrong. People get too greedy. Not that there's anything wrong with being greedy," she added, quickly. "It's just that you have to know when you can get away with it."

"If you're such an expert, then how come you're working the streets of a liberty port?" asked Dorn.

Katana fixed her once again with that implacable, crystalline gaze. "Because I choose to, *honey,*" she said, stressing the word purposely. "Good times aren't all I sell. I deal in information, too. Besides, *I'm* not the one who's grounded and stranded in K'trin, am I?"

"Take it easy," Riker said. "She's just a little tense, that's all."

"No, it's not all," Katana said, flatly. "You don't like me, do you, Thorn? You think I'm some kind of freak, don't you?"

"I didn't say that," Dorn replied, curtly. "You did."

"I *said,* take it easy," Riker interjected sharply. "Both of you. This isn't going to get us anywhere." He turned to Katana. "Look, you seem to know your way around here. And you said you deal in information. We don't have a lot of money, but we'd be willing to pay for a connection that would get us a ship off-planet."

"Yeah? And then what?" asked Katana. "With what you three pulled, any captain that would sign you on would either have to be desperate or crooked. If he's desperate, then you're history as soon as he can find replacements for you in another port, and then you're right back where you started. If he's crooked, he'd have to have his head examined to sign you on, because with your records on file, it would be like a red flag on whatever operation he's running. Face it, Stryker, you three just scammed yourselves right out of the Merchant Spacefleet."

"So what you're saying is there's nothing you can do to help?" said Riker.

"Are you *listening* to me, Stryker?" she replied. "Wake up and smell the coffee, hotshot. It's *over.* You three have flushed your careers right down the tubes. About the only chance you've got is to sign on with some rustbucket freighter skippered by an independent who can barely make ends meet, hauling toxic waste or something no one else will touch. You'll wind up on a route so far removed from merchant space lanes that the only liberty port you'll ever see will be some dome planted on an asteroid. Face it, you gambled and you lost."

"Don't hold back," said Riker. "Tell me what you really think."

She smiled. "I'm just giving you it to you straight, hotshot. But who knows, maybe it's not the end of the world."

"What do you mean?"

The cybrid shrugged. "Hell, this is the frontier. Look around. This is a wide-open Zone. There's a lot of opportunities here for people who know how to take advantage of them."

"You mean like those rollers who just tried to jump us?" Riker said. He snorted with derision. "That's not exactly my idea of a growth career."

"Hell, I wasn't talking about anything like that," Katana said. "That's strictly small-time. With your qualifications, I think you could do better."

"If you've got something in mind, I'm listening," said Riker.

The server brought their drinks, rewarded Riker with another sultry smile, and left.

"Drink up," Katana said, getting to her feet. "Let me go make a few inquiries."

"What's in it for you?" asked Riker.

She grinned. "I'm sure we can work something out. Don't go away. I won't be long."

They watched her move through the crowd. "You're not going to trust that cybrid bitch?" said Dorn.

"Only to look after her own interests," replied Riker. "And in this case, her interests might turn out to be ours, as well."

"Just so long as she keeps her hands where I can see them," said La Forge, uneasily. "That lady makes me very nervous."

"She's no lady," Dorn said.

"So far, she's the best lead we've got," said Riker.

"What do you think she's going to do?" asked La Forge.

"Try to broker a connection and collect from both ends," Riker replied.

"Yeah, but what kind of connection?" asked La Forge.

"We'll just have to wait and see," said Riker. "My guess is she's got an in to the local black market. Those drugs she loads into her built-in hyposprays are not easily available. Laboratory-grade morphetomine is a black-market pharmaceutical, and it wouldn't come cheap."

"You'd be surprised at what you can pick up in the Zone," said Dorn.

"Maybe," Riker said, "but you don't pick up exotic drugs like cerebrocain and ambrocide just anywhere. To manufacture those would require a state-of-the-art pharmaceutical laboratory. And something like that would be a little tough to hide."

"Unless you had a government that looked the other way," La Forge said.

"Or maybe a cloaking device," said Dorn.

"You mean Blaze's *ship?*" said La Forge.

"Think about it," Dorn said. "If J'drahn or T'grayn were allowing illegal drug manufacture on D'rahl or one of the other K'tralli worlds, they'd still have to worry about the problem of distribution. They'd have to ship the drugs from the plant to some distributing point, and from there, ship them off-planet."

"They could cut deals with crooked merchant fleet captains, or maybe small-time independents," said La Forge.

"Maybe," Dorn said, "but it would be risky. If anyone got caught, they could blow the whistle on the entire operation. On the other hand, if you subsidized a plant that was operating aboard a *ship,* then even if something went wrong, you wouldn't get caught with an illegal plant in your own backyard. And if you were charged with being an accessory, it would be difficult to prove. You'd have plausible deniability."

"You've got a very devious mind, Lieutenant," said La Forge.

"You hang around here long enough, you'll have one, too," she replied dryly.

"I suppose it's possible," said Riker, thoughtfully. "On a Constellation-class ship, he could get by with a smaller crew and fewer amenities, which would leave him space to convert crew quarters to laboratories. And he could trade hijacked cargo for the raw materials he'd need."

"And what better place to hide an illegal drug-manufacturing plant than aboard a cloaked ship?" asked La Forge.

"We may be reaching here," said Riker. "But either way, Katana's got to be getting her supplies from somewhere. And whoever her supplier is, he's not small-time. I think we may be on to something."

"How do you want to play it?" Dorn asked.

"We'll have to follow her lead," said Riker. "You can bet that whoever she's calling is going to have us checked out first."

"And what they'll find in the official records will back up everything we've said," La Forge replied. "We'll look like three crooked spacers who got caught and have flat run out of options." He grimaced. "I'm almost starting to believe it, myself."

"If we're going to pull this off, you'll have to believe it," Riker said. "We're moving into dangerous territory. We can't afford any slips."

A few moments later, Katana returned. "You may be in luck," she said. "It's just possible that my contact might have something for you."

"What are we talking about, exactly?" Riker asked.

"It's too early to talk about the details," she replied evasively. "I don't really know what my contact has in mind, but it sounded like he might have something that could interest you."

"What I'm interested in right now is knowing what I might be getting into," Riker said.

"Have a little patience, Stryker," she replied.

"These things don't happen right away. Calls and arrangements have to be made. As soon as I hear from my contact, we'll set up a meeting and you'll get all the details then."

"Suppose I don't like the details?" Riker asked.

"Then it goes no further," said Katana. "But it's not as if you have a lot of options, is it?"

"No," Riker said, "I guess it's not. Okay. What do we do in the meantime?"

"Keep yourselves available," she said. "You can get a room upstairs. It's liable to be a little noisy, but it's cheap, if you don't mind sharing. I can talk to the manager and have him move in a couple of extra cots. And you can get food from the kitchen. It isn't bad."

"And you get a kickback for renting us the room, right?" Riker said.

She shrugged. "Everybody's got to make a living. Of course, if you don't like the deal, you can always go someplace else. But it'll cost you more."

"And while we sit around and wait and spend our money, you just disappear, right?" said Dorn.

"I could," Katana agreed, "but then I'd lose out on what I'd get for making the connection. And that wouldn't be good business, would it?"

"How long will we have to wait?" asked La Forge.

She shrugged. "I'd say till tomorrow, or the next day, at the latest. But if my contact says he's got something, then he's got something. If you don't like the deal, then at most you're out two days' room rent. You'd have had to pay that anyway,

130

unless you don't plan on sleeping while you're here."

Riker nodded. "Okay, we'll take the room. But until I hear something more specific, that's all we're going to take."

"Fair enough," Katana said. "I'll go set it up. You can hang out here and get some food, or go upstairs. But don't go wandering off. If I get the word, things will move fast and I'll want you where I can find you."

She left the table once again to get a room for them.

"How do we know she's not going to set us up to get rolled?" asked Dorn.

"She could've done that outside," Riker reminded her. "Anyway, we're not going to get anywhere by playing it safe. What we do is try to minimize the risks. We make sure there's no one waiting for us in that room when we go in, then we check it out carefully and sleep in shifts, one of us awake at all times."

"I sure would feel better with a phaser," said La Forge.

"So would I," said Riker, "but if we're searched —and we can probably count on that to happen at some point—it would be hard to explain where we happened to come up with phasers." He glanced at Dorn. "You don't have any more surprises like that baton, do you? If you do, I want to know about it *now.*"

"I'm not packing anything else," she replied.

"If I find out you are, I'll have you brought up on charges of insubordination," Riker said.

"I said, I'm not packing anything else, *sir,*" she said.

"That wasn't smart, Lieutenant," Riker said. "You jeopardized the safety of this mission."

"She bought my explanation of how I got it," Dorn said, defensively.

"That's not the point and you know it," said Riker. "I don't have any tolerance for mavericks, Lieutenant. *Especially* on a mission like this. You understand me?"

"Yes, sir."

"She's coming back," said La Forge, spotting Katana returning to their table.

"Okay, it's all set," she said as she came up. "I got you a room on the fourth floor, so it shouldn't be too noisy. It's got a bed and a couple of extra cots. It's not exactly a luxury suite, but like I said, it's cheap."

"All right, let's go check it out," said Riker, getting up.

"No hurry. Stay and finish your drinks."

"We'll go now," said Riker.

Katana smiled. "What's the matter, you don't trust me?"

Riker smiled back. "Frankly, no," he said. "Lead the way."

They had to go through a door at the back, walk down a short corridor, and climb the stairs to get to the fourth floor. There was no lift. The stairwells were dimly illuminated and not very clean. On their way up, they passed one of the dancers coming back down, counting money as she went. She glanced at them and raised her eyebrows, but made no comment. Riker didn't have to guess what most of the rooms upstairs were used for.

When they came to the fourth floor, Katana led them down a hallway a short distance and stopped before a door about halfway down. "This is it," she said. She gave Riker the key.

He opened the door with it, then stood aside. "After you."

She glanced at him, no expression in those unsettling, artificial eyes. "Whatever you say." She turned to walk through the door and Riker shoved her through, then came in fast after her, knife drawn. There was no one in the room.

"Satisfied?" Katana said, wryly.

Riker looked around, noting that there were no connecting doors. He sheathed his blade, then signaled the others, and they gave the room a quick but thorough examination. "I guess it'll do," he said when they were finished.

"You don't take many chances, do you, Stryker?" said Katana, with a smile.

"Not if I can help it."

She nodded. "I think you'll do."

"I'll do for what?"

She smiled and came up to him. "You'll find out."

Two men suddenly appeared in the doorway behind her. Riker quickly reached for his knife, but she moved even faster. Her hand came up to his cheek and there was a soft, chuffing sound as she injected him with one of her built-in hyposprays. As La Forge and Dorn reached for their weapons, the men in the doorway fired stunners. La Forge and Dorn both collapsed to the floor.

"You . . ." Riker grabbed Katana by the throat, but she took his hand and effortlessly pried it away. He sank to his knees.

"Don't fight it, hotshot," she said. "If I give you a stronger dose, it'll only make you sick."

"Damn you . . ." Riker said, thickly, and then the room started spinning violently. His eyes rolled up and he fell to the floor.

Chapter Five

"I DON'T LIKE THIS, JEAN-LUC," Gruzinov said. "You're taking too much of a chance."

"Taking chances is what we're here for, Ivan," Picard replied, as they entered the transporter room. "Besides, I believe you are overestimating the potential risk involved."

"That may be, but I still don't like it," Gruzinov insisted. "You've got two landing parties down on D'rahl, including your XO, your chief weapons and security officer, your ship's counselor, *and* your chief engineer. If anything goes wrong, all your senior personnel are absent from the ship."

"Not so. I think you will find that Mr. Data is quite capable," Picard replied, "and Dr. Crusher has experience serving on the bridge, as well. Besides, the crew is more than qualified to deal with any emergency that may arise in my brief absence."

"Damn it, Jean-Luc, that's not the point, and you know it!" Gruzinov persisted. "You have no business absenting yourself from your ship under these circumstances! And you especially have no business beaming down alone! It's contrary to regulations!"

"Captain Gruzinov does have a point, sir," Data said. "Starfleet regulations clearly specify that—"

"I am well aware of the regulations, Mr. Data," said Picard, interrupting him. "But they do not happen to apply in these particular circumstances. I am not leaving the ship without an officer qualified to command in my absence. Captain Gruzinov will be in command while I am gone. And I am not beaming down into hostile territory. The risk factors in this situation are minimal."

"You are merely taking refuge in a technicality," Gruzinov said. "I command a *starbase*. I have never commanded my own ship. It has been years since I have even served aboard one."

"And you were an excellent officer, as I recall," Picard said, "more than qualified to man any bridge station, from weapons to navigation. I do not believe you could have forgotten all that."

"Perhaps not," Gruzinov said, "but it *has* been a long time. And I was repeatedly passed over for command."

"Ivan, I would not leave the *Enterprise* in your hands if I were not fully confident of your abilities," Picard replied. "In my opinion, the fact that you were not offered command of your own ship was merely an accident of opportunity and timing.

Had you not accepted command of Starbase 37, you might have been offered the *Enterprise* instead of me."

"I labor under no such illusions, Jean-Luc," Gruzinov replied. "Quite aside from that, what you are proposing to do could create a serious diplomatic incident. Z'gral's residence is guarded. Essentially, he is under house arrest. If your visit were exposed, J'drahn would have grounds to accuse you of interference with—"

"J'drahn would be in a very poor position to accuse me of anything," Picard replied. "He has publicly stated, to us as well as to his own people, that Colonel Z'gral is in poor health and has gone into voluntary retirement. If he were to make an official protest, then I would be able to refute those claims publicly."

"Unless they're true," Gruzinov said.

"You have assured me they are not," Picard replied.

"Well, I don't believe they are," said Gruzinov, "but Z'gral is an old man and it's been a while since he's been seen by anyone outside his residence. He might well have become sick. He might even be dead, for all we know."

"Then why keep up the pretense that he is still alive?" Picard asked. "J'drahn would have nothing to gain from that. Besides, when we spoke to T'grayn and he told us that Colonel Z'gral was in poor health, Counselor Troi received the distinct impression he was lying. I have never known her to state anything for a fact if she was in any doubt concerning the accuracy of her empathic impressions."

"All right, then let *me* go instead," Gruzinov said.

"No, Ivan, that would not be wise," Picard said. "If, for any reason, something *were* to go wrong, I would need to depend upon your knowledge of K'tralli law and politics. Conceivably, if I am caught, I could be placed under arrest, and then you would be the most qualified to keep J'drahn from doing something foolish. You know the situation here far better than anyone else. And if Colonel Z'gral is being held against his will, as we believe, then I intend to bring him back with me under the provisions of political asylum. Under the circumstances, it would be much better if I were to bear the brunt of the responsibility for that decision rather than you."

Gruzinov sighed, heavily. "All right, you've made your point. But in practical terms, what we are talking about still amounts to a jailbreak, so for God's sake, be careful. If you're caught, J'drahn could have you arrested and shot and then claim some overzealous guard thought you were an intruder."

"Which is why my communicator will remain on at all times, so that you and Mr. Data can monitor and record everything that happens," said Picard. "Even overzealous guards would hesitate to fire on someone in a Starfleet uniform, and if I am caught, I shall immediately advise them that they are being recorded. They would not risk harming a Starfleet captain, Ivan. At worst, they would take me into custody and inform Governor T'grayn, who would take no action without informing Overlord J'drahn. Do you perceive any flaw in my logic, Mr. Data?"

The android shook his head. "None, sir."

"Satisfied?" Picard said to Gruzinov.

"At least take a couple of security officers down with you," said Gruzinov.

"No," said Picard. "My presence alone may not be perceived as a threat, but more would increase the odds of someone getting nervous. I admit it's a calculated risk, Ivan, but I *have* weighed it carefully. And we need Colonel Z'gral."

Gruzinov nodded. "Yes, I am afraid we do. The old man simply wouldn't listen to anybody else."

"Then it's settled. Let's get on with it," Picard said, stepping up onto the transporter pads.

Data moved over to the control station.

"Have you got a fix on the estate, Mr. Data?" asked Picard.

"One moment, sir, I am entering the coordinates Captain Gruzinov specified right now. . . ." A moment later, he said, "I have a fix, sir."

"Scan for life-forms," said Picard.

"I am showing a fair number of life-forms on the grounds of the estate, sir, as well as in the outbuildings and on the first and second floors of the residence itself. However, on the third floor, in the east wing, I am scanning only one K'tralli life-form."

"That'll be Z'gral," said Gruzinov.

"Lock in those coordinates, Mr. Data, and stand by to energize," Picard said.

"Locked in, sir. Standing by."

"Energize," Picard said.

The moment Picard dematerialized, Gruzinov touched his insignia, activating his communicator. "Gruzinov to bridge," he said.

"Lieutenant Koski here, sir. Go ahead."

"Stand by to monitor Captain Picard's transmission," said Gruzinov. "We'll monitor from here, as well. Patch the signal through to the ship's data banks and begin recording now."

"Aye-aye, sir."

"Gruzinov out." He nodded to Data. "Put it through the board speakers, Mr. Data."

"Aye, sir."

"Keep a firm fix on the captain and stand by to get him out of there instantly if anything goes wrong," Gruzinov said. "And cross your fingers."

Data looked puzzled. "All of them, sir?"

Gruzinov smiled and held up his hand. "No, Mr. Data. Just these two."

Data looked puzzled, but did as he was told.

"Now let's just hope that nobody does anything stupid," said Gruzinov.

Picard materialized in a large, airy, and well-furnished sitting room on the third floor of Colonel Z'gral's residence. He glanced around quickly. The floor was exquisitely laid in rich, highly polished, contrasting woods, and the walls were hung with ornate tapestries. There were a number of comfortable reading chairs upholstered in some sort of dark, attractively textured animal hide placed around the room, and a large sofa upholstered in the same material roughly in the center, placed so that it faced an entertainment console built into the wall. There was a large, beautifully carved table with some chairs around it and a fresh bowl of fruit placed in the center, and Picard felt a soft breeze coming in from the open doors leading to the balcony.

It did not look even remotely like a prison. It looked more like the palatial estate of some aristocrat, which was exactly what it was at one time. Gruzinov had told him that before the revolution, this sprawling estate had been the private residence of a K'tralli prince. Now, most of the old estates and palaces were the private residences of governors and high-ranking bureaucrats in J'drahn's administration. There was a new order, but for the K'tralli people, nothing much had changed.

Picard heard the tapping sounds of someone working at a computer keyboard coming from the open doors to the bedroom. He moved so that he could look through the doors and saw a figure dressed in a richly embroidered robe seated at a large desk, with his back to him. The man looked old, for his hair was completely white, falling down well below his shoulders, and his head was bald on top. However, his shoulders still looked broad and powerful, and he sat erect in his chair. It was not the figure of a frail and sickly old man, thought Picard, but of a man who, despite his age, kept himself in excellent physical condition.

"Colonel Z'gral?" he said.

The man stopped typing and turned. His dark eyes registered surprise when he saw Picard, and he rose to his feet at once with a fluid motion. Again, Picard thought, not the reaction of a frail old man on his last legs. His features showed his age, but the eyes were bright and clear, and his posture was that of a soldier. "Who *are* you?"

"My name is Captain Jean-Luc Picard, of the Federation starship *Enterprise*. And it is my understanding that you are being held here against your will."

"A Federation starship?" said Z'gral. "By the gods! At last! I had almost given up hope. Has J'drahn been removed from power? Has the government fallen?"

"No, Colonel, I am afraid not," Picard said. "That is partly why I have come to see you."

"How many men have you brought with you?"

"I am alone."

"Alone? Are you mad? How did you get past the guards?"

"I transported directly from my ship," Picard replied. "The same way we can get you out of here, sir. However, for the sake of formality, it would have to be at your request."

"Oh, yes, of course," Z'gral said. "I must request . . . what do you call it? Political asylum?"

"That is correct, sir," said Picard.

Z'gral nodded. "Consider the request made, Captain," he said. "But I must first get these computer files." He sat down at the desk. "I have been writing my memoirs, with little hope of anyone ever seeing them. But it is all here, a complete record of all J'drahn's nefarious—" There was the sound of footsteps approaching from down the hall. Z'gral looked up. "Quickly, the balcony!"

Picard turned immediately and ran out onto the balcony, careful to sidle around the open doors, so that he would not be silhouetted in the light from the room behind him. He stood just outside, pressed against the wall, as the doors to Colonel Z'gral's room opened. Several guards came marching in, and Picard risked a quick glance inside. What he saw made his hand reach immediately for his phaser. The guards were wearing the uniforms of Romulan centurions.

Picard pressed himself back up against the wall, his mind racing. Romulans! Here, in Federation territory! He looked out over the balcony. It was dark outside, but in the illumination of the floodlights covering the grounds of the estate, he could make out the guards patrolling below. And they were all Romulans, as well.

"What do you want?" he heard Z'gral demand of the guards.

"Your life, Colonel," one of the Romulans replied.

"Hold it!" said Picard, coming in from the balcony. As the startled Romulans turned toward him, raising their disruptors, Picard fired with his phaser on wide beam. The Romulans fell without a sound.

"Are they dead?" Z'gral asked.

"No, merely stunned," Picard replied.

"Pity," said Z'gral.

"Enterprise to Picard!" Gruzinov's voice came over the communicator. "Jean-Luc, are you all right? What's happening?"

"Stand by, *Enterprise,"* Picard replied. "Colonel, we must go *now."*

Z'gral held up the chip on which he had stored his files. "I am ready now, Captain."

"Enterprise, two to beam up," Picard said.

He heard footsteps running down the hall. The sound of his phaser firing must have alerted the guards downstairs. Moments later, they came bursting in, but Picard and Z'gral were already gone.

"What happened down there? I heard you fire your phaser," said Gruzinov, rushing up to them with an anxious expression on his face.

"We have worse trouble than we thought," Picard said grimly, as he stepped down off the staging platform with Z'gral. "I was barely in time to prevent Colonel Z'gral's assassination. By Romulan centurions."

"Romulans!" Gruzinov said.

"Colonel Z'gral, I believe you know Captain Ivan Gruzinov, commander of Starbase 37?"

"Captain," said Z'gral, with a nod. "My thanks to you both. I owe you my life."

"It is indeed a pleasure to see you alive, Colonel," said Gruzinov. "But *Romulans? On D'rahl?* What about the guards?"

"The guards *were* Romulan," Picard said. "At least, the ones I saw were."

"They were all Romulans, Captain Picard," Z'gral said. "The entire complement of guards."

"The entire complement?" Gruzinov said, with disbelief.

"Can you give us any idea of their strength, Colonel?" asked Picard.

"Two companies of Romulan centurions," Z'gral said.

"Bozhe moi!" Gruzinov said, reverting to his native Russian in his astonishment.

" 'My God,' indeed," Picard said, gravely. "That's a full-scale assault force."

"The estate was more than merely my prison, Captain," said Z'gral. "With its extensive grounds, outbuildings, restricted airspace, and high walls, it was also an ideal barracks for them. And a place to conduct drills."

"What sort of drills?" Picard asked.

"Assault drills," replied Z'gral. "They often kept me awake at night, running on the grounds and through the corridors. There is a Romulan tribune in command. His name is Kronak."

"Then Governor T'grayn is in league with the Romulans?" Picard said.

"It would be more accurate to say he is their lackey," replied Z'gral, with disgust. "And J'drahn is involved with them, as well. He always was corrupt, but now he has turned traitor, selling out his people for his own gain."

"This changes everything," Picard said, with concern. "We must bring back our landing parties at once. Mr. Data, get in touch with Mr. Worf's team and have them return to the ship immediately. Then call Mr. Riker and—no, wait, cancel that last order. If we communicate with Riker, we risk exposing him and his team to danger. Bring back Worf's landing party, then get a fix on Riker's position and report to me on the bridge."

"Aye-aye, sir."

"Colonel, if you would be so kind as to accompany me . . ."

"My pleasure, Captain," said Z'gral.

They left Data behind in the transporter room and made their way to the turbolift.

"Colonel, how long has there been a Romulan presence on D'rahl?" Picard asked.

"I cannot say for certain," the old K'tralli soldier replied. "The K'tralli soldiers guarding me were all withdrawn and replaced by Romulan centurions just prior to last Liberation Day."

"That would be about three months ago," Gruzinov explained.

"Three months!" Picard said, astonished that they had been there for so long.

"However, I believe there must have been Romulan presence on D'rahl well before that time," Z'gral continued. "Contact had to be secretly established, arrangements had to be made. . . . I fear they have been coming here for some time, Captain. And with their cloaked vessels, they have easily been able to avoid detection."

"And our sensors could not differentiate between K'tralli and Romulan life-form readings," said Picard, grimly. "Together with the political situation, conditions could not have been more ideal for a Romulan infiltration."

"What I do not understand is why they had decided to kill me now, after all this time," Z'gral said.

"The *Enterprise*'s arrival here had to be the reason," said Gruzinov. "T'grayn must have panicked."

"Or else the Romulans forced his hand," Picard said. "And now, unwittingly, I have forced theirs."

"The question is, what will they do?" Gruzinov said.

"More importantly, where is their ship?" Picard added.

"There may not be a ship," Colonel Z'gral said. "When they first arrived, I observed them bringing in a large number of supplies. Enough to fill several of the outbuildings. And there have been no changes in personnel since then."

Picard took a deep breath. "We may be in luck, then," he said. "If they were dropped off by a Warbird, and then the ship departed, it would mean those troops were emplaced for a long-range mission."

"An advance force for an invasion?" asked Gruzinov.

"I shouldn't think so," said Picard, as they stepped out of the turbolift and onto the bridge. "Why start a war when you can achieve your objective by other means? It comes back to Blaze again."

"Blaze?" Z'gral said, with a puzzled frown.

"A freebooter we believe is being supported by Governor T'grayn," Picard explained. "One whose ship has been equipped with a cloaking device. In fact, Colonel, it is entirely possible that some of those supplies you saw consisted of equipment meant for Blaze."

"Of course!" Gruzinov said. "It all starts falling into place. They equipped Blaze to raid Federation shipping, knowing that a cloaked pirate vessel would bring a starship in response. Proving a link between J'drahn and the freebooters alone might not be enough to get him expelled from the Federation, but at the very least, it would result in sanctions being imposed, which would force him to turn to the Romulans. But proving that J'drahn was involved in helping equip Blaze with Romulan ordnance and technology would *guarantee* his expulsion. Then the Romulans would have an assault force already in place to make certain J'drahn does as he is told. Either way, the Romulans get what they want."

"Unless we were to destroy the *Glory* in combat," said Picard, with a frown. "If we happened to destroy Blaze's ship, along with its crew, then there would be no real proof. The Romulans could not have failed to take that possibility into account."

He shook his head. "There is still something we are not seeing."

"I take it that neither of you gentlemen have ever hunted game," said Z'gral.

They both turned to look at him. "No," Picard said, in a puzzled tone. He glanced at Gruzinov, who merely shook his head.

"I thought as much," Z'gral said. "Otherwise, you might have realized that if you plan to use a live beast as a lure to bring down a larger one, then you would first need to stake it down."

Picard exchanged glances with Gruzinov. "Of course, a Judas goat. They *intend* for us to take Blaze's ship," he said, as comprehension dawned.

"But . . . how?"

"We could have taken the *Glory* the first time, but for Blaze's cleverness in using the *Wyoming* as a shield," said Picard. "And when he attacked, he took us completely by surprise, with our shields down. Yet despite his reported skill, he nevertheless failed to deliver a crippling blow."

"A saboteur?" Gruzinov said, following Picard's train of thought.

"A Romulan agent, infiltrated among Blaze's crew," Picard said. "Placed there for the sole purpose of making certain that something aboard the *Glory* failed at the key moment, enabling us to capture it."

They were interrupted by a call from Data, in the transporter room.

"Picard here. Go ahead, Mr. Data."

"Sir, Lieutenant Worf's landing party is back

aboard the ship," said Data. "However, I am unable to locate Commander Riker's party."

"You mean they are no longer in the Zone?" Picard asked, with a frown. "Have you tried widening your sweep?"

"Sir, I have conducted repeated sensor sweeps of the entire city," Data replied. "They are no longer in K'trin. I have also conducted a series of wide-range scans, in addition to sending an ultra-high-frequency signal to their communicators in an attempt to track it. The signal has not been received, sir. It would appear that they are no longer on the planet."

Riker came to slowly, still feeling the aftereffects of the drug. He was lying on a bunk. He opened his eyes and blinked several times, trying to focus his vision. He heard a groan and sat up, a bit too quickly. The room started to spin. He propped himself up with one arm and closed his eyes, then opened them again. The room stopped spinning, but he still felt a bit groggy.

He heard a groan; then La Forge said, "God, my head hurts."

"Where the hell *are* we?" asked Lieutenant Dorn. She sat up in her bunk, slowly swung her legs down to the floor, and moaned, putting her head in her hands.

Good question, Riker thought. He looked around. "We're aboard a ship," he said.

Dorn glanced around, disoriented. "Are we in a *brig?*"

La Forge looked around at their surroundings, taking in the design and layout—the bulkheads, the lights, the vents, the forcefield that held them prisoner—and then his gaze settled on Riker. "Oh, no. Don't tell me. . . ."

"Yeah," said Riker, grimly.

"Don't tell him what?" asked Dorn.

The outer doors to the brig opened and Katana entered, followed by the two men who had surprised them at the Flying Dutchman. And there was a third man with them, tall, lean, and exotic-looking, outlandishly dressed, with long black hair, sharp features, and a patch over one eye. "Allow me to welcome you aboard the *Glory,*" he said. "My name is Captain Blaze. I apologize for your discomfort, and for relieving you of your weapons and communicators, but I wanted to make sure you did not attempt anything foolish."

"Captain Blaze?" said Riker. "I've heard of you. You're the freebooter who's been raiding all the shipping in this sector?"

Blaze smiled. "I see my reputation precedes me. But you see, *your* reputation precedes you, as well."

Riker tensed. "Is that right?"

"You are Bill Stryker, formerly executive officer of the merchant vessel, *Phoenix,*" Blaze said. "I've had you and your friends checked out, Stryker."

Riker felt relieved. For one bad moment, he thought their cover had been blown. "By her?" he said, glancing at Katana.

"And the Merchant Spacefleet Union," Blaze replied. "It was a simple matter to call them and request access to their database for crew applicants. In a busy port, it's such a routine request, they didn't even ask me who I was. Your files showed some rather interesting activity. Black-marketeering, insurance fraud, conspiracy. . . ." Blaze shook his head. "It seems you three have been busy."

"What do you want from us?" asked Riker.

"You said you were looking for a ship," said Blaze. "Well, it so happens I have one. And it also happens that I am in need of qualified personnel, especially a competent ship's engineer. My last one was killed in action recently. I am also in need of someone with medical training, and I could use a good ship's gunner. Would you be interested in applying for those positions?"

"You mean we have a choice?" said Riker.

"Well, no, not really," said Blaze. "I am in no position to accept a refusal, I'm afraid. I was merely trying to be polite. However, I suspect you would much rather accept voluntarily and become a part of an extremely profitable venture than suffer the unpleasant consequences of refusing."

"The words 'extremely profitable' have a nice ring to them," said Riker. "Much nicer than 'unpleasant consequences.' I guess we accept."

"Splendid," Blaze said. "Katana, release our new crewmates, if you would be so kind."

The cybrid cancelled the forcefield, and as they warily came out of the cell, she smiled at Riker and said, "Welcome aboard. I told you we'd work something out."

"Yes, you did," said Riker, "but this wasn't quite what I expected. Are you part of this crew?"

"First mate," she replied. "That's executive officer to you, Stryker. I outrank you."

"Do I call you 'sir'?" asked Riker, dryly.

"We do not stand on such formality aboard this ship," said Blaze. "You may address me as 'Captain'; and your fellow crew members you may call by name, as you get to know them. We do not use standard military rankings aboard this ship. Katana is first mate, my navigator is second mate, and so forth for the rest of my senior officers. We like to keep things simple."

"What about our property?" asked Riker.

"Ah, yes, that very handsome knife of yours," said Blaze, with a smile. "I must have it replicated. It is an excellent design. It will be kept in storage, along with your other weapons. Your communicators have been confiscated and destroyed. You will have no need of them, and as I understand the Merchant Spacefleet has offered a sizable reward for my capture, I wouldn't want any of my crew to be unduly tempted. All weapons are kept secured in the arms lockers and issued only when necessary. Only I and my trusted senior personnel carry weapons aboard this ship. And they do not have stun settings."

"I see," said Riker, noting the Romulan disruptor Blaze wore on his hip. He followed Blaze along with the others as he turned and left the brig. "What about the 'extremely profitable' part?"

"Ah, that interests you, does it?" Blaze said, as

they walked down the corridor. "You appear to be a man after my own heart. You will not receive any regular wages in the manner to which you have been accustomed. However, we do have a very generous profit-sharing plan, which I believe you will find much more advantageous. Each member of the crew receives equal shares of any profit realized in any of our ventures. You may spend it as you wish, when we make port, or else establish an account and save for your eventual retirement. You may even invest in a diversified portfolio, if you like."

"Right, and you control all that, of course," said Riker.

"Absolutely not," said Blaze. "I would be happy to advise you, if you so desire, or you may take advantage of the financial database we have on board and make your own decisions. Transfers of funds and assets are all done electronically, through financial institutions here in the K'tralli sector or in the Ferengi system, all of which conduct transactions by subspace communications without asking any questions. We believe in free enterprise aboard the *Glory*."

"Well, I'm all for enterprise," said Riker, with a smile. "However, was it really necessary to shanghai us? If you had made us a straight offer—"

"If I had made you a straight offer, you might have been in a position to refuse," Blaze replied. "And the nature of my business is not such that I can go around recruiting openly, as I'm sure you'll understand. Also, it is not every day that one encounters people with your particular qualifications, combined with such a decided bent toward larceny."

"You said your last chief engineer was killed," said La Forge. "What happened?"

"We had a minor disagreement with a Federation starship," Blaze replied. "You might say it ended in a sort of stalemate. I fully intend to have a rematch with the captain of that ship."

"You took on a Federation starship?" Riker said, feigning astonishment.

"Yes, the *Enterprise,* captained by Jean-Luc Picard," said Blaze. "A flamboyant name for a rather unflamboyant individual. But he knows his business, I'll say that for him. I shall not underestimate Captain Picard again."

"Underestimate him?" Riker said. "The *Enterprise* is a Galaxy-class starship. You're lucky you didn't get blown right out of the sky."

"Luck had little to do with it, Stryker," Blaze said. "If anything, luck was on the side of Captain Picard. I caught him with his shields down, completely unprepared. I should have disabled his ship with my first shot."

"Is that why you have a sudden vacancy for a gunner?" Riker asked.

Blaze glanced at him and arched an eyebrow. "According to your file, which I received courtesy of the Merchant Spacefleet Union, you scored at the top of your class in gunnery at Starfleet Academy, before being dishonorably discharged for a violation of the honor code. Stealing, was it not?"

"All right, so you've done your homework," Riker said. "But I haven't manned a weapons console since my days at the Academy. That's a long time ago. And you seem to have a rather low tolerance for poor marksmanship."

Blaze smiled. "Everyone is capable of making a mistake, Stryker. I can forgive that. What I do not forgive is disloyalty or treachery. My former gunner was too good a marksman to miss a shot like that. And his error nearly cost me my ship. Later, I discovered that the targeting system had been purposely misaligned. The man protested he was innocent, but he was the only one on board qualified for such an act of sabotage. Doubtless, he was tempted by the reward offered by the Merchant Spacefleet Union, and the promise of immunity from prosecution. It really was a pity. He was an excellent gunner."

"Well, I'm no gunner," Riker said. "I was second-in-command aboard the *Phoenix*. It took me years to overcome the stigma of my discharge and work my way up through the ranks. I'm not thrilled about the idea of serving as a lowly gunner."

"My gunnery mate is one of the most important crew members on this ship, Stryker," said Blaze. "And he commands respect. Besides, you are hardly in a position to quibble about your duty assignment. This is not the Merchant Spacefleet. This is the *Glory*. And we do things rather differently aboard this ship, as you will soon discover. There are no review boards to impress here. Only me."

"And if you want *my* job, hotshot," added Katana, "you're going to have to *take* it from me. Think you're man enough?"

Riker gave her a steady stare. "Maybe we'll find out," he replied.

"Any time you're ready," she said.

"If you two are done flexing your muscles," said La Forge, "I'd like to take a look at Engineering. If *my* welfare's going to depend on keeping this ship running, I'd like to see just what I've got to work with."

"And so you shall," said Blaze, beckoning them into the turbolift. "I will be pleased to show it to you personally, as I am anxious to see your reaction."

"I'm rather anxious to see your engineering section myself," said Riker. "They say you've got a cloaking device. If that's true, I'd like to know how you got one to work aboard a Federation ship. It's supposed to be impossible."

"It *is* impossible," La Forge said. "It would burn out the dilithium crystals."

"It would, indeed," said Blaze, "*if* we were powered by a Federation engine design."

"If?" said La Forge, playing along.

"The *Glory* is powered by modified Romulan drives," said Blaze.

"You can't be serious," said La Forge. "Where the hell would you get your hands on Romulan drives?"

"Why, from the Romulans, of course," said Blaze.

They stepped out of the turbolift and moved down the corridor to Engineering. It looked much the same as the engineering sections on other Constitution-class vessels, but this one had received a few modifications. La Forge immediately went over to the warp propulsion systems display and turned it on. The others watched as he stared at it with fascination for several moments, then gave a low whistle as he switched the display to examine the schematics of the engine nacelles and reactant injectors.

"Well, LaBeau? What do you think?" asked Blaze.

La Forge shook his head. "It's going to take time for me to familiarize myself with this system," he replied. "I've never worked with Romulan drives before. I've never even seen the schematics for them. Hell, no one has! But whoever put this system together for you was no shade-tree mechanic, that's for sure."

"Think you can figure it out?" asked Riker.

La Forge shook his head. "I guess I'll have to, won't I?"

"You will not be working entirely in the dark, LaBeau," said Blaze. "You've got full documentation on all of the modifications available in the data banks, and our engineering crew will be able to assist you. I did not expect you to know your way around an unfamiliar design at once." He raised his voice. "Ragnar!"

"Aye, Cap'n," came an answering reply from the upper engineering deck. It sounded like the voice of doom. Riker glanced, startled, in the direction of the sound. The owner of a voice like that had to be *big*.

"Get down here and greet our new chief engineer!" called Blaze.

The largest man any of them had ever seen came up to the railing and looked down at them, then started to make his way down the stairs.

"Jeez!" said Dorn, staring at him.

As he approached them, Riker found himself craning his head back to look at him. The man stood fully eight feet tall and had to mass well over four hundred pounds. He looked like an ambulatory tank. He had arms like tree trunks and legs almost as thick as Riker's entire upper torso. His bare chest and shoulders were thick and broad, corded with well-developed muscle on a scale unlike anything Riker had ever seen, and almost every square inch of skin was covered with intricate tattoos. His hair was so blond as to be almost white, cropped close to the scalp, and his eyes were a startling, improbable shade of sky blue. As he came toward them, his footsteps sounded like the beats of a kettledrum.

"That's not a man," said Dorn, in a low and awestruck voice, "it's a dinosaur!"

"This is George LaBeau, our new chief engineer," said Blaze. "LaBeau, meet your engineering crew chief, Ragnar Ragnarsson."

La Forge gulped, staring up at the leviathan, and extended his hand hesitantly. "Good to meet you, Chief," he said.

The cold, imposing, Viking countenance suddenly split into a wide grin, revealing absolutely perfect teeth, and the huge crew chief's face was instantly transformed. It was a smile so warm, so genuine, so open, and so friendly that it was irresistibly infectious.

"Welcome aboard, sir," he said, in that incredibly deep, basso profundo voice. He took Geordi's hand, enveloping it in his own gigantic paw, and shook it gently.

"Chief Ragnar will introduce you to the remainder of your engineering crew," said Blaze. "Then he will conduct you to your quarters. We've got a lot of work to do, LaBeau. We are currently conducting repairs after our encounter with the *Enterprise,* and we have just received some new engine components that have to be installed. Your job will be to get the *Glory* spaceworthy as soon as possible. There will be a bonus for you and the entire engineering crew if you can manage it within the next seventy-two hours."

"I'll do my best, Captain," La Forge said.

"Excellent. I will check back with you later. The rest of you come with me."

As they left Engineering, Riker said, "That was the biggest, scariest-looking man I've ever seen. Were did you find him?"

"Here aboard the *Glory,* Stryker, we do not ask questions about people's pasts," said Blaze. "But I can tell you that for all his size, Ragnar is generally one of the most placid souls I've ever met. Until he loses his temper, that is. And then he becomes absolutely homicidal and nothing short of a disruptor blast will stop him."

"How often does that happen?" Riker asked.

"Often enough to make the other crew members wary of him," Blaze replied. "However, you need have no concern for your friend, LaBeau, assuming he knows his business. The one thing Ragnar loves above all else are his engines. He dotes on them like a child with a beloved pet."

"What about the rest of the crew?" asked Riker. "We haven't seen many of them. Are most of them on liberty?"

"My crew does not take liberty in Federation ports," Blaze answered. "Even on D'rahl, where law enforcement is rather lax, it would entail certain risks, especially now that we are in the process of refitting. At the moment, most of them are engaged in unpacking and preparing to install the replacement components we have recently received."

"From where?" asked Riker.

"We have our sources," Blaze replied.

"In other words, you don't trust me and it's none of my business, right?" Riker said.

Blaze smiled. "Trust, Stryker, is something that has to be earned."

"Am I allowed to ask how many people constitute the crew, or am I going to have to go around and count?"

Blaze arched an eyebrow at him, amused at his

display of insolence. "At the moment, counting ourselves and LaBeau, our crew roster numbers twenty-six."

"Just over two dozen people?" Dorn said, with surprise. "That's all?"

"I could run this ship with half that number," Blaze replied. "These old Constitution-class vessels were very well designed. And I understand the Galaxy-class starships can be operated with only a skeleton bridge crew, if necessary. It really is a shame I can't get my hands on one of those. But who knows? An opportunity may yet present itself."

They stepped into the turbolift. "Bridge," said Blaze.

Riker exchanged glances with Dorn. "If I understand correctly," he said, "you were seriously damaged in your encounter with the *Enterprise*. I'm assuming we're in orbit above D'rahl, which means the ship has to be cloaked, otherwise you'd be visible on scanners. You told LaBeau that the repairs involve installing new engine components. That's a pretty big job. It also means you're going to have to go through a drive systems shutdown at some point."

"That is correct," said Blaze.

"But that means you won't be able to stay cloaked during that time," said Riker.

"No, we will not. It is unavoidable, but there will be a period of time during which we shall be exposed and vulnerable. It shall be up to your friend, LaBeau, to render that period of time as brief as practically possible."

"But what about the *Enterprise?*" asked Riker. "The minute you decloak, you'll show up on their scanners."

"Worried, Stryker?"

"You mean you're not?"

"We will deal with the *Enterprise* when the time comes," said Blaze.

They stepped out onto the bridge. For Riker, it was an eerie sense of déjà vu. He had been aboard Constitution-class starships before, so the bridge looked familiar, but modifications had been made here, as well. It appeared as if Romulan navigation consoles had been installed, and the communications console was different, as well. So was the bridge crew. An Orion was sitting in the captain's chair, which he vacated as soon as Blaze came on the bridge. The navigator was a human, but the helmsman was a K'tralli, as was the communications mate. And they were as rough-looking a lot as Riker had ever seen, dressed in a wild array of clothing that included bits and pieces of Merchant Spacefleet blues combined with outlandish civilian garb and K'tralli uniforms. Most of them were tattooed, and many had ears, noses, cheeks, and even eyebrows pierced.

"This Stryker, our new gunner," Blaze told the bridge crew. "And Thorn here, among her other duties, will be the one to patch you up should you start getting at one another's throats, so I suggest you treat her with respect." He introduced the bridge crew. "Navigator San Marco, Helmsman D'karr, Communications Mate T'gahl, and Bos'n Gol." The last was the Orion. "And here will be your station, Gunner's Mate," Blaze said, conducting him to the weapons console.

Riker saw that, unlike some of the other consoles on the bridge, this one was original equipment. Or, at least, it was similar to the original weapons console, which would have been removed when the ship was sold as surplus. Somewhere, Blaze had found another one to replace it. He looked it over carefully. It seemed to have been assembled from the components of several different consoles, but it was familiar enough that he would have no trouble operating it. However, he saw no point in letting Blaze know that.

"It's been years since I've even seen one of these," he told the freebooter. "And this isn't like the consoles we had back at the Academy. This one is an older model. What's more, it looks as if several separate consoles were cannibalized to put this one together."

"I can assure you that does not impair its function," Blaze replied. "I suggest you spend time familiarizing yourself with the equipment. It's programmed to conduct simulations, just like the ones you trained with. I will expect you to be able to operate it expertly by the time we are ready to leave orbit."

"And if I can't?" asked Riker.

"I have confidence in you, Stryker," Blaze replied. "However, if necessary, I can operate the weapons console myself. I said that I could use a gunner. I didn't say I *needed* one."

"Right," said Riker. He glanced at the crew, then turned his attention to the console as Blaze conducted Dorn from the bridge to show her the ship's medical facilities. As he pretended to concentrate on studying the layout of the console, he tried to rack his brain for a way out of the situation.

They had come to the Zone in order to seek intelligence about Blaze. Instead, they had been shanghaied aboard his ship. Their weapons had been confiscated, which made little difference one way or another, as they would have been pitifully inadequate against the disruptors carried by Blaze and his senior officers. More importantly, their communicators had been seized and destroyed. That meant there was no way they could call the ship, nor was there any way the *Enterprise* could attempt to trace them through signals sent to their communicators.

We're stuck, but good, thought Riker. He was thankful he had taken the trouble to be so painstaking in documenting their cover identities and making sure the files were placed in the Merchant Spacefleet data banks. Blaze had accepted them at face value as a result. Still, he was under no illusions that Blaze's trust would be won easily or quickly. He'll have us watched, he thought. There was even a good chance he might have their quarters monitored. They would have to find someplace safe to talk. Somehow, they had to get off this ship and alert the *Enterprise* to its location. But how?

If he could seize a moment or two at the navigations console, then he could determine the *Glory*'s current position. But even if there were some way he could manage to do that unobserved, there was still the problem of getting off the ship and conveying that information to the *Enterprise*. The transporters would be the only way. Assuming they would have a chance to get to them. Failing that, their only chance was in somehow alerting the *Enterprise* to the *Glory*'s presence, either by getting a signal out or through some act of sabotage. The only trouble was, Blaze would immediately realize who must have done it and they would still be aboard the ship when the *Enterprise* attacked.

One way or another, he would have to figure something out before the crew finished their repairs. And that was another thing. Installing new drive components was not something that could be done quickly, and it would require a drive systems shutdown. Since the cloaking device operated off the drives, then the *Glory* would not be able to remain cloaked during that time. Blaze knew that, and he wasn't worried. That bothered Riker. For the length of time it took to install the new drive system components, the *Glory* would be a sitting duck. Its phaser banks would remain operative off stored charges, but the ship would be completely unable to maneuver. There would be no way in hell

Blaze could hold off the *Enterprise* under such conditions. So why wasn't he worried?

"Need any help?" said San Marco, the navigator, coming up to stand beside him at the console.

"No, thanks. I think I'll manage," Riker replied.

"You're sure?"

"I think so."

"You'd better hope so, Gunner, for your sake."

Riker glanced at him and nodded. Yeah, he thought. Tell me about it.

Chapter Six

"Mr. Data, are you absolutely *certain* they are no longer on the planet surface?" asked Picard, with concern.

"I do not possess enough information to be absolutely certain, Captain," Data replied. "It is possible that Commander Riker and his party might have been removed to some location our sensors are not able to penetrate. However, we know that the K'trall do not possess the technology to interfere with our sensor scans, nor do they possess the knowledge to construct forcefields or structures which our sensors would be unable to penetrate."

"Yes, but the Romulans do," Picard said, grimly. "Commander Riker's party may have been taken prisoner, or even killed."

"I had considered that possibility, as well, sir,"

Data replied. "If that were the case, it would have been necessary for them to have been killed in such a manner as to preclude any attempt to communicate with us. A phaser or disruptor set on wide-dispersal beam might have accomplished that. However, I programmed the ship's sensors to scan for minute atmospheric traces of rapid nadion effect that would indicate any vicinity where a phaser or disruptor might have been discharged recently. I was able to pinpoint only one such locale, and the coordinates match those from which you recently beamed up with Colonel Z'gral. In other words, sir, despite the Romulan presence on D'rahl, the only one to have fired an energy weapon anywhere on the planet surface within the last twenty-four hours was yourself. Having eliminated that possibility does not, of course, mean that Commander Riker's party might not have met with violence by some other method, but lacking more detailed information, I am unable to draw any conclusions."

Picard took a deep breath. "Mr. Data, how many vessels are currently stationed in orbit above D'rahl?"

"Our sensors register eleven merchant freighters, sir," Data replied. "However, we are unable to detect any vessels on the other side of the planet."

"I want you to conduct sensor probes of all those vessels, Mr. Data, starting immediately," said Picard. "**Mr. Worf, contact Starbase 37 and the Merchant Spacefleet Union office on D'rahl and** request a complete listing of all vessels currently in port, along with scheduled departure times. Inform them that this is a Starfleet Priority request."

"Inform them also, Mr. Worf, that until further notice, all scheduled departures are canceled, as per my authority," Gruzinov added. "No vessel is to leave orbit without my personal authorization."

"Aye-aye, sir," Worf replied.

"I'll take the heat for that, Jean-Luc, don't worry," Gruzinov told Picard. "We'll get your people back."

"Assuming they are still alive," Picard said, grimly. "Commander Riker would not have left the planet surface voluntarily without communicating his intention to us. So either they have all been killed, or else they have been taken prisoner, most likely aboard a ship."

"Given the strength of the Romulan presence on D'rahl, it is entirely possible that they have a cloaked Warbird in the vicinity," Gruzinov said. "Perhaps even stationed in orbit and cloaked. We'd better notify Starfleet Headquarters."

Picard compressed his lips and nodded. "The Romulan presence on D'rahl leaves us with no other choice." He took a deep breath and exhaled heavily. "This may be the beginning of a war."

"Captain, I am receiving a message from the planet surface," Worf said.

"Onscreen, Mr. Worf."

Governor T'grayn's face appeared on the main viewscreen. He looked extremely agitated. "Captain Picard, I fear that I must lodge a formal protest. Word has reached me that you have abducted Colonel Z'gral and are holding him aboard your ship. I must demand his return immediately."

"Now, you listen to me, you fat, traitorous—" Z'gral began, angrily, but Picard took him by the arm and squeezed, firmly.

"Colonel . . ." he said, softly.

Z'gral fell silent at once. He was a soldier, and he understood that Picard was in command here.

"Governor," said Picard, "Colonel Z'gral came aboard this vessel voluntarily and has formally requested political asylum."

"Ridiculous," T'grayn replied. "Colonel Z'gral is not a dissident, nor is he a criminal. He is one of our most honored citizens! You invaded his home and—"

"Governor, let us drop this absurd pretense," Picard said. "You know perfectly well that I am fully aware of the conditions under which Colonel Z'gral was being held. Are you going to deny that there are currently at least two companies of Romulan centurions stationed at Colonel Z'gral's estate?"

T'grayn moistened his lips, nervously. "I . . . I have no idea what you're talking about, Captain. That is an absolutely outrageous allegation! You have no proof—"

"I saw them with my own eyes, Governor, and I have Colonel Z'gral to corroborate my testimony," said Picard. "Starfleet Headquarters is being notified of the Romulan presence on D'rahl even as we speak. Governor, this has gone beyond a mere question of clandestine support for freebooters and black-marketeering. This could mean *war."*

T'grayn looked shaken. "War?" He shook his head. "But . . . but that is absurd! I . . . I don't know what you're talking about! I . . . I don't know anything about any Romulans—"

"Enough of this," someone suddenly said, shoving T'grayn aside roughly. A new face appeared on the viewscreen. Picard tensed as he found himself looking at a man in the uniform of a Romulan tribune.

"Kronak!" said Z'gral, through gritted teeth.

"Captain Picard, you are in violation of K'tralli law," said Kronak. "Colonel Z'gral was being held prisoner, under house arrest, by the order of Overlord J'drahn. The conditions of political asylum do not apply to breaking a prisoner out of jail, as you very well know. I would strongly suggest that you return Colonel Z'gral to K'tralli custody at once."

"What nonsense is this?" Picard replied, angrily. "Under what authority do you presume to speak?"

"Authority? I was not issuing any orders or demands, Captain," Kronak replied, smoothly. "I was merely making a suggestion, as an interested party, you might say. The Romulan Empire certainly has a vested interest in preventing the spread of Federation hegemony. All this talk of war, for instance, is merely more evidence of Federation hostility and intimidation."

Picard stared at the Romulan with disbelief. "You have the unmitigated gall to accuse the Federation of hostility and intimidation when it is *you* who have broken the treaty of the Neutral Zone?"

"We have broken no treaty, Captain. There has been no hostile Romulan incursion into Federation territory. We are here at the invitation of Overlord J'drahn."

"Your very presence in Federation territory is in violation of the treaty, as you know perfectly well!" Picard replied.

"Is it your position that your Prime Directive allows you to dictate to the K'trall with whom they can or cannot conduct peaceful negotiations? I was under the impression that the Federation claimed to allow autonomy of government to its member planets. If the K'trall should decide to discontinue their alliance with the Federation and enter into a pact with the Romulan Empire, is the Federation threatening to go to war in order to prevent it? What is that, Captain Picard, if not hegemony and intimidation?"

"Is it your contention that Overlord J'drahn has 'invited' you here in order to conclude an alliance with the Romulan Empire and withdraw from the Federation?" asked Picard.

"You would have to ask Overlord J'drahn that question," replied Kronak. "I would not presume to speak for him."

"I see. And if Overlord J'drahn should request your departure, I suppose you will simply pack up and leave back across the Neutral Zone?" Picard said.

"Why, certainly, Captain," Kronak said. "We are not seeking to provoke a war. But, as I have said, you will have to take that question up with Overlord J'drahn."

"I fully intend to," said Picard. "In the meantime, there is a landing party from my ship that has turned up missing. I don't suppose you know anything about that?"

"Why should I?" Kronak asked. "It is not my job to keep track of your people, Captain Picard."

"Then you deny having them in custody?"

Kronak frowned. "What sort of game is this?" he asked.

"Answer the question!"

"I am not holding any of your people, Captain," Kronak said. "What possible reason would I have to do so? Let us speak frankly, Picard. You and I both know the situation here favors a resolution to my benefit. Why would I weaken my position by seizing Starfleet personnel and holding them hostage? That would constitute a clear initiation of hostilities. The very last thing I would wish to do is offer you any justifiable provocation. In fact, to demonstrate my sincerity in that regard, I am more than willing to have my centurions aid in the search for your missing landing party."

Picard stared at him, coldly. "I will take the time to consider your courteous offer," he said, with thinly disguised sarcasm. "Meanwhile, Colonel Z'gral will remain aboard this ship, as he is here of his own free will and Governor T'grayn has already stated for the record that he is neither a dissident nor a criminal. Picard out."

He gave Worf the cutoff signal.

"Counselor, what was your impression of Tribune Kronak?" Picard asked Troi.

"I sensed that he was telling the truth, Captain," Troi replied. "He seemed genuinely surprised when you implied that he might be holding Commander Riker's party. And I believe he was sincere in his offer to help search for them. He seems very confident of his position, and my impression was that he believes he can prevail without forcing a conflict."

"How can she possibly know that?" asked Z'gral, with a frown.

"Counselor Troi is half-Betazoid, and possesses strong empathic abilities," Picard replied. "If she believes Tribune Kronak was sincere in his denial of holding our people, then I am inclined to accept her judgment." He sighed, heavily. "Besides, the situation *does* favor a resolution to his benefit. If he can demonstrate that he is, in fact, here at the invitation of Overlord J'drahn, then it is J'drahn who bears the responsibility for violating the treaty. Given those circumstances, Kronak would have nothing to gain by holding our people. He has no need of hostages. If we took any action against him now, then he could claim that we were the ones who had initiated the hostilities."

"But they *have* crossed over the Neutral Zone, sir," Worf said.

"Yes, Mr. Worf, technically, they *are* in violation, but we are in something of a gray area here, thanks to Overlord J'drahn and Governor T'grayn. And after so many years of conflict, the Federation Council will not wish to risk a war. If the price of a continued truce is giving up the K'tralli Empire and extending the boundaries of the Neutral Zone, then I believe the Council would grudgingly pay it. Especially since J'drahn's involvement with the Romulans brings interpretation of the Prime Directive into question. We are in a very dangerous and highly volatile situation." He turned to Z'gral. "And you, Colonel, may be the only one who can help resolve it."

Z'gral nodded. "J'drahn must be removed from power," he said. "And H'druhn is the only one who can accomplish that. I must speak with him at once, Captain."

Picard nodded. "That was my intention," he said. "But it would mean leaving here and going to N'trahn."

"And you are concerned about the fate of your missing landing party," said Z'gral. "I understand. It is your decision, Captain."

Picard grimaced. "Mr. Data, have you completed your sensor probes of the ships in this vicinity?"

"Affirmative, Captain," Data replied. "But there is no sign of Commander Riker and his party being held aboard any of those vessels."

Picard took a deep breath. "Mr. Worf, have we

received the information we requested from Starbase 37 and the Merchant Spacefleet Union?"

"Aye, Captain," Worf replied. "There are currently twenty-three ships in port, stationed in orbit above D'rahl. Subtracting the eleven we have already scanned, that leaves twelve stationed in orbit on the opposite side of the planet."

"Not counting Blaze's ship," Picard said, "assuming it is here and cloaked, or the possible presence of a Warbird." He shook his head. "I cannot believe that Kronak would be so confident without a ship to back him up, and in the time it would take for us to make a half-orbit around D'rahl to scan those vessels, he could make his move. If Blaze's ship is here and cloaked, our sensors will not detect it. We could be under his guns even as we speak. Or under the guns of a Romulan Warbird."

"Or both," said Gruzinov. "Our shields would not stand up under fire from both ships, and Kronak could easily claim that we were attacked by Blaze alone. You're right, Jean-Luc. Now that Kronak's hand has been exposed, the longer we remain here, the more vulnerable we are."

"It concerns me that Kronak does not seem to be worried about General H'druhn," Picard said. *"Why* isn't he worried?"

"By the gods!" Z'gral said, suddenly.

"What is it, Colonel?" Picard asked, glancing at him sharply.

"I am an old fool!" Z'gral said, in an angry,

self-recriminating tone. "The Romulans often kept me awake conducting drills at the estate. I had simply assumed they did it to prepare against the possibility of an assault. There are still soldiers in the army who are loyal to me, and I merely thought T'grayn was not taking any chances. But now it all suddenly takes on a new perspective. The estate where I was confined had been built by a wealthy aristocrat as a replica of the Summer Palace on N'trahn!"

"General H'druhn's residence!" Gruzinov said. "Of course! They plan to seize the Summer Palace and assassinate him!"

Picard took a deep breath and decided. "Mr. Koski, set course for N'trahn and take us out of orbit."

"But what about your people, Captain?" asked Z'gral.

"We cannot afford to waste any time looking for them now," Picard said. "Small wonder Kronak was willing to help us search for them. Anything that would keep us at D'rahl, a formal protest over Colonel Z'gral or a search for our landing party, would only play into his hands and buy him time to put his plan into effect."

"I still have one operative cruiser stationed at the starbase," said Gruzinov. "I could dispatch it to D'rahl at once and make certain none of those ships leave orbit."

Picard shook his head. "No, Ivan, I wish it could be so, but with the possibility of a cloaked Romulan

Warbird in the area, we don't dare leave Artemis VI unprotected."

Gruzinov made a wry grimace. "It wouldn't be very much protection," he said. "A Warbird would make short work of my light cruiser. And even if they are not holding our people prisoner, any one of those vessels in orbit above D'rahl could be used to ferry an assault force over to N'trahn."

"Unless they already have troops in place," Picard said. He shook his head. "No, I cannot take the chance. The colony on Artemis VI must be protected. Dispatch your cruiser there at once and have them stand by on yellow alert."

Gruzinov nodded. "Mr. Worf, get me Starbase 37."

"Aye-aye, sir."

"If Kronak has a Warbird, then by now they are aware we have left orbit," said Picard. "And you can be sure that they will follow us. Yellow alert, Mr. Worf."

"What have you done?" T'grayn said, wringing his hands in anxiety. "You have exposed me as a liar and a collaborator! You have exposed J'drahn! You have ruined everything!"

"Be silent," said Kronak, as he rapidly punched in a code on the viewscreen console.

"You could have withdrawn your troops!" T'grayn said. "I could have denied everything! It would have been their word against mine!"

"I said, *be silent,* you miserable slug!" said Kronak.

"What . . . what are you going to do?" T'grayn asked, fearfully.

The face of a K'tralli appeared on the viewscreen.

"This is Tribune Kronak. I wish to speak with Overlord J'drahn at once," said Kronak.

"Overlord J'drahn has retired for the night, sir," said the K'tralli.

"Then *wake* him! *Now!*"

"One moment, sir. . . ."

"Is everyone in this bloody culture an idiot?" said Kronak. There was a signal on his communicator. He removed it from his belt and snapped it open. "Kronak," he said.

"Your Excellency, the *Enterprise* has left orbit."

"Predictable," said Kronak. "Stand by to beam me back aboard the ship." He turned back to the console. "What's keeping that fool?"

J'drahn's sleepy-looking face appeared on the screen. "What is so important that it could not wait until morning, Kronak?" he asked, petulantly.

"Picard has Colonel Z'gral," said Kronak. "He is aboard the *Enterprise,* which has just left orbit and is undoubtedly on its way to N'trahn even as we speak."

J'drahn grew pale. Suddenly, he was wide awake. "B-but . . . h-how is that possible?" he stammered. "You *assured* me that Z'gral was going to be taken care of!"

"Regrettably, Picard reached him first and rescued him," said Kronak. "I did not think he had the nerve, but he is more clever than I thought. If you wish to maintain your position as overlord of the K'tralli Empire, then I suggest you see to it immediately that H'druhn is in no position to remove you from office."

"You mean . . ."

"I mean, *kill* him."

"But . . . my own father?" said J'drahn.

"Your own father, when confronted with your actions by Z'gral and Picard, is liable to have you executed for treason. I certainly would, if you were my son."

"No, he could never do that," J'drahn protested. "I have my loyal troops—"

"And he has his," said Kronak. "At the very least, he will bring a civil war down on your head, and as he is considerably more popular than you, I would not give great odds for your chances. You know what you have to do, so do it. *Now.*"

"But the *Enterprise* . . ."

"Leave the *Enterprise* to me," said Kronak. "Now stop wasting time. You have precious little of it left."

Kronak cut off the transmission and called his ship on his communicator. "Prepare to leave orbit," he said. "Beam me up now."

"But . . . what am *I* to do?" T'grayn asked, miserably.

"I could not care less," said Kronak, with contempt. "I have no further use for you."

The transporter from the Warbird locked on to him, and an instant later he was gone.

T'grayn stood alone, wringing his hands, his

chest rising and falling with his panicked, labored breathing. Sweat stood out on his high forehead. This was not how it was supposed to be, he thought. It was supposed to be nothing more than easy profits, letting the freebooters take all the risk . . . and all the blame. But everything had changed when J'drahn brought Kronak into it. Kronak and Blaze.

He had been a fool not to see this coming. Blaze was uncontrollable. And that had suited Kronak's purposes perfectly. T'grayn now saw that Blaze had been nothing more than a lure to bring the Federation starship. That was what Kronak had wanted all along, and J'drahn had been too greedy and too full of his own self-righteousness to see it. Or perhaps he truly didn't care if the Romulans took over. Perhaps he really believed they would retain him in his position as overlord of the K'trall. T'grayn knew better now. Kronak would discard J'drahn just as he had now discarded him. He could easily have killed me, thought T'grayn. Except that he did not even think that I was worth the trouble.

He had to get away. He had to escape while there was still time. If the Federation prevailed somehow, it would be all over for him. J'drahn's government would fall and they would both be tried for their crimes. And if the Romulans prevailed, as seemed likely, then every citizen of D'rahl would be howling for his blood. There would not be a safe place for him anywhere in the K'tralli Empire.

He sat down at the console and reached for the keyboard, his fat, beringed fingers trembling. He swallowed hard, moistened his lips, and punched in a code. When his call was answered, he took a deep breath, trying to steady his nerves, and said, "This is Governor T'grayn. I must speak with Captain Blaze at once."

Riker got out of the turbolift on Deck 7 and made his way quickly to sickbay. When he got there, Dorn was busy tending to a couple of the *Glory*'s crewmen, applying sealant to their wounds.

"I'll be with you in a moment," she said, glancing at Riker as he entered. She turned back to the crewmen and gave each of them a hypospray injection. "There, all finished."

"Thanks, Doc," the crewman said.

"Don't call me 'Doc,' I'm not a doctor," she said. "And I'm a little rusty at this, so try to finish each other off next time and save me the trouble of patching you up again."

"You're all right, Doc."

"Get out of here. I've got another patient and I'm still not finished taking inventory. Go."

"*Doc?*" said Riker, as they left.

"It seems I'm the closest thing they've got to a ship's doctor," Dorn said, wryly.

"What about Katana, with her built-in pharmacy?"

Dorn sneered. "You think she *gives* anything away? Besides, she's a shooter. All she knows how to do is inject drugs and biogens. And the stuff she's loaded with is worse than any pain you might've got."

"What happened to those two?" Riker asked.

"They got into a fight down in the cargo bay while they were unpacking some of the supplies. Went at each other with pry bars, for God's sake. Multiple contusions and lacerations, some minor fractures, a broken nose, and several missing teeth. Somebody broke it up before they killed each other. By the time they got here, it was all a big joke. They don't even seem to remember what started it." She shook her head and snorted. "Boy, this is some bunch. Merchant-fleet and military rejects, criminals and borderline psychopaths . . . Yet Blaze has somehow managed to make a crew out of them."

"You almost sound as if you admire him," said Riker.

"I suppose I do, in a way. He's got something. He's a charismatic individual, you've got to give him that."

"It sounds as if maybe he's been turning some of that charisma on you," said Riker.

"He's a very handsome man. And I think he's attracted to me," Dorn said, with a grin.

"You think that's funny?" Riker asked, frowning.

"Well, isn't it? I mean, considering the circumstances . . ."

"I *am* considering the circumstances. Where is he now?"

She shook her head. "I don't know. He brought me down here, gave me the grand tour, then told me to take inventory and make a list of anything I think the sickbay needs. And he wants it in a hurry, too. He doesn't plan on staying around here long."

"Well, neither do I," said Riker. "I don't have much time. I told the bridge crew I was just coming down here to get something for a headache."

"And they bought that?"

"It wasn't far from the truth," said Riker. "I'm getting a migraine trying to figure out how we're going to get out of this mess."

"Any ideas?"

"The transporter's our best shot," said Riker. "He's got two shuttlecrafts aboard this ship, but if we tried taking one of them, they could blast us before we got a hundred yards."

"Have you seen La Forge?"

Riker shook his head. "Not yet. I think he's still down in Engineering. And I haven't managed to get a fix on our position yet. But as soon as I do that, we'll have to move fast. We've got to get back to the *Enterprise* before Blaze can complete his repairs. We're going to have to arrange someplace to meet."

"Most of the crew is quartered on Deck 5," Dorn said. "Blaze and his senior personnel are on Deck 4. Deck 6 is vacant. We could meet in one of the empty cabins down there after most of the crew has gone to sleep."

"Assuming Blaze doesn't keep them working around the clock to get all the repairs completed," Riker said. He thought about it for a moment, then shook his head. "No, Deck 6 won't do. It would be the first place they'd look if they discovered we were missing, and it would be too easy for us get pinned down. Can you get to the aft Jeffries tube?"

"Shouldn't be any problem. There's a tube entry hatch just down the corridor from my cabin."

"Good. When it's time to make our move, take the Jeffries tube down to Deck 14. At the aft end of the horizontal intermix chamber is a double-sliding door leading to the landing bay control room. From there you can get down to the landing bay level on Deck 16. The chief engineer's office is down there. That's where we can meet up with Geordi. From there we can make our way down the stairwell to Deck 17 and the secondary hull's emergency transporter facility. Geordi can bypass the bridge controls and make sure they can't cut the power off from there."

"Right," said Dorn. "Then what? We can beam down to the planet surface, but how do we get in touch with the *Enterprise* without our communicators?"

"I'll try to get ahold of one, if I can," said Riker. "But by now it's been almost twenty-four hours since we checked in. Even if we can't signal the *Enterprise,* they'll be looking for us and they should be able to get a fix on us as soon as we're back down on D'rahl."

"Meanwhile, Blaze can get our transporter coordinates off the emergency transporter console after we're gone and beam down a party to come after us," she said.

"I didn't say it was going to be easy," Riker said.

"But if we can't get our hands on a communicator, we can call the *Enterprise* or Starbase 37 from the Merchant Spacefleet Union. Once we've reached the spaceport, we're in Starfleet jurisdiction."

"And I can get every security man under my command down there," said Dorn. She nodded. "It's a good plan. When do we move?"

"I don't know yet," Riker said. "As soon as possible. I'll have to talk to Geordi first. If he can figure out some way to sabotage Blaze's cloaking device, then we can disable the relay boards for the phaser bank controls and the photon torpedo launchers before we leave. That'll leave them essentially defenseless."

"Blaze will probably figure that out," said Dorn. "And he may have replacement components. I'd be surprised if he didn't."

"Maybe not, if we're lucky," Riker replied. "But even if he does, the repairs should tie up essential personnel and buy us and the *Enterprise* some time."

"We could use a diversion," Dorn said. "If I could disable the automatic fire control system on Deck 6 and get a blaze going, I'd still have plenty of time to make it to the Jeffries tube before the general alarm went off."

"It's risky, but it's worth a shot," said Riker. "Especially if they've got a drug laboratory set up down there."

"If they do, Blaze hasn't mentioned it. I asked him what he does with all the empty space down on

Deck 6 and he said they just use it for additional storage. If that's true, maybe we can pick up a communicator or some weapons down there."

"With a crew like this, I doubt he'd leave equipment like that lying around unprotected. In any case, there's not going to be much time to look for it." Riker shook his head. "No, forget the idea of going down to Deck 6. A diversion would be nice, but it's going to take time for you to get down to Deck 14 through the Jeffries tube. It's just not worth the risk."

"I can make it," Dorn said.

"I said no, forget about it," Riker said. "That's an order, Lieutenant. There won't be any time to wait for you. And it just adds to the chances for something going wrong. I'd better be getting back. I've still got to talk to Geordi. Sit tight until you hear from me. I'll get word to you somehow. If I can't do it any other way, I'll take the chance of calling you on the ship's intercom. We'll need a coded signal of some kind."

"You can call and ask me if I've found that medication yet," said Dorn. "If anybody asks, tell them it's something for your bad back and I couldn't find it when you came down before. I already told Blaze this place was a mess when he first brought me here, and it would take some time to organize everything."

Riker nodded. "Okay, that should work. But when you get the signal, don't waste any time. Got it?"

"Got it."

"And watch yourself with these people."

"I can take care of myself."

"Just remember, we can't afford any slips." Riker took a deep breath and exhaled heavily. "Keep your fingers crossed. With any luck, we'll get out of this thing in one piece."

"If not, we'll take as many of them with us as we can," said Dorn.

"Let's hope it doesn't come to that," said Riker.

"I hear you. But if it does, remember this: That cybrid bitch is *mine.*"

Chapter Seven

"Sir, subspace communication coming in from Starfleet Headquarters," said Worf, glancing up from his console.

"Onscreen, Mr. Worf," Picard said.

The logo of Starfleet Command appeared on the main viewscreen, along with the time and stardate, and a moment later, the image of Fleet Admiral Creighton appeared on the screen, seated behind his desk.

"Enterprise, your message regarding armed Romulan presence on the Federation-allied planet of D'rahl, in the K'tralli sector, has been received and submitted to Emergency Plenary Session 2351-B of the Federation Council. Pursuant to the Council Finding of this date, and Starfleet regulations regarding the provisions of the Treaty of the Algeron, the *U.S.S. Enterprise,* Captain Jean-Luc Picard, commanding, is herewith authorized to

take whatever steps deemed necessary, in the discretion of the commanding officer, to enforce the Treaty. Additionally, as of this date, Federation starships *Intrepid* and *Serapis* have been dispatched to the K'tralli sector, to rendezvous with the *Enterprise* and enforce the provisions of the treaty. Captain Jean-Luc Picard is hereby authorized to assume overall command on their arrival and make whatever command decisions he deems necessary regarding the dispositions of the joint expeditionary force. Signed and executed this date, by order of Federation Council, the Honorable Bokar Dirvak Singh, Chairman."

Creighton put the Finding he was reading from down on the desktop and gazed directly into the monitor. "There you have it, Jean-Luc. That's the official line. Note the language of the Finding, however. It does not, repeat, *not* constitute a formal declaration of war. The Council is suspending judgment on that issue, pending the actions of the Romulans. You're formally charged with enforcing the provisions of the treaty. Period. If that means engaging the Romulans and blowing them to kingdom come, then you are authorized to do it. And it doesn't necessarily mean you have to wait for them to initiate hostilities. In the opinion of the Council, they have already done that by crossing over the Neutral Zone and establishing a presence on D'rahl. They must vacate immediately and return to their own territory, or else suffer the consequences. No discussion."

Creighton took a deep breath, exhaled heavily,

and then continued, grimly. "There is, however, one fly in the ointment. The Council has, at least for the present, declined to vote on the question of expelling Overlord J'drahn from the Federation. The K'tralli Empire is and must remain Federation territory. From a strictly legal standpoint, that means K'tralli autonomy must be respected. You are not empowered to take any actions that would be in violation of a strict interpretation of K'tralli law, and you are not authorized to remove J'drahn from power." He paused. "But if a way could be found to remove J'drahn *unofficially,* the Council would not be unduly distressed. They didn't say that, however, and neither did I. You are hereby ordered, under the provisions of the Official Federation Secrets Act, to keep no record of this communication and you and any members of your crew who may be privy to it are never to discuss it with anyone. The only official record of this Finding will exist here, at Starfleet Command. And that goes for my supplementary remarks, needless to say. Good luck, Jean-Luc. End transmission."

The logo appeared on the viewscreen once again; then the screen went blank. For a long time, everyone on the bridge of the *Enterprise* remained absolutely silent as the import of Creighton's words sank in. Finally, Gruzinov broke the silence.

"Am I imagining things, Jean-Luc, or did I just hear Creighton tell you to—"

"You have just heard Admiral Creighton order us not to discuss the Council Finding with *anyone,*" Picard said, quickly interrupting him. "I interpret that to mean that we are not to discuss it among ourselves, as well."

Gruzinov stared at him, with astonishment. Picard's expression was unreadable. "My God," Gruzinov said, in a low voice. "Jean-Luc, what about the Prime Directive we're talking about—"

"One more word on this subject, Captain, and I shall be *forced* to have you placed under arrest and removed to the brig," Picard said, fixing Gruzinov with an unflinching gaze. "This is *my* responsibility, Ivan," he added.

Gruzinov stared at him for a moment, then swallowed hard and nodded. "Of course. I understand. But must you carry it alone?"

"Estimated arrival time at N'trahn, Mr. Koski," said Picard, curtly.

"Approximately ten minutes, sir."

"Captain," Troi said, "I must have a word with you. In private."

"My quarters, Counselor. Captain Gruzinov, you have the bridge in my absence."

"Yes, sir."

The moment the turbolift doors closed, Troi turned to Picard with concern and said, "Captain, you cannot possibly be considering—"

"I said, *in my quarters,* Counselor," Picard repeated.

"Yes, sir," she replied, and they went the rest of the way in strained silence.

The moment they entered Picard's quarters, he waited till the door had closed, then turned to her. "Now that we are safe from any possibility of being overheard, Deanna, allow me to anticipate you. No, I am most definitely *not* considering assassinating J'drahn. Surely, you did not think me capable of such a thing?"

Troi sighed with relief. "No, Captain, but considering what Admiral Creighton said—"

"Admiral Creighton *said* the Council would not be unduly distressed if J'drahn were removed unofficially," Picard replied. "That comment is, of course, open to interpretation, as Admiral Creighton fully realizes. I choose to interpret it very literally, as a simple statement of the Council's feelings concerning Overlord J'drahn, and not as any sort of order, direct or otherwise."

Troi nodded. "I understand. But Captain . . . what are you going to do?"

Picard sighed heavily and sat down at the table. He drummed his fingers anxiously on the tabletop. Troi watched him, her face full of concern. She could sense his inner turmoil.

"I don't know yet," he replied, after a moment. "But I am *not* going to start a war, if I can possibly help it. I wish to God that Will were here. And La Forge. To be confronting the possibility of engagement without my executive officer and chief engineer . . ." His voice trailed off and he simply shook his head.

"That is not all you are concerned about," said Troi.

Picard nodded. "No, it is not. I fear for their safety, Deanna, but I cannot afford to give any thought to that right now. I must consider the fact that *Intrepid* and *Serapis* cannot possibly arrive in time. We may well have a general engagement on our hands long before they get here. It all depends on just how far Kronak is willing to go. And if there is an engagement and we should lose, then *Intrepid* and *Serapis* will be arriving not merely to enforce the Treaty of Algeron, but to fight a full-scale war. I've got to prevent that at all costs."

"But the Council has practically tied your hands behind your back," said Troi. "If General H'druhn proves unable to remove his son from power, then how can you possibly fulfill the mission without contravening K'tralli law?"

"I cannot," Picard replied, "and the Council knows that perfectly well. They are practicing the fine art of brinkmanship. They have their official Finding as evidence of the fact that we were merely ordered to enforce the provisions of the treaty with all due respect for K'tralli autonomy. Never mind how ludicrous that may be in reality. As a policy decision, it possesses the proper ring of diplomacy."

There was a signal from the bridge. Picard activated his communicator. "Picard here."

"Captain, we are approaching N'trahn," Gruzinov said.

"I'm on my way," Picard said, getting to his feet. He turned to Troi. "This has been a privileged conversation, Counselor."

"Yes, sir," she said, with resignation. "I understand."

* * *

Riker got back to the bridge in time to catch the tail end of a communication from Governor T'grayn. He had not been part of the landing party that had visited the governor of D'rahl, so he did not recognize T'grayn's face on the screen when he came onto the bridge, but in the course of the conversation, it quickly became obvious who he was. Fortunately, his inability to recognize T'grayn also meant that T'grayn couldn't recognize him. In any case, T'grayn's attention was entirely on Blaze as Riker came onto the bridge. If T'grayn noticed him at all, thought Riker, it was probably merely as a body moving in the background. The K'tralli governor was overwrought and on the edge of hysteria. Riker took up his position at the weapons console and listened to the exchange.

"You have *got* to help me, Blaze!" T'grayn was saying. "You *owe* me!"

"I owe you?" Blaze said, his calm tone a marked contrast to T'grayn's agitation. "What, exactly, is it that I owe you, T'grayn? You have become rich from the bribes I've paid you, and you have raked off a generous percentage of all my profits in return for the dubious security you've granted me. There is nothing you have done for me for which I did not pay dearly."

"But I . . . I . . . I could have charged you a great deal more!" T'grayn protested.

"If you thought you could have, Governor, I have no doubt you would have done so. And then it is *you* who would have been the pirate and not me."

"But I have also given you valuable information!" said T'grayn. "I told you that the *Enterprise* has departed for N'trahn! If not for me, you never would have known that, stationed where you are!"

"Well, no, not really, Governor," said Blaze. "It is true that I have taken care to keep the planet between me and the *Enterprise,* even while cloaked, because I had no intention of underestimating Picard again. However, the fact is that Tribune Kronak contacted me only moments earlier and informed me of the *Enterprise*'s departure. He wanted me to join forces with him and pursue Picard to N'trahn, but regrettably, I have not yet completed my repairs. He was most displeased to hear that. He felt that I owed him something, too."

Riker tensed. In one brief, overheard exchange, he had just learned information that was absolutely staggering. Not only would the *Enterprise* be unable to help them, because it had departed for N'trahn, but there was a Romulan Warbird in pursuit. Moreover, the presence of a Romulan tribune could only mean one thing—not only a Romulan ship, but Romulan land assault troops. Only where? And how many?

"Without Kronak and myself, where would you have . . . Wait, what are you saying? *You mean you cannot leave?*" T'grayn asked, with alarm, as the full import of Blaze's words sank in.

"The repairs should be completed before long," Blaze replied. "Especially now that the *Enterprise* is gone and I can safely order a drive systems shutdown and decloak. But I estimate that it will take at the very least another twenty-four hours, and probably longer."

"How long?" T'grayn asked, moistening his lips nervously.

"A conservative estimate would be approximately seventy-two hours," Blaze replied.

"Three days?" T'grayn said, with despair. "In three days, we could be in the middle of a war!"

"Then I will try to get it done in two," said Blaze. "I have no desire to get caught between the Federation and the Romulans."

"You *must* take me with you, Blaze! Please, I *beg* you. . . ."

"Why?" asked Blaze. "Of what possible use would you be to me aboard this ship? You would merely be unwanted cargo. Unless, of course, you were in a position to make it profitable for me to take you. I do not imagine you would wish to leave all your ill-gotten gains behind."

"I . . . I was going to ask your help in transferring my assets," said T'grayn. "You have contacts in the Ferengi system, I know you do. I would gladly pay—"

"Half," said Blaze.

T'grayn's jaw dropped. *"Half?* But . . . that is *outrageous!"*

"Half," said Blaze. "Or you can remain on D'rahl and take your chances. A similar argument to the one you used on me when we made our arrangement."

"A third," T'grayn ventured, tenuously.

"Half," said Blaze, emphatically. "And be grateful I am considering it at all. I could simply leave, you know. However, for a fifty-percent fee, I will undertake to transfer all your assets to the Ferengi system and convey your miserable, fat carcass anywhere you wish to go. Do we have a deal?"

T'grayn swallowed hard. "Yes, damn you!"

"Splendid. Call me when you're ready."

He gave the cutoff sign and the viewscreen went blank. He turned around and saw Riker at the console.

"Ah, Stryker," he said. "I was told you went to sickbay. Feeling better?"

"I've got to check back with Thorn later," Riker said. "She couldn't find the proper medication for my back pain. She says it's a disorganized mess down there."

"Well, I trust she will soon organize it," Blaze replied. "How are you coming with the weapons systems?"

"It's coming back to me," said Riker. "But you never told me there was a Romulan Warbird in the area, in addition to a Federation starship. Nothing like a little pressure, is there?"

Blaze smiled. "You strike me as someone who works well under pressure. Besides, both the Warbird and the *Enterprise* have departed for N'trahn. With any luck, they'll blow each other to pieces. If not, we should be long gone before the victor can return."

"What if we're not? What happens then?"

"I suppose that would depend on who prevails,"

said Blaze. "But I suspect we have outlived our usefulness to Tribune Kronak. Henceforth, he will consider us a liability rather than an asset. I suggest you practice, Stryker. You have six hours before I run a test simulation for you."

"What happens if I fail the test?"

"The best gunner in his class at the Starfleet Academy fail a simple simulation run? I would be very much surprised and disappointed. But not as disappointed as you would be, I promise you."

"In that case, I'd better get down to Engineering and make sure the phaser bank relays and modulators are properly calibrated," Riker said. "And I'll want to check on the photon torpedo launchers, as well."

"You can do that from here," said Blaze, with a frown.

"But I won't know if I'm getting an accurate reading unless I check at the source," said Riker. "And LaBeau has his hands full directing the repairs."

"True," said Blaze, nodding. "Very well, go ahead then. And while you're at it, tell LaBeau to prepare for a drive systems shutdown in one hour. I will want all systems installed and fully operational six hours from now."

"Six hours?" Riker said. "But I thought you told T'grayn—"

"Six hours, Stryker. In six hours, I want to be ready for a shakedown cruise. And twelve hours from now, I intend to be out of this sector entirely. Let's hope LaBeau is up to the task, for his sake."

"Aye-aye, sir," Riker said, wryly. He left the bridge and took the turbolift down to Engineering. *Six hours?* Blaze was dreaming. To shut down, install new drive system components, restart, and recalibrate in that length of time would be one hell of a stretch even for a crack engineering crew such as the one Geordi had back aboard the *Enterprise*. For a crew of misfits such as this, it was impossible. Geordi was one hell of a chief engineer, the best Riker had ever seen, but he wouldn't be able to do it all alone. And that wasn't their biggest problem, Riker thought. Not by a long shot.

The plan had been to get off the ship. But now the *Enterprise* was gone, and even if they could get their hands on a communicator, the signal from a personal communicator could not reach to N'trahn. Somehow, Riker thought, I've got to warn them about that Warbird. But how? If they could reach the Merchant Spacefleet Union, he could send a message from there to Starbase 37, and have them warn the *Enterprise*. But in the time it would take for them to effect their escape from the *Glory,* it might already be too late. He would have to try and risk sending a message from the ship. And there was no way to do that without alerting the bridge crew. To warn the *Enterprise* in time, he thought, we're going to have to blow our cover.

Main Engineering was a madhouse. Most of Blaze's small crew was hard at work installing the replacement components and patching up damage. "Patching up" was the operative term, thought Riker, as he glanced around at all the activity. Any damage repair that wasn't absolutely essential to the operation of the ship was simply being ignored. He looked around for Geordi.

Riker was accustomed to the calm, steady efficiency of the *Enterprise*'s engineering crew. This was another story. Everywhere he looked, Blaze's ragtag crew members were hard at work, some bare-chested with their colorful tattoos covered with a sheen of sweat, others wearing only vests, or cutoff uniform shirts and trousers. The noise was almost deafening. Laser welders, power drivers and riveters, and plain old hammers and wrenches added to the din of the crew members' cursing and shouting at one another. The giant Ragnar was in the center of it, herding them along, every now and then adding a kick or a swat to the back to punctuate his booming orders. Finally, Riker spotted La Forge and waved to him. Geordi made his way over to him. He looked harried and tired.

"How's it going?" Riker asked.

"Do you have to ask?" La Forge replied, with exasperation. "If it wasn't for Ragnar, I think these guys would've killed me by now. And we've only been at it for a few hours. To top it off, I'm working with unfamiliar drive system components. But these drives are something else. The Romulans must have been planning a conversion like this for years. My guess is they were hoping to capture a Federation ship and use it as an infiltrator. These babies were custom-built, and whoever engineered them really knew his stuff. I'm telling you, the way they—"

"Geordi," Riker said, leaning close to make sure that no one else could hear them, not that there was much chance of that with all the noise, "are you actually trying to *fix* this thing?"

La Forge sighed, wearily. "I've got to at least go through the motions," he replied. "Ragnar's pretty sharp, but I'm still not sure how much he knows. I've got a few ideas, but I can't afford to do anything to sabotage this bird and have him catch me at it. Then we'd all be in for it."

"We're already in for it," Riker said. "I figured out a way we might get off this ship, but I just found out the *Enterprise* has left for N'trahn. And there's a Warbird in pursuit, with a Romulan tribune in command, no less."

"My God," said Geordi. "That means they've got assault troops. What are we going to do?"

Riker quickly outlined his escape plan.

Geordi nodded. "It should work, if we can time it right," he said.

"The trouble is, we could get down to the planet surface, but we'd still need to reach the *Enterprise*," said Riker. "And by the time we can get to the Merchant Spacefleet Union, it might already be too late."

"Mr. LaBeau!" Ragnar shouted. "We need you back here!"

"I'll be right there!" Geordi shouted back. He turned to Riker. "What other options do we have?"

"Just one. We try to signal the *Enterprise* from here," said Riker, grimly.

"How can we do that without blowing our cover?"

"We can't."

Geordi stared at him, then exhaled heavily. "Right," he said.

"Mr. LaBeau!"

"I'm coming!" Geordi turned back to Riker. "The *Enterprise* has to come first. We both know that. Do what you have to do, Commander."

"All right, Blaze is ordering a drive systems shutdown in one hour. If we can make our move just before he gives that order, we might have a shot at pulling this thing off. Try to get to the emergency transporter just before Blaze orders the shutdown. Tell Ragnar you've got to check something in the horizontal intermix chamber, make up whatever excuse you can, and then get down there so you've got enough time to preprogram the escape coordinates. You have to be ready to transport the moment Dorn gets down there."

"Got it. But what about you?"

"Don't wait for me. If I can, I'll use the main transporters on Deck 7, otherwise I'll send the message and move like hell to reach Deck 17. If you've already got the transporter preprogrammed, all I'll have to do is energize and jump up on the pad. But I might not make it, and there's no point in all of us getting caught."

"I understand," La Forge said. "Good luck, Commander."

"Yeah," said Riker. "You, too. We're gonna need it."

Riker went back out into the corridor. He was thinking fast. He didn't see how Blaze could get his ship operational within six hours, and without Geordi, he might never get it done. If they could just succeed in getting off the ship, he thought, Blaze would be effectively stymied. The question was, how to send a message to the *Enterprise* and still have time to get to the emergency transporter?

The timing would have to be perfect. He would have to allow enough lead time for Dorn to get down to Deck 14 and reach the emergency transporter facility two decks below, just aft of his present position. It shouldn't take her longer than three or four minutes to get from Deck 14 down to Deck 17, assuming she moved quickly and wasn't spotted, but how much time would she need to get down to Deck 14 from Deck 7 through the Jeffries tube? If she moved fast—and didn't get caught— then twenty minutes? A half hour, to allow her enough time to get away from sickbay? The best he could do was guess, and he couldn't afford to guess wrong. He would have to allow her as much time as possible and gamble that she wouldn't be missed too soon.

Dorn would represent the X factor. If he was absent from the bridge for an hour, it shouldn't arouse any suspicion. It could easily take much longer than that to check the relays and the calibration on the phaser banks and the torpedo launchers, especially if adjustments were necessary. Geordi could easily come up with an excuse to leave Main Engineering and check on something, then get to the emergency transporter one deck below within minutes. Dorn would have to traverse the entire dorsal length of the ship through the Jeffries tube. Riker checked the time. Best to give her the signal now, he thought.

He found a bulkhead intercom and called sickbay, using the prearranged code just in case anyone else was listening.

"Sickbay," Dorn replied.

"This is Stryker. Have you located that medication yet?"

"Not yet, but I still haven't checked through all the stores. You'll just have to be patient for a little while. I'll give you call as soon as I've inventoried all of the supplies."

"Okay, thanks," said Riker, "but don't take too long." He clicked the intercom off. The plan was in motion. She would be on her way down the Jeffries tube as soon as she could get to the access hatch. He had about forty-five minutes left before shutdown to get a call out to the *Enterprise* and head for the emergency transporter. Fortunately, Blaze would not expect him back on the bridge any time soon.

Riker had a pretty good idea just what Blaze was planning. He would have T'grayn prepare an authorization for his K'tralli banks to execute a coded subspace transfer order of all his assets to the Ferengi system, undoubtedly to one of Blaze's own accounts. Then he would tell T'grayn that he was waiting for a subspace confirmation of the transfer before taking him aboard. And while T'grayn waited to hear from him, Blaze would simply leave. T'grayn undoubtedly had considerable assets, and Blaze's mind would be on getting hold of them, especially since he had contributed so heavily to T'grayn's wealth in the first place. But even though Blaze would be preoccupied with hijacking T'grayn's accounts, there still wasn't any time to lose.

Riker knew his best chance to get a message out quickly would be to do it from Auxiliary Control on Deck 7. That would also put him within close distance of the main transporter rooms. Blaze would undoubtedly have someone stationed there. The armory was also on Deck 7. It would be locked, and probably guarded under normal circumstances, but with a small crew and every available crewman needed for the repair details, there was a chance there might be no one posted at the armory. But he didn't want to have to bet on that.

If he could reach Auxiliary Control, it would almost certainly be vacant. Getting there would be only the first problem, however. Once inside, he could compose his message in advance on the computer, then lock out the bridge controls and broadcast it on Starfleet frequency, so that it would reach both Starbase 37 and the *Enterprise*. There would be little point in taking time to code the message. Just sending it would blow their cover, and then Blaze would realize who sent it and exactly what it contained.

As Riker made his way back to the upper decks, he tried to estimate how much time he would have from the moment he started to transmit the message. The moment he keyed "transmit," it would be picked up on the bridge immediately, unless they were all asleep up there. Not much chance of that, he thought, wryly. It would take only a moment for the communications mate, T'gahl, to register the transmission command on his console, see where it was coming from, and warn Blaze. Another moment for Blaze to order crewmen to auxiliary control.

The bulk of the crew were working on repairs, but aside from those on the bridge, Blaze had to have at least some crewmen posted at key stations throughout the ship. Someone would have to be stationed at the main transporter rooms, and probably at the armory, as well. They would be closest, so he should probably count on at least two people within easy reach of him on Deck 7. The rest would be up on the bridge or working down in the aft section of the ship. Some of the crew would EVA with workbees as soon as Blaze ordered the drive systems shutdown, so they could start work on the exterior of the hull. Geordi would probably assign as many of them to EVA detail as he could reasonably get away with before he made his move, and he would try to make sure the rest of them were tied up with work, as well.

In any case, thought Riker, it would take much longer for crewmen to reach him at auxiliary control from the aft section of the ship than it would if they came down directly from the bridge. Blaze would realize that, of course, which meant that Blaze would probably come after him himself, with some of the bridge crew. The turbolift could take them directly from the main bridge to Auxiliary Control in about a minute or two. That wasn't much time.

He could get to the main transporters in about a minute or two if he ran, but if he was slowed down by having to overpower anyone in his way, and then having to program his escape coordinates, it would give those coming from the bridge enough time to catch up with him. He decided he couldn't take the risk. He might be able to overpower one or two men in a couple of minutes, if he was lucky, but he'd never have enough time to program the transporter. And Blaze would undoubtedly realize he would be heading there.

No, thought Riker, the main transporters were out. He'd have to do it the hard way, and hope like hell they didn't catch on soon enough. Send the message, then race full-tilt down the length of Deck 7 to the vertical intermix shaft, take one of the one-man lifts that ran along the shaft down to Deck 15, and race down the companionway through the horizontal intermix chamber to the landing bay control room. From there, he could take the stairs down to Deck 17. That was a long way to go. And if Blaze figured out where he was heading, he'd have plenty of time to get on the ship's intercom and order crewmen up from Engineering to cut him off. Where? The most likely places for him to get trapped would be either in the horizontal intermix chamber or on the stairs, coming down from the landing bay control room.

"Options, Number One," Picard would say at a time like this. "I want options." Well, Riker thought, there just flat weren't that many. Try for the main transporters on Deck 7 and he would be caught while trying to overpower the transporter operator or program the escape coordinates, or else try to make it down to Deck 17, where Geordi would have the transporter all set to go, and take a chance on getting caught between the horizontal intermix chamber and the emergency transporter facility in the secondary hull. Either way, there was a good chance he'd never make it.

What I wouldn't give for a phaser right now, he thought, as he stepped out of the turbolift on Deck 7. Or even that bowie knife. As he passed sickbay, he quickly glanced inside. Dorn was already gone. Good, he thought. Move it, Lieutenant. Fly. He kept on walking down the corridor, past the armory and the main transporter rooms. He couldn't tell if anyone was on duty in the transporter rooms, because the doors were closed. No one was stationed outside the armory, but it was locked, which meant that anyone trying to break in would alert whoever was stationed at the transporters. Assuming there was only one transporter operator on duty, that meant he only had one man to get past once the bridge gave the alarm. He was tempted to check, but he didn't want to risk the transporter operator becoming suspicious and checking with the bridge to see what he was doing there. He was supposed to be clear at the other end of the ship.

No, he couldn't risk it. He had to get the message out first.

He made it to the auxiliary bridge and entered. No one there. Blaze wasn't very careful about security. But then, under the present circumstances, he couldn't afford to be. He was far more vulnerable uncloaked and with his drive systems shut down. He had to use every crew member he could spare for the work details to get the job done as quickly as possible.

Riker sat down at the computer console and punched up duplicate readouts from the navigation station on the bridge. It was safe enough to do that, he thought, it wouldn't alert them up there. He noted the position of the *Glory,* then started to compose his message. Keep it short and to the point. "Riker to *Enterprise,"* he typed. "Landing party shanghaied aboard *Glory,* in orbit above D'rahl." He entered the position coordinates. "Unknown number Romulan forces present in area. T'grayn/J'drahn in collusion. Warbird on your tail, in pursuit. Red alert. Will try to effect escape. If unsuccessful, give 'em hell. End message."

He sat back and stared at the screen. That should do it, he thought. He checked the time. Roughly twenty minutes before Blaze gave the shutdown order. They would have already started preparing for it on the bridge and down in Engineering. That meant Geordi would be making his move in about ten or fifteen minutes. Riker wished he could take advantage of that time to simply program the auxilliary communications console to send the message in ten minutes and then start making his way back down to Deck 17, but unless he locked out the bridge controls, there was a chance that they could interrupt the signal from the bridge. And the moment he locked out the bridge controls, he'd give himself away. He grimaced. Nothing to do but sit tight for at least the next ten minutes. Then lock out the bridge controls, send the message, and run like hell.

Dorn climbed quickly down the ladder running the length of the aft Jeffries tube. It was a long way down and she had to move fast. There was just one problem, something she hadn't told Riker about. Something she had never told anyone about.

She had received a commendation for the mission in which those renegade cybrids had been killed, the same mission that had seen the entire landing party under her command wiped out. Those cybrids had fought harder than anyone expected. The authorities on Artemis VI were supposed to aid her people, but they'd had enough. Starfleet was on hand, and they wanted Starfleet to take care of it. The three cybrids had holed up in a warehouse at the spaceport. They had probably hoped to commandeer a shuttle and try to get off-planet, but they had run out of time. The warehouse was surrounded, but none of the colonists were willing to go in and get them. The job fell to the landing party.

They went in, and it was horrible. The cybrids

took out three of them before they knew what hit them. And Dorn had panicked. She had found an empty shipping crate and crawled inside, fastening the lid, and there she had cowered, in the dark, in the cramped, closed-in dark, while the cybrids stalked and systematically took out the remainder of her command. She had been completely paralyzed with fear, waiting for them to find her. She heard her crewmates calling out for her, and was too terrified to respond, too terrified to move. The last one to die had been Ensign Mathieson. But as the cybrids moved in for the kill, the dying young ensign had set his phaser on overload and the cybrids were killed in the resulting explosion. When it was all over, she was the only one left alive, and she got the credit for what Ensign Mathieson had done. And she could never admit what had really happened. She had carried the guilt in secret ever since. And she had also carried something else . . . something she had gained while cowering in that cramped, dark shipping crate. She had developed claustrophobia.

The Jeffries tube was narrow, and it was very close in there. As she climbed down the ladder, she felt the terror mounting and was helpless to do anything to stop it. All she could think of was getting *out* of there. Her breathing came in short gasps and she felt her stomach knotting up.

"Come on, come on," she told herself, as she climbed faster. "I've got to get out. I've got to get . . . out. . . ."

She slipped and almost fell. She grabbed on to the

rungs of the ladder and clung to it for dear life. She had to go on, but the panic was starting to overwhelm her, and if she gave in to it, she was liable to fall while trying to scamble madly down the ladder.

She took great, gulping, deep breaths, desperately trying to steady her screaming nerves. And then the lights in the tube flickered.

"Oh, no . . ." she said.

They must have been doing something with the power down in Engineering. A moment passed, and the lights flickered again.

"Please, no . . ." she said.

And then the lights went out.

"No, no, *nooooo . . ."* she wailed, as the darkness enveloped her. "No, please," she moaned. "Come on, come on, come back on, *please. . . ."*

But the darkness persisted. She began to whimper. She tried to will herself to move, but her fingers would not let go of the rungs. She was frozen with fear. The minutes passed, and it grew worse and worse. She could feel the cold sweat trickling down her spine.

"Got to get out," she whispered. "Got . . . to . . . get . . . *out!"*

With an effort, she managed to climb down another rung, but her entire body had started trembling violently.

"Come on," she urged herself. "Come on, you . . . lousy . . . damn . . . good for . . . nothing . . . *coward. . . ."*

She moved a little farther, but it was slow, agonizingly slow, going, and it was all she could do to keep herself from screaming. Too long. It was taking too long.

"Move it, Dorn!" she said, through gritted teeth. *"Move* it, damn you!"

Little by little, she started making progress. But it was too slow, much too slow. It seemed like an eternity had passed before the lights came on again. She sobbed with relief. And suddenly, the fear had left her. Just like that, it was gone. She started moving quickly once again, but she had no idea how much time had passed. And as she clambered down the ladder to Deck 14, she thought about Riker and La Forge, and wondered how she would be able to live with herself if her fear resulted in their being caught.

"Ragnar, get the workbees ready for EVA," said Geordi. "We'll be going to shutdown in about five minutes. I've got to go check on the flow regulators in the horizontal intermix shaft. We want to make sure we're getting the same readings down here. I'll be back in time for shutdown."

"Right, Mr. LaBeau," said Ragnar, nodding. He raised his booming voice. "All right, workbee detail, report to landing bay and prepare for EVA!"

Geordi hurried out of Main Engineering and headed quickly down the corridor, not toward the horizontal intermix chamber, but in the opposite direction, toward the landing bay control room and the stairway down to Deck 17. He knew he had to move fast. He hoped Dorn had made it all right. She should already be there. But his main concern was for Riker. He hated leaving without him. But then, Riker might not make it. They both knew that. If he was captured, then Blaze probably wouldn't kill him. He'd know the message had gone out to the *Enterprise* and Riker would be valuable as a hostage. Geordi pushed the thought from his mind. Don't think about it, he told himself. Riker's gonna make it. He's got to.

He hooked his legs over the railings of the stairway and slid down to the lower landing, then slid down again to the lower deck. Moments later, he had reached the emergency transporter facility doors. He went inside. Dorn wasn't there. *Damn,* he thought. Where *is* she? He rushed over to the console and started to compute the transporter coordinates for the spaceport on D'rahl. *"Come on, Lieutenant, come on,"* he said, under his breath. He checked the time. Two minutes. Where the hell was Dorn?

The coordinates were now locked in. All it took was throwing the switch to energize and they could be off the ship in seconds. But there was still no sign of Dorn. He waited, tensely, wondering what could have gone wrong. He didn't have any details working in the Jeffries tube that ran along the dorsal fin of the ship. If she was able to get out of sickbay and make it to the access hatch, she should have a clear shot all the way down to Deck 14. He had made sure there was no one working up there, so that she could get to the stairs that led down to the rear of the horizontal intermix chamber on Deck 15. From there, she just had to get through a short corridor to the stairs leading down to Decks 16 and 17. If she ran into anyone along the way, it would be there, but he had assigned as many of the crew to EVA duty as possible, using the reasonable excuse that more personnel would get the job done faster, and everyone else would be tied up in Main Engineering. Should he risk going to check?

He was out of time. *"Dammit,"* he swore. He couldn't leave without her. The moment he energized the transporter, it would show up on the bridge, and if she came in after him, they could alert the men in Engineering and catch her before she could beam down. Either they went together, or she would be left behind.

They would be starting the drive systems shutdown. There would still be power to the transporters, but by now everyone would be wondering where he was. *What was keeping Dorn?*

It was time. Riker locked out the bridge controls, keyed the transmit command, and then bolted through the doors, running at full speed. The sound of his running footsteps in the empty corridor alerted the man on duty in the transporter room and he came out almost as Riker drew even with the doors. Riker didn't even slow down. He smashed into the man at full speed, bowling him over, then paused only long enough to deliver a sharp blow to his jaw as he tried to get back up. He quickly checked to see if the unconscious man was armed. He wasn't. Riker swore and took off running once again.

They would be coming down from the bridge right now, and Riker knew there would never be enough time to enter one of the main transporter rooms and program the escape coordinates before they got to him. But the unconscious man lying in the corridor might buy him some time. They would assume that he had gone into one of the main transporter rooms, and they would check inside each one before they realized that none of the transporters had been activated. With luck, that would allow him enough time to get down to the horizontal intermix chamber. It was about to get real dicey.

If Blaze was smart, he'd leave someone behind in Auxiliary Control to remove the lockout on the bridge, and then they'd have access to the ship's PA. Unfortunately, there was no way Riker could disable it from Auxiliary Control. The best he could do was prevent them from using it up on the bridge. But as soon as the lockout was removed, they'd be able to get on the PA from auxilliary control. If Blaze figured out where he was going, he could alert the crew in engineering and there were two places where they could cut him off. If they came up the stairs forward of the landing bays, they could cut him off as he was coming through the horizontal intermix chamber. His only chance was to get through the chamber first. Otherwise, they could cut him off between the landing bay control room on Deck 15 and the emergency transporter on Deck 17, forward of the landing bay.

Riker was gambling that if they realized where he

was headed, they'd figure on his taking the shortest and most direct route, down the stairs forward of the landing bay to the engineering deck, then along the corridor and down the forward stairs to Deck 17. Instead, he planned to race straight through to the landing bay control room at the extreme aft end of the ship, then down the stairs to Deck 17 and across the landing bay. If he could just manage to get through the horizontal intermix chamber before they cut him off, then he could flank them. They'd be coming up the stairs forward of the landing bay while he was coming down from the landing bay control room.

He gritted his teeth and tried to will the lift to move faster down the shaft. It seemed maddeningly slow. He was almost down to the level of Deck 14 when he heard Blaze's voice on the ship's PA echo throughout the shaft.

"Attention, all hands! Attention, all hands! Find and apprehend Stryker, LaBeau, and Thorn immediately! Repeat, find and apprehend Stryker, LaBeau, and Thorn immediately! Cut off all access points to the cargo bay transporter and the secondary hull emergency transporter facility! I want them alive! Repeat, I want them alive!"

"Son of a bitch!" swore Riker. He leaped off the lift as it approached the level of Deck 15 and dropped the rest of the way down.

He landed hard, rolled, and came up running, sprinting hard along the length of the horizontal intermix shaft. He had been a track star back in high school, but that was a long, long time ago and the doors at the other end of the chamber seemed impossibly far away. He pumped his arms and kicked hard, running all out and gasping for breath. Thirty more yards . . . twenty . . . ten . . .

His shoulders barely cleared the opening doors as he plunged through. He heard shouts and running footsteps coming up the stairs from below. Another few seconds, and they would have cut him off. But all the noise they were making would easily drown out the sound of his running footsteps. He kept on going toward the aft end of the ship, got to the stairs at the landing bay control room, hooked his legs over the railings and slid down to the first landing, just as four crewmen were coming up from the floor of the landing bay. For a moment, they were startled as they saw him suddenly appear on the landing just above them, and Riker took advantage of that instant of surprise to launch himself in a headlong dive down the stairs, directly at them.

He hit the first man and they all went down like dominoes, tumbling in a heap to the floor of the landing bay below. Riker came up fighting. The man at the bottom caught the worst of it, and had apparently been knocked out. But that still left three others. The burly crewman Riker had struck first clamped his arms around him in a crushing bear hug. Riker butted him in the face with his head, breaking the man's nose. As the man let go and howled with pain, Riker rolled free. As he scrambled to his feet, so did the remaining two crewmen.

One of them came at him with a roundhouse

right. Riker caught his wrist and, using the man's own momentum against him in an aikido move, sidestepped and flipped him over onto his back, breaking his wrist in the process. As the second man came rushing at him, Riker dropped to one knee and threw the man over his head. He landed hard, but as he came up, Riker was ready for him. He moved in quickly and grabbed the man's head as he was getting up, jerking it down sharply as he raised his knee to meet his chin at the same time. The crewman crumpled to the deck, unconscious.

As Riker turned to start across the wide expanse of the landing bay, he saw Katana standing in front of the doors across from him, holding a disruptor aimed straight at his midsection.

"Not bad, hotshot," she said. "But not good enough."

Riker simply stood there, breathing hard from his exertions, and his heart sank. There were at least twenty yards separating them. No chance of disarming her at all.

"My judgment must be slipping," she said, approaching him, the weapon dead steady in her hand. "I had you figured all wrong. So you're a Federation agent."

"I'm a Starfleet officer," said Riker.

"Is that right?" she said, coming closer at a leisurely pace. "So what's your real name, hotshot?"

"Commander William Riker, executive officer, *U.S.S. Enterprise.*"

"My, my," she said, coming closer still, the

disruptor never wavering for an instant. "And here I thought you were just a small-time hijacker and fraud artist. But a Starfleet officer . . . Well, that'll work out just fine. They'll find you dead, and when the cloaking device fails at the crucial moment, Blaze will assume you must have done it."

Riker stared at her, and then it sank in. "So then it was you who misaligned the targeting system," he said. "It never was the gunner. You're the saboteur! You're working for the Romulans."

"You ought to thank me," she said. "If not for me, the *Enterprise* would have been taken out of action. But Kronak doesn't really need Blaze anymore. Or the *Enterprise,* for that matter. The game plan's changed. Either way, I still get paid."

"How do you figure on living to collect?" asked Riker.

"I've got my escape prepared," she said. "Too bad you're not going to make yours." Her gaze flicked quickly from him to the men lying unconscious on the deck and back to him again. "I've got to admit, you're pretty good. Let's see just how good you are."

And to Riker's amazement, she tossed the disruptor aside. He watched it fall and skitter across the deck, its impact-resistant casing preventing it from firing.

"There it is, hotshot," she said. "I'll be a sport. Let's see if you can get to it."

Riker lunged for the weapon, but the cybrid was faster. She cut him off and chopped out with her robotic arm. Instinctively, Riker went for an aikido move, but trying to capture and exert leverage on a metal joint was pointless. She reversed his grip neatly, breaking his hold in the process, and trapped his elbow, exerting pressure upward, against the joint. Riker grunted with pain, but before he could react with any move of his own, she slammed her fist into his stomach. The wind went whistling out of him. She released him and, at the same time, smashed him in the face with her natural hand. Riker staggered backward feeling blood spurt from his cut lip.

She was fast, thought Riker as he backed away, fighting for breath, and she could punch like a prizefighter. But she was only playing with him. If she had hit him that hard with her robotic hand, she would have demolished his entire jaw. What was more, she could shoot him full of nightmarish narcotics with her built-in hyposprays, or else extend the needles from the fingernails of her other hand and give him a dose of bioengineered glandular secretions that would give him a cerebral embolism, fry his nerve synapses, and stop his heart, all at the same time. Only she wasn't going for it. That would be too easy.

"Come on, hotshot," she taunted him. "Let's see what you've got."

Still doubled over slightly, Riker suddenly dropped to the deck and swept her feet out from under her. As she fell, he cocked his leg and uncorked a kick from prone position, straight at her head. Her neck snapped back with the impact, but she shook it off and kicked up to her feet, landing lightly. Riker barely scrambled up in time. Bad move, he thought. That alloy casing on her skull absorbed most of the impact. A head shot was not the way to bring her down. Go for the body.

As she swung, he ducked underneath the blow and hammered her with two hard, fast shots to the midsection, one to the stomach, one to the ribs. She grunted and straightened him out with an uppercut, then a shot to the chest with her metal hand. It felt as if he'd been hit with a sledgehammer. He was knocked about six feet backward, right off his feet. Those two blows to the midsection hadn't even slowed her down.

"Is that all you've got?" she mocked him, as he struggled back up, clutching at his chest. It felt as if at least three or four ribs were broken. "Come on!"

He suddenly realized they had gained an audience. Some crewmen had come down from the landing bay control room, behind him, and others came through the doors of the landing bay behind Katana. They started shouting encouragement to both of them. They wanted to see a fight. Well, he was just in the mood to oblige them. At least Geordi and Dorn had gotten clear.

She came at him, swinging. He slipped the first blow, ignoring the pain in his chest, and blocked the second, then drove a palm heel strike straight up into her jaw. As her head snapped back, he followed it up with a hard left to her chin, putting everything he had into the blow. She went down, but rolled as she fell and came back up again.

Gasping for breath, Riker rolled his eyes and

shook his head with disbelief. What the hell was she made of? He had given her his best shot. He had just about nothing left. She came at him again and he couldn't move fast enough to slip the blow. He tried a forearm block instead, and it felt as if his arm had come in contact with a wooden club. And then she let him have it with her metal hand, an openhanded swipe across his head. It knocked him sprawling.

It felt as if a gong had gone off inside his skull. His vision had gone blurry. He tried to get up, supporting himself with his hands, but she kicked him in the side and he went down again.

"Come on! Get up!" she shouted, over the din of the cheering crewmen.

Riker shook his head, trying to clear his vision. He blinked several times, and as his gaze slowly focused, he saw Blaze standing in front of the crowd near the entrance to the landing bay. To his despair, he saw Geordi and Dorn beside him, each being held by a couple of crewmen.

"Katana!" Blaze shouted.

She glanced back at him over her shoulder. The others all fell silent at the sound of their captain's voice.

"I want him alive," said Blaze.

"What for?" she said, and launched another kick at Riker. He saw it coming, but he couldn't get out of the way. He felt it connect and groaned with pain. He rolled over onto his back. His mind was screaming at him to get up, but his body simply would not obey.

"Back off, damn you!" Blaze shouted. "He's had enough!"

"Not yet he hasn't," she said, raising her arm and extending the needles from her fingernails.

"Katana!"

Riker focused everything he had on trying to get up, but only managed to make it to his knees. And as everyone watched, distracted, Dorn suddenly broke away from the men holding her and launched herself at the cybrid with a scream. As Katana turned, Dorn leaped and brought her down. They both fell to the deck together, but Katana clamped her metal arm around Dorn's waist, rolled her over, and plunged her needles to the hilts into her neck.

"No!" Geordi shouted, struggling against the men who held him.

Dorn cried out and stiffened. Her eyes opened wide and her body jerked as Katana withdrew the needles. And then Dorn said something inaudible and spat directly in the cybrid's face.

As Katana got up, wiping her face with the back of her hand, Riker heard the high-pitched sound of disruptor cycling, and the cybrid suddenly became wreathed in light. An instant later, she was gone, disintegrated.

There was complete silence in the landing bay. Then Blaze spoke. "I *said* I wanted them alive."

Riker crawled over to where Dorn lay, her entire body spasming.

"I'm . . . sorry, sir . . ." she said, trembling violently and struggling to get the words out. "I . . . guess I . . . blew it. . . ."

Those were the last words she ever spoke. Riker put his head down on her chest and moaned.

"Help him up," he heard Blaze say.

He felt hands on him, lifting him to his feet. He felt his arms being draped over shoulders on either side, as he was supported between two men. He looked up and saw Blaze standing in front of him.

"I am genuinely sorry about that," Blaze said to him. "Katana disobeyed orders, and she paid the price."

"Is that supposed to make it even?" Riker said, weakly.

"No," said Blaze. "But I will not have my orders disobeyed. It looks like you'll require medical attention. Unfortunately, your friend was the closest thing we had to a doctor aboard this ship. The next closest, I'm afraid, is me. Let's hope your injuries are not too serious. I may only wind up making them worse. Ragnar, take him to sickbay."

The huge engineering chief came up to Riker and took him from the men supporting him, lifting him up in his arms as easily as if he were baby. And Riker felt just about as helpless.

Chapter Eight

"MESSAGE COMING IN from the planet surface, Captain," Lieutenant Worf said.

"Not now, Mr. Worf," Picard said.

"Sir, it is from Overlord J'drahn."

"Let him wait," Picard said, curtly. "Let him sweat a little. Have we received those transporter coordinates from Starbase 37?"

"Received and entered, sir," Worf replied.

"Is the landing party standing by in the main briefing room?"

"Standing by, sir."

"Very well, Mr. Worf, we will conduct the briefing from here. Put us up on the screen in the main briefing room."

Worf punched a few buttons on the console, then looked up. "Ready, Captain."

In the main briefing room, the screen came on, showing a view of the bridge. The personnel selected for the landing party, hand-picked by Worf for their proficiency, settled down to watch and listen.

"Attention," said Picard. "We are about to begin the mission briefing. The session will be conducted by Captain Gruzinov. Captain?"

"Thank you, Captain," said Gruzinov. "We have received transporter coordinates from Starbase 37 from my last visit to the Summer Palace, the residence of General H'druhn. They will bring us down into the courtyard in front of the main entrance. Mr. Data, can you bring up that map we generated on the computer?"

"Aye, sir," Data replied, and punched up the simple, blueprint-style map he had drawn on the computer, following Gruzinov's directions. It appeared on the main viewscreen and on the viewscreens in the briefing room at the same time, a simple white drawing against a black background.

"Superimpose the magnified scanner image, please, Mr. Data."

A high-resolution photographic image of the Summer Palace, taken from orbit, appeared superimposed over the blueprint.

Gruzinov approached the console and activated the touch-sensor on the console screen. As he touched a spot on the console screen with his finger, a corresponding cursor appeared on the main viewscreen and the viewscreens in the briefing room.

"This is where we'll be coming in," he said. "Between the fountain in the center of the plaza, here . . ." He pointed on the screen. ". . . and the steps leading up the palace entrance, here. There will be guards stationed here, here, here, and here. . . ." He pointed out the locations on the map. "However, there is no guarantee that the disposition of the guards has not been changed since my last visit, so be prepared. We will be going in by the front entrance, here. Those of you assigned to rear guard duty will take your positions here . . . and here. Delete scanner image, Mr. Data."

The exterior image disappeared, leaving only the outlined blueprint map of the interior.

"The rest of us will proceed into the main hall, down this corridor. There are two wide corridors branching off to the north and south wings, here and here. I want those covered; Lieutenant Worf will assign the personnel on-site. Now, lacking a genetic matrix scan on General H'druhn, we cannot simply beam him up out of the palace because, obviously, sensors will not be able to differentiate his readings from those of other K'trall in the palace. If we are not admitted to the palace, we're going to have to force our way in, locate him fast, surround him so the transporter sensors can get a fix on him, and then beam the hell out of there. We go in fast and hard, and get out as quickly as we can.

"Now, here comes the tough part. We won't have any way of knowing for certain which part of the palace the general will be in. His private quarters are on the upper floors, but since I've never been there and only met with him in the main hall, I have no idea where they are. We cannot communicate with the palace, because we don't want to alert them that we're coming. So, if we're refused entry, we'll just have to do it the hard way.

"We will conduct a fast and systematic search throughout the palace for the general. If we can get someone to tell us where he is, so much the better; otherwise we'll simply have to do a room-by-room search. There's a main staircase leading to the upper floors here, by the main hall just off the entrance. Squads Alpha and Bravo will take the north wing, squads Charlie and Delta will take the south. Phasers on stun *only*. Repeat, phasers on *stun*. When General H'druhn is found, he is to be treated with respect befitting a man of his position. He is not to be manhandled in any way. Find him, secure him, and call the others. Any questions?" Gruzinov waited. None were forthcoming. "Very well, that concludes the briefing. All members of the landing party are to report to the transporter rooms immediately and stand by to beam down. Bridge out."

Gruzinov turned and nodded to Picard. "Very well, Mr. Worf," Picard said. "Is Overlord J'drahn still waiting?"

"Aye, sir."

"Let us see what he has to say then. Onscreen."

The image of Overlord J'drahn appeared on the main viewscreen. He did not look happy. "I am not accustomed to being kept waiting, Captain Picard."

"Forgive me, Your Excellency, it was unavoidable," Picard replied. He said nothing else, leaving the next move to J'drahn.

"I see you have returned from D'rahl," J'drahn said. "Was your mission there successful?"

"Not entirely," Picard replied. "We encountered an impediment in the form of two companies of Romulan centurions. And their commander, Tribune Kronak, insists that he is here at your personal invitation."

"And what if he is?" asked J'drahn.

"In that event, Your Excellency," Picard said flatly, "you are in violation of your treaty with the Federation, and the Romulans are in violation of the Treaty of the Algeron. Am I to understand that is the case?"

"The Romulans are our neighbors across the Neutral Zone, Captain," J'drahn said. "Being on the frontier of Federation territory such as we are, it is clearly in our interests to establish a diplomatic understanding with the Romulan Empire. Otherwise, in the event of any breakdown in the truce, we would be the first to suffer. Tribune Kronak is here on a purely diplomatic mission, and it is my right to conduct diplomatic talks with whomever I please."

"And does this diplomatic mission of Tribune Kronak's include establishing an armed camp in the city of K'trin and holding a high-ranking K'tralli citizen prisoner?" asked Picard.

"I assume you are refering to Colonel Z'gral," J'drahn said, smoothly. "Colonel Z'gral has long been a vocal critic of this government, Captain, and has made numerous slanderous and unsubstantiated accusations against myself and Governor T'grayn. He was judged to be a disruptive influence, fomenting insurrection, and under our laws, could have been tried as a criminal. Out of respect for Colonel Z'gral's age, however, which was doubtless instrumental in his actions stemming from diminished faculties, and out of consideration for his past service to the K'tralli people, it was determined that it would be best to simply place him into forced retirement, rather than subject him to the rigors of a trial and risks of the penalties he would doubtless incur under our laws. Your abduction of him poses a serious threat to the security of the K'tralli Empire and our relations with the Federation. I must insist that he be returned at once."

"I fear I must refuse," Picard replied. "Colonel Z'gral has asked for and been granted political asylum under the provisions of Federation law. And your remarks just now have clearly labeled him as a dissident. As for the issue of the Romulans, I must demand that you request their departure from Federation territory immediately."

"Demand?" J'drahn said, in a tone of outrage. "Who are you to demand anything of the overlord of the K'trall? You have overstepped your authority, Picard! And you have violated our laws and interfered with the legal functions of our government. It is you who are in violation, Picard, of your own Prime Directive! If you do not return Colonel

Z'gral to our custody immediately, then I will lodge a formal protest with the Federation Council and demand that you leave K'tralli space at once!"

"I am afraid that under the circumstances, Your Excellency, I cannot comply with your demands," Picard said. "I will have to communicate with Starfleet Command and advise them of the situation, then await their instructions. I will let you know as soon as I have received a response. *Enterprise* out."

He turned to Gruzinov. "That should buy us a little time," he said. "Let's go. Mr. Data, you have the bridge."

"Aye-aye, Captain."

They entered the turbolift.

"You know him best," Picard said to Gruzinov. "What do you think he's going to do?"

"I don't think he has the faintest idea what to do," Gruzinov replied. "He has been playing both ends against the middle and now he's stuck. I think he's scared, and I think he's desperate. And we both know what scared and desperate people are capable of doing."

Picard nodded. "That is how I read the situation," he said. "Even though it will not solve all of his problems, to secure his position he must remove the only man capable of taking it away from him. I can only hope that we are not too late."

They stepped out of the turbolift and marched quickly to the transporter rooms, where the landing party of two dozen crew members was awaiting them, along with Colonel Z'gral, Counselor Troi, and Dr. Crusher.

"Captain," said Z'gral, "I must be allowed to accompany you to the Summer Palace!"

"Sir, we have tried to convince him of the risks, but he remains insistant," Troi said.

"Captain, unless I am present with your landing party, General H'druhn may regard this as an attack," Z'gral said. "Your people will be at risk. I must be allowed to go with you."

"Captain, with all due respect to Colonel Z'gral, I cannot approve," said Dr. Crusher. "Given the possibility of an armed confrontation, his age places him at considerable risk."

"Nonsense!" said Z'gral, angrily. "I was leading troops into battle when you were nothing more than a mewling infant!"

"My point, exactly," Crusher replied, wryly.

"Colonel, I can understand your sentiments, and I appreciate your offer," said Picard, "but I am afraid I must refuse. You have accepted political asylum aboard this vessel, and that makes you my responsibility. Aside from which, without you, we might not be able to convince General H'druhn to remove his son from power. As heroes of the revolution, both you and General H'druhn enjoy the support of the K'tralli people. For their sake, we cannot risk your well-being. We will bring the general back here, and that is when you will be needed most. I hope you will understand."

Z'gral nodded reluctantly. "Yes, I understand,

Captain." He sighed heavily. "Very well. Good luck."

"Thank you, sir," Picard replied. He checked his phaser. "All right, gentlemen, prepare your details for transport."

Riker came to lying on a bed in the sickbay of the *Glory*. That was the second thing he realized, however. The first thing he realized was that his entire body hurt. He started to raise himself, but felt a sharp, stabbing pain and fell back on the bed with a groan.

"Don't try to sit up," he heard Blaze say. "Your ribs are broken."

"My whole body feels broken," Riker said, weakly.

"It should be," Blaze replied, stepping into his field of vision and looking down at him. "You did very well, considering."

"Considering what?"

"Considering the fact that you were grossly overmatched. An ordinary human is no match for a cybrid. Katana was the best fighter on this ship. She killed at least seven men."

"At least?"

"Well, I cannot speak for what she may have done before she joined my crew."

"Why don't you ask the Romulans?"

Blaze raised his eyebrows. "The Romulans?"

"Katana was your saboteur. Your gunner's mate was innocent." Riker grimaced. "Of sabotage, at least."

"Interesting," said Blaze. "How did you discover this?"

"She admitted it, just before you arrived with your men," said Riker. "She planned on killing me, and then blaming whatever she did to your cloaking device on me."

"I will have Ragnar examine it. But why tell me about it?" Blaze asked. "Doesn't that work counter to your purposes?"

"I figure it's a moot point," said Riker. "If my ship doesn't come after you, the Warbird will. And without La Forge, you'll never get the *Glory* operational in time. It's over, Blaze. All you can do now is sit here and wait it out."

"Perhaps," admitted Blaze. "But I do have you as hostage."

Riker shook his head. "That won't get you anywhere. La Forge won't succumb to that kind of pressure. Neither will Captain Picard."

Blaze raised a hypospray.

"What's that?" said Riker, apprehensively.

"A painkiller. I think."

"You *think?*"

"I'm not exactly sure. It's been a while since I've performed any first aid. I'm a little rusty. And your friend Thorn, or whatever her true name was, did not really organize the sickbay as she promised. This could easily have been mislabeled."

"Dorn," said Riker, emptily. "Her name was Dorn. Lieutenant Angela Dorn."

"A member of your starship crew?"

"Starbase 37."

"Ah. One of Gruzinov's people. A good man, Gruzinov. Wasted in a backwater like this."

"I'm sure he'd be delighted to hear your fine opinion of him," Riker said, then grimaced with pain.

"Here, let's see if this helps," Blaze said, and injected him with the hypospray. "So Katana played me false. Well, that does make me feel less regretful about killing her. She was often difficult, but she was a valued member of my crew. I fear I shall not be able to replace her."

"Yeah, it might be tough to find another homicidal cybrid," Riker said.

"It would be impossible," said Blaze. "She was the last of her kind."

"How's that?"

"How much do you know about the cybrids, Stryker? . . . Excuse me. It's Riker, isn't it?"

"Yeah. I know the general story."

"Then allow me to fill in the details. After the cybrids made their escape, they were hounded all over the galaxy, pursued and persecuted wherever they went. They were incredible fighters, but it's tough to win when the entire universe seems to be against you. A handful of them managed to survive and they came here. This was just before the revolution. When it was discovered who and what they were, and specifically, how good they were, they were offered a permanent, safe haven here in return for their help in fighting the revolution. They accepted, and were a strong, relentless force in the conflict. At the end, only six of them were left. And every promise that was ever made to them was broken. They were ostracized and treated like pariahs. They were just too different. Too alien. One of them was murdered. Another committed suicide. Three of them made their way to your colony on Artemis VI, where they were treated no better than they were treated here. I know all about bigotry and prejudice, Riker. I've suffered from it all my life because of being half of one race half of another. Not from everyone, of course, but enough to know what it's like. For the cybrids, it was even worse. They were attacked by some of the colonists on Artemis VI. They defended themselves. And as a result, they were hunted down as murderers."

"What about Katana?"

"She remained behind on D'rahl, which was where I found her, prostituting herself and selling shots to jaded spacers."

"Shots that you supplied her with," said Riker.

"I am pirate, Riker, not a drug dealer. Katana received her drugs courtesy of T'grayn's wide-ranging distribution network. And doubtless that was how she made her arrangement with the Romulans, as well."

"T'grayn?"

"You thought it was me?" Blaze shook his head. "You do me an injustice, Riker. T'grayn was operating a drug manufacturing laboratory. In the basement of his palace, no less. He so loved his precious gardens. The aromatic flowers and ornamental vines concealed plants of a much more interesting variety. They brought him a great deal of profit. As did I, of course. But all that is over now. In a short while, T'grayn will be nothing more than an unsavory memory."

"And what about us?" asked Riker. The pain was starting to ebb. Apparently, it was a painkiller in the hypospray, after all. "Where's La Forge?"

"Ah, yes, your chief engineer. He's really remarkably skilled. Ragnar is tremendously impressed by his abilities. At the moment, he is directing the final stages of the repairs on the drive systems."

"What?" said Riker, sitting up. He grunted. *"Aaah!* Damn!"

"Well, as long as you're up, let's tape those ribs," said Blaze. "Regrettably, I can do no more than that. My skills as a medic are rather limited, you know."

"What do you mean, he's directing the repairs? What did you do to him?"

"Nothing at all," said Blaze. "We simply struck a deal."

"You *what?"*

"A deal, a negotiated settlement," said Blaze. "I knew that holding you hostage would not have insured his cooperation, and I want my ship repaired properly, not sabotaged in some clever way, something I am sure he would be more than capable of doing. To do the job right, he needed an incentive. I provided one."

Riker stared at him with disbelief. "No way," he said. "No way in hell would Geordi ever accept a bribe. You're lying."

"I never said I offered him a bribe," said Blaze. "I said that I provided an incentive. We struck a bargain. He gets the *Glory* fully operational in record time, and I take the ship to N'trahn to aid the *Enterprise.*"

Riker simply stared at him. "And he *believed* you?"

"I gave him my word."

"And I suppose you intend to keep it," Riker said, derisively. "The way you're going to keep it with T'grayn?"

"T'grayn would never keep his word with me if our positions were reversed," said Blaze. "Why should I keep my word with him? Your friend, La Forge, on the other hand, *is* keeping his word. He knows there is no guarantee that I shall follow through, but he's taking a chance on trusting me. Not many people would do that. He's got my entire crew, save myself and those on the bridge, working at an absolutely feverish pace, and much more efficiently than I have ever seen them work before. It really is too bad. He's very good. I'm going to miss him."

Riker tensed. "What do you mean?"

"When I return you to the *Enterprise,* of course," said Blaze. "Assuming that we are not too late and Kronak has not blown her to her bits. In that event, I will simply deposit you at some convenient Federation port. That was our deal."

Riker gazed straight into his eyes. "You're serious," he said.

"Why not? As you quite correctly pointed out, without your friend La Forge, I would be at the mercy of Kronak when he returned. Or of your Captain Picard, if the *Enterprise* proved to be victorious. I would not care to find myself in either of those situations. My first concern is for my ship. Hold still, damn you. There, that should do it."

Riker swung his legs down from the bed, gingerly. It still hurt, but at least he could move without excruciating pain. "I don't think even Geordi can have this ship up and running in time," he said. "Whatever's going to happen, it'll be over long before we get there."

"I wouldn't be so sure," said Blaze. "If Kronak merely wanted to attack your ship, he would have done so when you first arrived at D'rahl. His Warbird has been cloaked and stationed in orbit all this time. He's after bigger game. He wants the K'tralli Empire. And there's a good possibility the Federation will simply let him have it by default. All he needs to do is make sure J'drahn remains in power and is exposed for his dealings with me, T'grayn's black market, and the Romulan Empire. He knows Picard has Colonel Z'gral, the only man capable of convincing General H'druhn of his son's treachery, but without H'druhn himself, Picard will be able to do nothing. Kronak will wait and see how it plays out."

"How can you be so sure?" asked Riker.

"Because I know him. I understand the way he

thinks. Kronak will wait to see if J'drahn can manage to assassinate his father before Picard can get to him. If not, and J'drahn is deposed, then Kronak will accuse the Federation of violating its own Prime Directive, toppling the legal government of the K'tralli Empire to prevent J'drahn from concluding an alliance with the Romulans and leaving the Federation. And *then* he will attack. But it would be a much more interesting victory for him if he could maneuver the Federation into expelling J'drahn. Then he would gain the K'tralli Empire without ever firing a shot. Imagine the standing that would give him with Romulan High Council."

"Yeah, it would be one hell of coup," admitted Riker. "He'd win using our own laws against us. The trouble is, I don't know how the hell he can be stopped."

"We still have time, Riker. Don't underestimate my crew. They're an unruly bunch, I'll grant you that, but they know their business. I'll match them against any ship in Starfleet, even your *Enterprise.*" He grinned. "In fact, I already have. Ironic, isn't it? I thought I was preparing for a rematch with Picard. Instead, I'll be going to his aid."

"What are you hoping to gain from this, DeBlazio? A pardon?" He shook his head. "You know we can't offer you that. It's beyond our authority."

"I will settle for a good head start. I will count on your influence with your captain to grant me one."

Blaze smiled. "You think you can operate a weapons console with your chest taped up?"

"You just watch me, mister," Riker said.

The landing party materialized in the plaza of the Summer Palace, between the large, multi-tiered fountain and the front entrance. The palace guards posted at the entrance were taken by surprise. It was not the first time Federation personnel had arrived in this manner to visit the general, but the sight of a large armed party took them aback and they were not sure how to react. As Picard and the others crossed the plaza and approached the steps leading to the front entrance, the guards glanced at one another uneasily and raised their weapons cautiously, though they did not point them at the advancing party.

Picard knew that the next few moments, while they were still all grouped together and exposed out in the open, would be the most dangerous. He had considered having the landing party open fire as soon as they materialized, stunning the guards before any of them could have a chance to react and then storming the palace. That would have been, perhaps, the safest course to follow, because while the phasers of the landing party were all set on stun, the guards would have no way of knowing that and their weapons could only shoot to kill.

However, if there was any chance that they could get to General H'druhn without having to use force, Picard knew he had to take it. If they fired on the guards, there was always the chance that someone would be killed, and Picard wanted to do everything possible to avoid that. He only hoped that J'drahn had not placed an assassin in among his father's personal guard. In that event, the assassin would almost certainly be able to reach H'druhn before they could.

The captain of the guard came out and stood at the top of the steps, his hand held close to his sidearm. "Halt!" he commanded.

Picard had already started up the steps, but he stopped at the guard captain's order.

"Identify yourselves and state your business!" said the guard captain.

"I am Captain Jean-Luc Picard, of the Federation starship *Enterprise*," Picard said. "We are here to see General H'druhn on a matter of the gravest urgency."

"I was not informed of the general expecting any visitors," the guard captain replied.

"He is not expecting us," Picard said, "but it is imperative that I speak to him at once. It is a matter of life or death."

"Indeed?" the guard captain said. "Tell me what you wish to speak with him about, and I will convey the message."

"I must speak with the general personally," Picard replied. "I have reason to believe there may be an attempt upon his life."

"By whom?" the guard captain asked, frowning.

"I will divulge that only to the general himself," Picard said.

The guard captain stared at Picard for a moment,

then looked beyond him, at the landing party. Picard could see that he was weighing the possibilities, and didn't like what he saw.

"Wait here," the guard captain said. "I will see if the general will receive you."

He turned and spoke to the guards briefly, then went back inside the palace. The guards stood ready with their weapons. They no longer looked uncertain. Picard knew that they had received instructions to fire if the landing party made any further moves toward the entrance. He turned and saw that some of the guards by the gates beyond the fountain were coming up, as well. "Mr. Worf," he said, softly.

"I see them, sir," said Worf. He directed his squad to face about. The guards that were approaching from the gates stopped a respectful distance away, but still within firing range.

"This is not a good position to be in," Gruzinov said, uneasily.

"I know. But we will not force our way inside unless it is absolutely necessary," said Picard. He touched his insignia. "Picard to *Enterprise.*"

"Data here, Captain. Go ahead, sir."

"Have you got a fix on me, Mr. Data?"

"Yes, sir."

"Very well, stand by," Picard replied. "I will leave the frequency open. If I am admitted to see General H'druhn, then the moment I am in his presence, I want you to lock on to us both and beam us up on my word. Have all transporters standing by to beam up the remainder of the landing party. Is that clear?"

"Affirmative, Captain."

"Ivan," Picard said, "if I am allowed inside, then you will be in charge here. I don't need to tell you that you will be in a precarious position. If I am successful in getting back to the ship with General H'druhn, then we will have the rest of the party beamed back up immediately. But if you are forced to defend yourselves—"

"I know," Gruzinov said. "Stun only." He grimaced as he glanced at the guards. "I don't suppose you could tell them the same thing?"

Picard smiled. "Let's hope for the best," he said. "But if the alarm is given, don't wait for them to fire first."

"What if they don't admit you?"

"Then we proceed with the planned assault," Picard said.

The captain of the guard came back out. "General H'druhn will see you," he said. "You alone, Captain Picard. The remainder of your party will wait here."

"As you wish," Picard said, and started up the steps.

"One moment, please, Captain," said the guard. *"Without* your weapon."

Picard turned and handed his phaser to Gruzinov.

"Very well," said the guard captain. "If you will follow me, please?"

Picard nodded to Gruzinov, who nodded back, and then he turned to follow the guard captain. He hoped the transporter operators were on the ball. The moment he beamed up with the general, the landing party would be at risk. They would have to move fast. But at least they didn't have to force their way in. That was something. It would gain them time, if nothing else.

The guard captain conducted him to the stairway leading to the upper floors. They climbed up to the third floor, then turned right down a long corridor. Picard noted that a pair of guards had followed them from the first floor, and there were guards posted outside the general's private quarters, as well. They weren't taking any chances.

The guard captain nodded to the men posted at the door. One of them opened it to admit them and preceded them inside. The guard captain motioned Picard to enter and then came in behind him. This wasn't good. It meant that there would be at least two other K'trall in close proximity to him when he met the general.

"I was hoping to speak with the general in private," said Picard, to the guard captain.

"Anything you have to say to me can be said in front of my men, Captain Picard," H'druhn said, coming into the room through a connecting door. He was wearing a dressing gown. "It is a bit late for such an unannounced visit. Now, what is this nonsense about an attempt on my life?"

As H'druhn approached, Picard started to step forward, but felt the guard captain take him firmly by the arm, restraining him. H'druhn stopped a short distance away.

"We have discovered that there are at least two companies of Romulan centurions present on D'rahl," Picard said. "And there may be a cloaked Romulan Warbird in the vicinity, as well."

"Romulans?" H'druhn said. *"On D'rahl? Impossible!"*

"We have proof that Governor T'grayn is in collusion with them, General," Picard said. "They had been holding Colonel Z'gral prisoner at his own estate, but he is now safe aboard the *Enterprise* and most anxious to speak with you."

"Z'gral? A *prisoner?* But why?"

"Because they knew he was the only man who would be able to convince you that your son is corrupt, in league with the freebooters and with the Romulans," Picard said.

H'druhn stiffened. "You dare accuse my own son of such things? I have heard similar allegations leveled against J'drahn before, Captain, by the commander of Starbase 37. But not even Captain Gruzinov had the temerity to suggest that my son would betray his own people and be a party to a plot against my life."

"General, I know how incredible this must sound to you—" Picard began, but H'druhn interrupted him.

"It is not only incredible, Captain, it is outrageous!" the old general said furiously, stepping closer to Picard. "When I concluded my alliance with the Federation, it was with the clear understanding that our autonomy would be respected and preserved. J'drahn explained to me how Captain Gruzinov was frustrated in his repeated attempts to extend his authority into K'tralli territory, and I see that now he has enlisted you in his despicable machinations. I am amazed that you should—"

Picard was about to give Data the signal, but suddenly there was the sound of phaser fire from outside, coupled with the sharp, staccato popping sounds of K'tralli weaponry. H'druhn turned quickly toward the window.

"Now, Mr. Data!" said Picard.

The transporter locked on immediately and beamed Picard, H'druhn, and the two guards flanking Picard up to the *Enterprise*. As they materialized in the transporter room, security personnel quickly stepped up and disarmed the startled guards.

"What is the meaning of this, Picard?" H'druhn demanded, in a tone of outrage. *"Have you lost your senses?"*

"Not now, General, if you please," Picard said. He activated his communicator. "Picard to landing party! What's happening? Report!"

"Gruzinov here. We're under heavy fire. The palace is under attack by K'tralli soldiers. We have sustained casualties."

"What is your current situation?" Picard asked.

"We have retreated inside the palace and are fighting a holding action together with the palace guard," Gruzinov replied, over the sounds of firing.

"Lieutenant Worf and a squad of men got pinned down by the fountain when they advanced to aid the guards stationed by the gates. Most of those guards were killed when the attack commenced. We have at least five dead and about half a dozen wounded among our own personnel. We're trying to lay down covering fire to allow Worf and his squad to get back to the palace."

"K'tralli soldiers? Attacking *my* palace?" said H'druhn, with disbelief.

As he spoke, the doors to the transporter room opened and Counselor Troi came in, along with Colonel Z'gral. "General!" Z'gral said. "Thank the gods you're safe!"

"Stand by, Ivan," Picard said. He turned to the transporter operator. "Have you got a fix on Lieutenant Worf and his party?"

"Aye, sir."

"Picard to Lieutenant Worf."

"Worf here, Captain."

"Stand by, Mr. Worf. We're going to get you out of there."

"Standing by, sir."

"Lock on and energize," Picard said.

"Commencing now . . ." said the transporter operator.

A moment later, Lieutenant Worf and the five survivors of his squad appeared on the transporter pads. Several of them were supporting their wounded crewmates.

"Report, Mr. Worf," Picard said.

"We were attacked by two transports of K'tralli

soldiers, Captain," Worf said. "They came in over the gates and fired as they landed. We sustained most of our casualties at that time. I advanced with my squad to assist the surviving guards, and Captain Gruzinov retreated to the palace with the remainder of the landing party. The palace is under heavy fire, but they have not yet broken through."

"Get those people to sickbay at once," Picard said, "then join me on the bridge."

"Aye, Captain."

"Picard to landing party."

"Gruzinov here, go ahead."

"Ivan, how is your situation? Can you hold?"

"We're holding them, Jean-Luc."

"Very well, stand by. Picard out." He turned to H'druhn. "If you require any more proof, General, I am about to provide it for you. Come with me, please. Counselor, would you please escort our guests?"

They made their way quickly from the transporter room down the corridor to the turbolift.

"There has to be another explanation for all this," H'druhn said, as the turbolift took them to the bridge. "I cannot believe that K'tralli soldiers would attack their own men! Or that J'drahn could be behind it!"

"Believe it, General," said Z'gral. "J'drahn controls the army now. I have seen the sort of men he has been promoting to positions of command in our regiments, and when I dared to criticize him and his policies, he had me confined to house arrest at my own estate under the pretense that I was ill and incapacitated. And to insure that none of the men who guarded me would suffer from divided loyalties, he had them all replaced with Romulan centurions."

"No," H'druhn said, "there must be some mistake, Z'gral. J'drahn would never betray me, much less his own people. Someone else is behind all this, someone who is trying to discredit my son."

"General, we have *proof* of J'drahn's involvement with the Romulans," Z'gral insisted.

H'druhn shook his head, unable to accept it. "No, I cannot believe that. Not my own son . . ."

As they came onto the bridge, Data got up from the captain's chair and took his own post at the navigation console. Counselor Troi assumed her place at the captain's side. Picard immediately contacted Gruzinov.

"Picard to landing party. Report."

"Gruzinov here. We're still holding. They have attempted another assault and been repelled. They tried having their transports fly over the palace and fire on the upper floors, but we shot one of them down and the other one pulled back out of range. I've assumed responsibility for ordering lethal settings on the phasers. The attackers are keeping their distance for the moment. However, they may be expecting reinforcements. The palace guard have taken heavy casualties. They're confused, but I've assumed command, and for the present we seem to have the situation under control."

"I want them to think the general is still inside the palace," said Picard. "Hold on for as long as you can, but if your position looks untenable, let me know at once."

"Affirmative," Gruzinov said.

"Picard out."

The turbolift doors opened and Lieutenant Worf came back onto the bridge and took his post.

"Mr. Worf, get me Overlord J'drahn," Picard said.

"Aye, Captain."

Picard turned to Z'gral and H'druhn. "General, if you would be so kind as to stand over there, please? I would prefer your son not to see you when we make contact."

The old general still looked shocked by what had happened, but he complied without comment. Z'gral stood beside him. Moments later, Worf reported that he had gotten through.

"Onscreen, Mr. Worf," Picard said.

J'drahn appeared on the screen, his expression tense. "Captain Picard," he said. "I am truly astonished at your arrogance. I am aware of the force you have dispatched to my father's palace in an attempt to hold him hostage and I demand its *immediate* withdrawal! I further demand that you immediately surrender yourself to K'tralli custody to await trial on charges of—"

"Trial?" said Picard, interrupting him. "It is *you* who should be standing trial. And I intend to see to it. The palace guard will testify that it was they who were attacked by your men, in an attempt to storm the palace and assassinate General H'druhn."

"The palace guard will testify to nothing,"

J'drahn replied, contemptuously. "In a short while, they, along with your Starfleet personnel, will all be dead. And my officers will testify that they were killed defending the palace from an attack by *your* people, Picard. It will be my contention that you attempted to seize my father and hold him hostage in order to engineer a coup designed to topple my government. And there will be no witnesses left alive to contradict me."

"You seem to have forgotten one thing," Picard said. "Your father knows the truth. Or do you intend to have him killed, as well?"

"It will be reported that my father died heroically, commanding the palace guard in defense against your cowardly attack," J'drahn said. "And with his death, the people will rally behind me. You cannot win, Picard. But I am willing to give you one last chance to withdraw your people and depart K'tralli space."

"And leave the K'tralli Empire to the Romulans?" Picard said.

"Our alliance with the Romulans will make us stronger than we ever could have been under our treaty with the Federation," said J'drahn. "And there is nothing you can do about it, Picard. But you can still leave and save yourself, before it is too late. Think about your own fate, and leave the destiny of the K'tralli Empire to me."

"I would sooner see you dead," H'druhn said coldly, stepping up to stand beside Picard.

J'drahn started with shock and the color drained out of his face. *"Father!"*

"That you can still call me 'Father' without choking on the word astonishes me," H'druhn said, bitterly. "They told me of your treachery, but I did not want to believe it, not even when I heard it from Z'gral. Yet now you stand condemned out of your own mouth, a craven traitor to me and to our people. I curse the day that you were born, and I will die before I see you betray everything I ever fought for!"

"Then you will die," J'drahn said flatly, and cut off the transmission.

H'druhn seemed to collapse into himself. "My own son . . ." he said, with despair, and his legs buckled. Z'gral caught him.

"Counselor, please escort the general to sickbay," Picard said. "Colonel Z'gral, if you would be so kind as to accompany him . . ."

"Certainly, Captain."

As they left the bridge, Picard contacted Gruzinov. "Picard to landing party. . . ."

"Gruzinov here."

"Stand by to beam up. We'll be bringing the palace guard up along with you," said Picard. "Have them be prepared."

"Standing by," Gruzinov said.

"Mr. Worf, have the transporter rooms start beaming up the landing party and the palace guard."

"Captain, Romulan Warbird uncloaking!" Worf said, suddenly.

"Cancel that last order! *Shields up! Red alert!*"

Chapter Nine

"Captain, we are being hailed," said Worf.

"Onscreen, Mr. Worf."

A moment later, the face of Tribune Kronak appeared on the main viewscreen. "Captain Picard. I am advised that you have an armed force on the planet surface, currently engaging elements of the K'tralli military. I must insist that they be withdrawn at once."

"So that you may attack the moment we lower our shields?" Picard said. "I think not, Tribune."

"I stand to gain nothing by firing on your ship, Picard," said Kronak. "I have already won the battle."

"Indeed?" Picard replied. "And just how have you accomplished that?"

"You have accomplished it for me," Kronak replied, with a smile. "You have both Colonel Z'gral and General H'druhn aboard your vessel, do you not? J'drahn may have failed to eliminate his father, but that is really of little consequence now. You have effectively removed the two men who posed the greatest threat to J'drahn's position. If they are aboard your ship, then they can do no damage on N'trahn. All that remains is for you to withdraw your landing party and depart. I will communicate with J'drahn and have him break off his assault on the palace so that you may remove your people safely."

"You expect me to trust you?" said Picard.

"That is entirely up to you," Kronak replied. "The attacking forces at the palace are about to receive reinforcements, and it is doubtful that your people will be able to hold them off for long. It really makes no difference to me, one way or the other, but it would be a pity if they were to die for nothing. Take them back aboard your ship, Picard, and then you will be free to leave unmolested."

"And what if I refuse?"

"That would be most unfortunate for you," said Kronak. "Observe your scanners."

"Captain, a second Warbird is uncloaking!" Worf said.

"Onscreen, Mr. Worf."

The image on the viewscreen changed, switching to exterior scanners. As they watched, a *third* Warbird uncloaked.

"They have us boxed in!" said Worf.

Picard compressed his lips into a tight grimace.

"As you can see, Captain," Kronak's voice came on, over the image on the screen, "I have received reinforcements, as well." The image on the screen changed as Worf switched back to visual on the communication. Kronak smiled. "And whether you trust me enough to lower your shields or not is really immaterial. You must realize that even with your shields up, you would never withstand the combined firepower of three D'deridex-class Warbirds, I will give you some time to consider my offer. Meanwhile, I will have J'drahn break off his attack. It would be a shame if your people were killed while you were trying to make up your mind."

The screen went blank.

Picard exhaled heavily. "Damn that smug, arrogant . . ." His voice trailed off. He clenched his fists in frustration. "Inform the transporter rooms to prepare to beam up the landing party, Mr. Worf, and stand by to lower shields."

"Captain!" Worf said. "Sir, with all due respect—"

"I gave you an order, Mr. Worf!"

"Aye-aye, sir."

Picard took a deep breath. "He *wants* us to get them back on board. That way, he can be sure to eliminate us all. General H'druhn, Colonel Z'gral, Captain Gruzinov . . . he gets us all in one fell swoop. And then he can be sure there will be no one to contradict whatever J'drahn claims afterward. He has us both outgunned and outflanked. But we will not make it easy for him."

"Transporter rooms standing by, Captain," Worf said.

"Maintain red alert, Mr. Worf, and stand by phasers and photon torpedoes," Picard said. "Mr. Data, stand by for evasive maneuvers on my order."

"Aye-aye, sir," Data said.

"Have the transporter rooms report the moment the landing party is safely back aboard the ship," Picard said, "and then restore shields immediately and stand by for engagement. The moment he sees our shields go back up, he's going to open fire."

"Aye-aye, sir," Worf said, passing the order along to the transporter rooms. He glanced up. "Ready, Captain."

Picard tensed. "Lower shields and energize," he said.

"Shields down," said Worf, grimly.

"Come *on,* come *on,*" Picard said, under his breath.

"Landing party safely aboard, sir. Shields up!" said Worf. A second later, he added, "Warbirds powering up to fire!"

"Evasive maneuvers, Mr. Data!"

"Aye, sir."

"Warbirds firing!" said Worf.

The *Enterprise* rocked as the fire from one of the Warbirds struck its shields.

"Shields holding!" Worf said.

"Fire photon torpedoes, full spread!"

"Torpedoes away," said Worf. "Warbirds taking evasive action."

The *Enterprise* rocked again as the fire from another Warbird struck the shields.

"Damage to aft port shield!" said Worf, as Data maneuvered the *Enterprise* in an attempt to avoid the fire coming from all three Warbirds. "Shield at fifty percent!"

"Fire phasers!"

The *Enterprise* rocked once again as it was struck by more enemy fire. The turbolift doors opened and Gruzinov came rushing onto the bridge. He staggered as the ship was struck by disruptor fire and only managed to keep from falling by grabbing onto an equipment console.

"Damage to forward shields!" Worf said. "Aft port shield has failed!"

"The bastards are shooting us to pieces!" said Gruzinov.

"Take communications!" said Picard. "I want damage-control reports!"

"Right."

With Gruzinov's help, Worf was now free to concentrate solely on the weapons. The *Enterprise* rocked again as fire from one of the Warbirds scored a hit.

"Fire at will, Mr. Worf!"

"Aft starboard shield at fifty percent!" Gruzinov said. "Damage to port shield!"

Worf fired the phasers once again. "Direct hit!" he said, triumphantly.

The Warbird they struck had sustained serious damage, but it was still capable of firing. Picard knew that it was only a matter of time. They could not hope to outmaneuver all three of them.

"Full about, Mr. Data!"

Kronak was on their flank, but there was another Warbird at their exposed rear, where one of their shields had failed completely and the other was only at fifty percent. One more hit there and it could finish them.

Suddenly, one of the Warbirds was struck by three photon torpedoes, one after another, in rapid succession. The first took out its shields, the second and third scored direct hits, and the Warbird exploded into a massive sheet of flame.

"What the hell . . . !" Gruzinov said. "That wasn't us!"

A ship came swooping in at a steep angle, raking the other Warbird with phaser fire as it passed so close to it that they almost brushed. Picard recognized the familiar lines of a Constitution-class vessel.

"I'll be damned," he said. "It's the *Glory!*"

"Starboard helm, bearing one-point-three mark four!" said Blaze.

"Cutting it a little close there, weren't you?" Riker said, looking up and wincing with pain as the ship banked sharply enough to make him grab the weapons console for support.

"She's still not responding very well," said Blaze. "Blame your friend, La Forge."

"He got this bucket running, didn't he?"

"Yes, if she doesn't shake herself apart," said Blaze. "Full about! Let's see if you can't shoot a little better this time, gunner. Engineering, I need more power on starboard engines!"

"I'm giving you all I've got!" La Forge replied, over the intercom. "One more maneuver like that and the entire nacelle's liable to give from the stress!"

The ship rocked as it was grazed by disruptor fire.

"Damage to Decks 4 and 5!" Communications Mate T'gahl shouted. "Hull integrity breached!"

"Seal off Decks 4 and 5! Damn you, La Forge, I need more power to the shields!" Blaze shouted.

"What shields?" La Forge replied.

"We don't have shields?" Riker said.

"La Forge!" Blaze shouted.

"What the hell do you expect?" Geordie replied. "It was all I could do to get these damned Romulan drives operative! You want miracles?"

"Right now, it wouldn't hurt," said Blaze. "Engage cloaking device!"

"Cloaking device engaged," said Helmsman D'karr.

"Port helm, bearing three-point-five mark two! Stand by phasers!"

"Phasers standing by," said Riker.

"She's cloaked!" Gruzinov said.

"Full about, Mr. Data!" Picard said. "Stand by photon torpedoes!"

"Sir, if we fire now, we could hit the *Glory,"* Worf said.

"Not if Blaze does what I think he's going to do," Picard replied. "Fire!"

Worf fired as they lined up on the ship Blaze had

just attacked. It was coming about to meet the new threat, but instead wound up exposing its flank to the *Enterprise.* The torpedo slammed into its aft section and exploded.

"Direct hit!" Gruzinov said.

"Enemy is withdrawing, Captain," Worf said.

"Let them go, Mr. Worf," Picard said. "Let's see to our friend, Kronak. Stand by phasers!"

"The Warbird is coming about to fire, Captain," Data said.

"Maintain heading," said Picard. "Stand by . . ."

As the Warbird's forward disruptors came to bear, the *Glory* suddenly uncloaked, directly behind Kronak's ship.

"Fire!" said Picard.

Both the *Enterprise* and the *Glory* fired simultaneously. Caught in the deadly crossfire, the Warbird's shields gave way and the ship exploded into a giant fireball.

"We got him!" Gruzinov shouted.

"Secure from battle stations," said Picard, exhaling heavily. "Maintain yellow alert. I want a full report from Damage Control as soon as possible."

"Message coming in from the *Glory,* Captain," said Gruzinov.

"Onscreen," Picard said.

Blaze appeared on the screen, sitting casually kicked back in his captain's chair, as if he were merely taking his ease instead of just having fought a pitched battle. "Nicely done, Captain," he said.

"We got that bastard trapped between the hammer and the anvil. But tell me, how did you manage to anticipate my move? Or was it merely luck?"

Picard smiled. "I seemed to recall that you had a tendency for putting other ships between us."

Blaze grinned. "Touché, Captain." He gave Picard a cavalier salute. "I shall remember that in the future. But for the present, I was pleased to be of assistance."

"I must admit to being curious," Picard said, with a puzzled frown. "You had no stake in this, and you stood to lose everything. Why take the risk?"

Blaze shrugged elaborately. "Life without risk is merely existence, Captain. I never trusted Kronak, anyway. I knew that he considered me expendable, and that I would be expended, so to speak, as soon as he had no further use for me. Besides, the odds against you were three to one, hardly a fair fight. And I always did have a weakness for the underdog."

"Well, my compliments to your weapons officer," Picard said, ignoring the dig. "I owe the survival of my ship to his superb gunnery skills."

Blaze smiled. "I am sure he would be delighted to hear that, Captain. Why don't you thank him yourself?"

"I would be happy to," Picard said. "Where is he?"

"Right here," said Riker, stepping out of the turbolift.

Picard turned around, an expression of astonishment and delight on his features. "Will!" he said.

The others on the bridge looked equally delighted and relieved to see him, but were concerned at his appearance. His face was badly bruised and cut, and his uniform shirt had been cut away, revealing his taped ribs.

"It's good to be back, sir," Riker said. "I sent Geordi to his quarters to get some badly needed sleep. He was absolutely exhausted. He was working round the clock trying to get the *Glory* operational in time for us to get here. We just barely made it."

"You were aboard the *Glory* all this time?" Picard said, with astonishment.

"You mean you didn't get my message?" Riker asked, with a frown.

"We received no message," said Picard, looking puzzled.

"Hmm," said Blaze. "Apparently, my long-range communication equipment is not in proper working order, either. You really did cause an annoying amount of damage to my ship, Picard. All things considered, it was a miracle we managed to arrive at all, much less participate in the engagement."

"Well, I am very grateful that you did," Picard said.

"Don't be so quick to thank me. We were already committed when your man La Forge informed me that aside from handling like a lopsided asteroid, my ship had no shields. Had I known *that,* I might have just laid off and watched those Warbirds batter you to pieces. Which is doubtless why La Forge failed to inform me of that pertinent little detail. Still, I suppose I shouldn't complain. He did manage to get my ship operational in record time, even if he did cut a few corners. A pity I couldn't induce him to remain with me. He is an absolutely brilliant engineer."

"What about Lieutenant Dorn?" Gruzinov said.

Riker looked grim. "I'm afraid she didn't make it, sir. She died saving my life. But for what it's worth, Blaze got the one who killed her. It was a Romulan agent."

"I regret the loss of your comrade, Captain Gruzinov," Blaze said. "It may not mean very much coming from me, but I am truly sorry, just the same."

"Well . . . this puts me in a somewhat awkward position," said Picard. "By rights, I should be taking you into custody, but I am in debt to you for coming to our aid. And at the moment, neither of our ships is truly fit for another battle. In fact," he added, pointedly, "I am not at all convinced that our engagement with the Romulans renders my ship capable of giving pursuit until the damage is fully repaired. However, if a certain freebooter continues to harass Federation shipping, I will be obliged to pick up where we left off."

Blaze grinned. "I was thinking that things have become a bit too hot for me in this sector, anyway. I hear that Romulan merchant vessels often carry a rich cargo. And I do have rather expensive tastes. However, there is still the matter of some unfinished business."

"What do you mean?" asked Picard, warily.

"I was referring to J'drahn," said Blaze. "I do not imagine that he will give up his position easily. And correct me if I'm wrong, Captain, but as I understand Federation law, you would be legally unable to assist General H'druhn in removing his son from power."

"What are you getting at?" Picard asked, with a frown.

"Well, I was merely thinking that my ship is still in need of some repair," said Blaze. "And I do so admire Chief Engineer La Forge's skills. For General H'druhn to depose his son without your assistance, he would need to raise troops, and that would take time, even for a hero of the K'tralli revolution. It could easily result in civil war, and a great many lives would be lost. On the other hand, if we moved quickly, my crew could assist the general in setting matters right, and you could be present merely as observers, so to speak."

"And in return, I lend you La Forge and the assistance of our engineering crews to finish repairing your ship," Picard said.

"Something like that," said Blaze. "Of course, none of this need show up in any official reports. And, technically speaking, I *am* still a K'tralli citizen. I would merely be doing my patriotic duty in supporting General H'druhn. In return for certain considerations, of course."

"Do you believe this?" Gruzinov said, with astonishment. "What colossal nerve!"

"An interesting offer," said Picard. "I will pass it on to General H'druhn."

"You're not serious!" said Gruzinov. "The man's a criminal!"

"I will not dispute that," replied Picard. "However, as a K'tralli citizen, he must be held accountable under *K'tralli* law. Mr. Worf, will you ask General H'druhn and Colonel Z'gral to come to the bridge, please? And Mr. Riker, you report to sickbay and have Dr. Crusher see to those wounds."

"Where the hell is Blaze?" J'drahn asked.

T'grayn's face on the screen looked worried. "I do not know, Your Excellency," he replied.

"What do you mean, you do not know? Have you been in communication with him or not?"

"I have not spoken with him in over twenty-four hours," T'grayn replied, anxiously. "At that time, he was still trying to complete the repairs on his ship."

J'drahn angrily struck the console with his fist. "Well, have you tried to raise him?"

"Repeatedly, Your Excellency. However, it is possible that he is unable to respond. If it was necessary for him to shut down his power in order to effect repairs, then he may not be capable of receiving any signals."

"How very convenient for him," said J'drahn, with disgust.

"What about Tribune Kronak? Surely, he should have arrived by now and—"

"Kronak's dead," J'drahn said. "Or else he's fled back across the Neutral Zone. There was an engagement, that's all I know, and since then I have heard nothing from him."

"The *Enterprise?*" T'grayn asked, anxiously.

"Ominously silent," said J'drahn, tensely. "They managed to get to my father before my men could take the Summer Palace."

T'grayn's face registered dismay. "Then it is over."

"Nothing is over!" said J'drahn. "They may have my father and they may have Z'gral, but if Picard attempts to help them overthrow me, he violates the Federation's Prime Directive and destroys his own career."

"But with H'druhn safe aboard the *Enterprise,* Z'gral can return to N'trahn or any of the colony worlds and raise troops against you," said T'grayn.

"Perhaps," J'drahn agreed, "but that will take time. And in that time, I could prepare. My protest could be registered with the Federation Council, and the Romulans would have time to return with more ships. Picard may have the upper hand for now, but he shall not retain it long."

"I wouldn't be too sure about that, Your Excellency," said Picard.

J'drahn spun around and saw Picard seated in a chair across the room. *"You!"* he said, with shock. "You *dare* transport into my own private quarters? *Guards!"*

270

"I think you will find that your guards are rather busy at the moment," said Picard, sitting casually with his legs crossed and his hands folded in his lap.

J'drahn simply stared at him with disbelief; then the sounds of shouting and weapons firing erupted from downstairs, in the main hall.

"Your Excellency! Your Excellency, what's happening?" T'grayn asked anxiously, from the screen.

"I believe the proper term for what is happening, Governor, is *coup d'etat,*" Picard replied. "A violent change in government. Although it is my hope that the violence, in this case, will be minimal. In any event, it will be much less violent than a full-scale civil war. The K'tralli Empire does not really need another bloody revolution."

J'drahn reached for his sidearm.

"Careful," said Picard, revealing the phaser he was holding in his lap. "If my life is threatened, I can still defend myself without violating the Prime Directive."

J'drahn stopped in the act of reaching for his weapon, staring at Picard uncertainly. "You have already violated the Prime Directive," he said. "If you think that you can get away with an assault upon the palace—"

"There is not a single crew member of the *Enterprise* involved in what is happening," Picard said. "I am here merely as an interested observer. I felt it incumbent upon me, as a Starfleet officer, to be present so that I could report upon the incident to my superiors. However, as you quite correctly pointed out, I cannot become personally involved."

"What sort of double-talk is this?" J'drahn demanded. "You expect me to believe that you had nothing to do this?"

Picard simply shrugged. "What you choose to believe or disbelieve is none of my concern," he said. "However, for the record, I will state again that no Starfleet personnel are involved in what is going on in any way."

"You're lying! If not your people, then who . . . ?"

"Me," said Blaze from the doorway, where he stood leaning casually against the doorframe, a disruptor held loosely at his side.

"Blaze!"

"It really is a pity your palace guards are not equipped with Romulan disruptors," he said. "I suppose Kronak did not trust you enough to supply them. Not that he trusted me, particularly, but then again, he didn't really see me as a threat. Unfortunately for him."

J'drahn stared at him with amazement. *"You?"* he said, with disbelief. His hand inched toward his holstered sidearm.

"Oh, please do," said Blaze, raising his disruptor casually. "Not that I need an excuse, but it would be nice if you provided me with one."

Picard remained seated, watching the exchange with a broad, satisfied smile.

"Picard! *Do* something!" said J'drahn.

"What would you have me do?" Picard asked,

innocently. "This is clearly an internal matter. I cannot become involved."

The sounds of battle had decreased significantly.

"It sounds as if your palace guards are not offering much resistance," Blaze said. "Wise of them, considering their weapons are no match for these." Blaze raised the disruptor slightly. As J'drahn backed away, Blaze crossed over to stand near the communications console. "Ah, T'grayn," he said, as he saw the governor's stricken face on the screen. "You will be glad to know that your transfer of assets to my accounts in the Ferengi system has gone through. The funds will be available there for you to draw upon anytime you can arrange transport to the Ferengi system. Of course, under the present circumstances, that may prove rather difficult. I understand you're going to be facing serious charges. I do hope you've kept enough in your accounts to arrange for legal representation."

"But . . . nothing remains in my accounts!" T'grayn stammered. "You have it all! You promised to take me, Blaze! You *promised!*"

"You cowardly, miserable wretch!" J'drahn said. He snatched a fruit from the basket on the table and hurled it at the screen. It exploded into sparks and smoke and shards of glass.

The sounds of shooting had died away completely and, a moment later, several of Blaze's crewmen, together with Colonel Z'gral and General H'druhn, came into the room. J'drahn saw them and his face fell. He glanced around, seeking some avenue of escape, but there was nowhere to run.

H'druhn stood looking at his son with contempt. "Have you nothing to say?" the old general demanded.

J'drahn merely stared at him sullenly, then dropped his gaze.

"Well, since you have nothing to say to me, then I have only one thing to say to you," H'druhn said. "My only regret is that you did not die fighting, like a soldier. That way, I would have been spared the humiliation of seeing my own son stand trial for crimes against the people and the Empire. Take him away."

Blaze's crewmen stepped up and disarmed him, then led him out of the room. Blaze raised his eyebrow at Picard, then turned to follow them.

"As of this moment," said H'druhn, "I formally resume my title as overlord of the K'trall, pending the holding of democratic elections to choose a new government. I would appreciate it, Captain Picard, if the Federation were to send diplomatic advisors to help us organize a transition to a different form of government, where all power no longer rests in one man's hands."

"I am sure the Federation would be more than willing to assist you in that regard," Picard said. "I would—"

There was shouting from outside the room, then the sound of something falling heavily.

"What the devil?" said Picard, moving toward the door, but just then Blaze came through it.

"I'm afraid there's been an unfortunate accident, General," he said. "I am deeply saddened to report your son is dead."

"What happened?" said Picard.

"He tried to break away, but slipped somehow and fell down the stairs," said Blaze, with a perfectly straight face. "I'm afraid he broke his neck. Pity. It appears there won't be a trial, after all."

"Were there any witnesses to this?" Picard asked, tensely.

"Oh, my crewmen will corroborate what happened," Blaze said, innocently.

"My son's death will be reported as an accident suffered while attempting to escape," H'druhn said, flatly. He took a deep breath and exhaled, heavily. He turned to Blaze and looked as if he were about to say something more, but hesitated, then said, "We will speak no more of this." He turned to Picard. "As to the matter of Captain Blaze, also known as Diego DeBlazio, a court will be convened at the earliest opportunity following the upcoming elections to determine the exact charges to be levied against him and to set a date for a trial. In the meantime, Captain Blaze will be free on his own recognizance, provided he can post a bail of ten thousand K'tralli marks."

"Ten thousand?" said Blaze.

"Eight?" said H'druhn.

"Five."

"Seven."

"Done."

Picard shook his head. "A man haggling over his

own bail. Now I've seen it all." He touched his insignia, activating his communicator. "Picard to *Enterprise*. One to beam up."

"How did you enjoy your 'liberty,' Mr. La Forge?" Picard asked.

"It was a little tiring, sir," La Forge replied with a sigh.

"Well, I shall not ask what you and your maintenance crews did after you beamed down to D'rahl," Picard said, poker-faced. "After all, what you do on your own time is none of my concern."

"Right," said Geordi.

"Message coming in from the *Glory*, Captain," Worf said.

"Onscreen, Mr. Worf."

Blaze appeared on the screen, sitting in his command chair on the bridge of the *Glory*. "Greetings, Captain. I did not wish to leave without saying good-bye. And thank you for—"

"For the record, Captain," said Picard, "I would just as soon you not be specific in your thanks."

Blaze grinned. "I understand. Oh, and, uh, about that clever little transmitter that someone installed in my cloaking device . . . Chief Ragnar found it."

Geordi sighed. "I tried," he said, with a shrug.

"Well, I had best be on my way," said Blaze. "My long-range sensors have detected the approach of two Federation starships. They should be here within a few hours, and I would rather not have to explain my presence. I think I'll go see what the

Romulan merchant fleet has to offer. Bon voyage, *Enterprise*. Blaze out."

The screen's image changed to the exterior scanners as the *Glory* pulled out of orbit.

"There he goes," said Riker. He shook his head. "The Romulans outfitted his ship, and now he's going to use it against them. That's what I call nerve."

"It's what I call poetic justice," said Picard.

Riker raised his eyebrows. "Do I detect a note of admiration?" he said.

"No, Mr. Riker, certainly not," Picard replied. "I do not admire pirates. However, I do appreciate panache." He smiled. "Set course for Starbase 37, Mr. Data. I am overdue for a drink with an old friend."